AN INVITATION TO DANCE

Just then Phoebe felt a touch at her elbow. She turned around and beheld Alan Stanfield regarding her with an uncertain smile.

"Do forgive me, Phoebe. I know you said you were engaged for the first set, but I thought perhaps . . ." He hesitated, then went on quickly. "It occurred to me when I saw you sitting there that your partner might not yet have arrived—owing to some unavoidable delay, no doubt. And if that was the case, I thought—well, I hoped that perhaps you might not mind taking the floor with me until he does arrive?"

Phoebe felt a strong desire to kiss him. Any gentleman might have seen her sitting there looking forlorn and guessed she lacked a partner. But how many gentlemen would have broached the matter as he had, tactfully assuming that her partner had merely been delayed and phrasing his invitation so she might accept or decline it without losing face? Phoebe felt no other gentleman in the world would have been so sparing of her feelings. Looking into Alan's eyes, Phoebe felt once again that sense of *something*—the sense that they understood each other. Smiling, she gave him her hand.

"I should be very pleased to dance with you, Alan," she said. "And I don't think we need be concerned about my other partner. Now I consider it, our engagement was not a positive one, and I would rather dance with you anyway."

A smile lit up Alan's face. Taking her hand, he led her out onto the floor. . . .

From "At First Sight" by Joy Reed

BOOK YOUR PLACE ON OUR WEBSITE AND MAKE THE READING CONNECTION!

We've created a customized website just for our very special readers, where you can get the inside scoop on everything that's going on with Zebra, Pinnacle and Kensington books.

When you come online, you'll have the exciting opportunity to:

- View covers of upcoming books
- Read sample chapters
- Learn about our future publishing schedule (listed by publication month *and author*)
- Find out when your favorite authors will be visiting a city near you
- Search for and order backlist books from our online catalog
- Check out author bios and background information
- Send e-mail to your favorite authors
- Meet the Kensington staff online
- Join us in weekly chats with authors, readers and other guests
- Get writing guidelines
- AND MUCH MORE!

Visit our website at
http://www.kensingtonbooks.com

MY SWEET VALENTINE

SHANNON DONNELLY
ALICE HOLDEN
JOY REED

ZEBRA BOOKS
Kensington Publishing Corp.
http://www.kensingtonbooks.com

ZEBRA BOOKS are published by

Kensington Publishing Corp.
850 Third Avenue
New York, NY 10022

All Kensington titles, imprints, and distributed lines are
available at special quantity discounts for bulk purchases for
sales promotion, premiums, fund-raising, educational or in-
stitutional use.

Special book excerpts or customized printings can also be
created to fit specific needs. For details, write or phone the
office of the Kensington Special Sales Manager: Kensington
Publishing Corp., 850 Third Avenue, New York, NY 10022.
Attn. Special Sales Department. Phone: 1-800-221-2647.

Zebra and the Z logo Reg. U.S. Pat. & TM Off.

First Printing: January 2002
10 9 8 7 6 5 4 3 2 1

Printed in the United States of America

CONTENTS

SILVER LINKS

Shannon Donnelly

ONE

"Think carefully before you answer, Olivia, for your honesty or dishonesty now will determine the future of everything between us."

Olivia looked up. She had been staring at her wedding ring, twisting it round on her finger. She still was not accustomed to the heavy gold band with its single square-cut emerald. And she was not accustomed to hearing the grim anger that quivered in her husband's voice. It set her stomach to quivering as well.

But she had nothing to fear. She had done no wrong. Or had she? Her mind scampered madly over the past fortnight, but she could find nothing to which he could object.

Nothing. And everything.

Since they had returned to London earlier that month, after spending the holidays at Duncastle, everything seemed to have changed between them. Now she stared across the room to her lord husband, wondering what had happened to the gentleman with the sweet smile who had walked with her along the wild shores of her native Devon, dodging the lapping white foam. The man who had courted her so ardently. The man who had vowed to love her forever.

They had met and married, all within a scandalously short time. A fall courtship, and then two months of separation as political duties pulled him away. He had returned to her with his ring and his promises, and they had wed in February. On the day of love, on St. Valentine's.

They had not yet even celebrated one anniversary.

And already she did not recognize this dark, unsmiling

man, austere in his black-and-white evening clothes, handsome in the candlelight of his study, but so forbidding that her heart thudded against her chest and her throat tightened.

Tonight he looked like Lord Duncastle, a dark-haired man with a lean, narrow, aristocratic face. A man with a cold, intimidating intelligence in his gray-green eyes. She sought for some glimpse of her dear, laughing, charming Layton Carlisle, but that man seemed to have vanished.

Lifting her chin, as if that might also lift her courage, she met the guarded stare from her husband's eyes. A touch of panic fluttered in her stomach. She saw no love in those eyes.

"I have never lied to you," she said, indignant that he should presume she would deceive him.

He frowned. When Olivia had entered the room, Duncastle had been standing beside the fire, his hands folded behind his back and staring down into the flames. He had turned away from the white marble fireplace when she entered, but he had not unfolded his hands. Nor had he invited her to sit in one of the brown velvet-covered chairs in his study.

She had not often been in this room. Duncastle kept it for his work, for the political meetings and diplomatic affairs that formed his life. In truth, this room, with its walls of leather-bound books with Greek and Latin titles stamped in gold, and its dark wood paneling, daunted her. This room made her feel a country nobody. It made her feel a frippery woman without education. It made her feel as if she did not belong here, though she had tried desperately to make a place for herself at her husband's side.

I have done nothing wrong, she thought again, seeking some reassurance and remembering all the parties she had learned to give, and the polish she had fought to achieve. She needed those few threads of comfort. She found none in her husband's implacable stance.

He moved at last, unfolding his hands, taking a step toward her. That put one of the high-backed chairs between them. He rested one hand on the chair back so that the gold signet ring he wore on his right hand glinted in the candlelight.

"Then tell me the truth now. Did you tell Lady Albers that it is part of our plan in negotiating peace with the French to exploit the weakness of their envoy for gambling?"

Olivia hesitated. His tone held so much hostility and contempt that the urge to deny everything leapt at once to her tongue. She wanted to lie. She, who had never before told him any untruth, wanted desperately to blurt one out now. But what was so wrong with what she had done?

Swallowing the dryness in her mouth, she gripped one hand tightly within the other to keep them steady. Then she wet her lips and said, "And what if I did? She had a right to know. It is Lord Albers, after all, who has lost so much money to the Comte Guillium, and . . ."

"And did you not think that Lord Albers would keep his wife informed if he wished her to know of such things?"

Her cheeks burned, but she met her husband's accusing stare. *I did nothing wrong,* her mind protested. But her stomach nevertheless twisted with guilt and shame.

"The poor woman was fretting that her husband should lose so much to the Comte," she told him, her voice sharp. She let her dislike of being confronted as if she were a child mask the fear that lay just underneath. "Besides, I did not see why his gaming should have any effect on your negotiations, anyway."

His mouth tightened and his eyes narrowed, and then he said, "I would tell you why it does if I thought I could trust you."

A sharp pain twisted in her chest at such a deliberate insult. He did not trust her. The muscles in her legs seemed to turn to liquid. Desperate to sit down, she would have moved to one of the chairs, but that meant moving closer to him. And she could not bring herself to do that.

She was afraid of him. Of that implacable tone in his voice, of the lack of emotion in his eyes, of the loathing he seemed now to bear for her.

Oh, what had she done?

Duncastle went on, his voice flat and as cold as the room had become for her. "I shall tell you, however, that Lady

Albers confided in Guillium that her husband was intentionally losing to him."

Stunned, Olivia could only stare at her husband. A foolish denial rose in her. Lady Albers could not have done such a thing. She had vowed not to mention this to another soul. Olivia had trusted her.

Dear Lord, I have been an idiot.

Pride rose to her defense. And anger. Anger at Lady Albers for misleading her. Anger at herself for having thought that lady her friend. Still, she clung to the thought that she had acted in the best interest of a woman who had been kind enough to offer kindness and support last spring. Olivia had been a new bride then, and new to London society. Lady Albers had shown her how to go on, and had become a friend. A good friend, she had thought.

Lady Albers had also had a right to know that her husband—for whatever reason—was intentionally gaming away his fortune, and could therefore be counted upon to put a stop to it before it went too far. It had not been simply gossiping to tell her ladyship. It had not!

Giving Duncastle back a chilly stare, Olivia sought for a righteousness as haughty as his own. "You did not say I should not mention this to anyone."

Duncastle arched one eyebrow. "I did not think I would have to mark what occurs between us in the marriage bed as something that is between us alone."

The cruel truth of his words dug into her, and she did not know how to answer. Ashamed now, she only knew that she had to get away from here. She had to get out before the tears that stung her nose and blurred her vision began to fall, disgusting him with her frailty and turning her into a swollen-red-eyed wretch.

Thankfully, he turned away from her so that she had time to swipe at her eyes and pull in a shaking breath before he stood beside his desk and faced her again.

"I am sorry if you think I did wrong," she said, praying that he would relent just a little. Just enough so that she might know that he could forgive her if she asked it of him.

"Sorry that you did it, or sorry that I think it?" he asked, his voice still indifferent and his eyes still guarded.

Both, she wanted to say. However, she only answered, with her chin high, "It shall not happen again, my lord."

He looked down at the papers on his desk, lifting one as if it now interested him more than she did. "You need not worry, Olivia. I know it shall not happen again. I shall keep temptation from your tongue."

Shaking inwardly, she waited for more from him. For that anger she sensed inside him to be unleashed. She braced for arguments such as she had heard as a child between her own parents over her mother's inability to manage the household accounts and her father's inability to be faithful.

Duncastle continued to look at his papers, and then he glanced up, his eyes now an icy gray. "Is there something else you have to say?"

The quivering apology almost burst out. But the last scraps of her pride stopped it. In his present mood, would he accept anything from her? Even the most abject repentance? He had certainly not accepted her reasoning. And he had made it completely clear that he no longer held any trust for her.

Cold bands tightened around her heart. Had she ignored the signs that his love had not lasted? That he now cared more for his papers and his diplomacy and his meetings— for he certainly spent more time with them than with her.

She shook her head. If he would not bend to her even a little, why should she bend to him?

Turning, she walked to the door. She let herself out, shutting the latch softly behind her, although she wanted to slam the heavy oak door until it shook the foundation of the house.

Oh, Lord, what had she done? And was this the beginning of the end of their love?

Duncastle watched his wife walk from the room, her slender back straight and her head proud. Gold lights glinted from the fashionable crop of short, curling, light brown hair. Under the blue and white stripes of her elegant gown, her hips swayed and the desire for her flashed hot in him as it did every time he watched her.

He tamped down such traitorous impulses.

He must learn to school his desire. He must learn to temper feeling with caution. He must remember that he could not trust himself with her. Nor could he trust her.

When the door clicked shut, he put down the paper that he had been blindly staring at and sank into his chair. Propping his elbows on his desk, he put his face into his hands and shut his eyes, but still the look in Olivia's eyes haunted him.

Those guileless, seemingly innocent blue eyes. They had darkened with hurt, a pain he had put there. He hated himself for that. The tears that had glistened in her eyes, making them luminous, had nearly undone his determination to do what he must.

Yes, she was an innocent. Or she had been when he had married her. But she had learned much this past year.

He had watched with pride as she had mastered the art of holding political affairs, inviting the right mix of people, and insuring their attendance with tempting delicacies, a free flow of wine, and entertainment. He had seen her acquire polish and poise, and he had loved her even more for it. But over the past few weeks, he had also watched her tongue sharpen and her wit grow more cutting. He had overheard her pass along other things that had been told to her—things she ought to know how to keep to herself. And he had heard her and Lady Albers just last week quite happily tear apart the character of another lady, and all without a thought as to how words could harm.

His country innocent, the woman he had loved, had become a London lady. And a part of him mourned the transformation.

Where was the generous, sweet woman he had loved? Where was the woman he had trusted? Was this what happened when love died, and only the shell of a marriage was left?

And was it his fault for neglecting her and allowing her to learn that worst vice of London—a thoughtless and therefore dangerous tongue?

With a frustrated oath, he rose and took up the poker to jab viciously at the fire.

How could she have done this? How could she so easily betray a confidence between them? He could have forgiven her anything. But not this tattle-mongering.

Gossips. He loathed their vicious rumors, their eagerness to reveal secrets, their need to feed on the wrongs—real or supposed—of others. He had watched his father succumb to such malicious mutterings, and all started from a careless phrase let loose by his mother.

She had been a sweet woman, but without sense and unable to keep her tongue between her teeth. She had noted to a friend how her husband had access to important dispatches, and so could use such information to make wise investments for himself and his friends. She had seen nothing wrong with the idea of using official secrets for personal gain, and it mattered not that her husband had never abused such a trust. No, the damage was done in the implications uttered.

All too soon, whispers had become talk. Layton could recall being at school and hearing another boy say something, and knocking that boy down with his fist. He had been sent down for brawling, and his father had patiently explained the danger of justifying such rumors with defense. Only Layton had watched and had seen that making no defense at all was as good as admitting guilt.

He could still recall his father coming home one day, ashen-faced, deep lines bracketing his mouth and forehead. He had called Layton into the library and had told him that he had resigned his post. Layton had not understood then why an innocent man should be required to give up everything of importance to him because of nothing more than talk. But Layton soon learned how easy it was to ruin a reputation, and how difficult it was to repair it. He watched that task break his father's health.

Dragging a hand through his hair, Layton turned away from the fireplace and tried to turn his mind from the past. His father was dead, and his mother lived now in infirmity and childlike grace in the dower house at Duncastle. To this day, she seemed to have no awareness that her need to tell the world about her husband's remorse, and his heavy drinking, had undone every effort made to quell the gossip about her lord's unreliable nature. She had not been able to keep anything to herself, and Layton had watched and learned how to keep his own council. His own secrets.

But now he seemed to have married a woman who could not keep a confidence.

Perhaps it was a curse with all Carlisle men. Perhaps he could not help but repeat his father's pattern. Only it was not just his own career at stake. If it were, he could have given Olivia a second chance. His heart ached to do so. But reason warned him that he risked far more than his future.

England had been at war with France for six long years. But Bonaparte, as First Console, had gained control over a country that had once gone mad and murdered its monarch. There seemed hope that a peace could be made. Too many more would die if this war went on. It was not just Layton's diplomatic career that mattered; it was England's future.

Which meant that he must follow his mind, not his heart. He must learn to shut out his wife from the most important parts of his life. Even if it cost him her love to do so.

And he very much feared it would cost him that. And much more.

Olivia paced her bedchamber, twisting her wedding ring upon her finger, her muslin skirts stirring around her ankles. She had learned from her mother to be strong, to bear up under adversity. And she needed now to think, to plan, to find some way out of this.

Turning, she paced back to the windows.

Grosvenor Square lay in moonlight and shadows under her view, the trees of the square stark and bare under winter's cold touch. She wished that she heard not the echoing of carriage wheels and hooves on cobblestones and the cries of the night watch, but the muttering rhythm of endless waves giving hushed embraces to Devon's shore.

She ached for home. For her mother's counsel. For words to soothe her and advise her. For her father's rough, hard grip, which could make the world seem a safe place, even though she knew it was not.

Only her place was here, beside a husband who no longer

trusted her. And how could his love last for much longer if there was no trust to nourish it?

The thought chilled her.

Rubbing her bare arms, she knew that she ought to put on a woolen shawl over the thin muslin of her high-waisted gown. Such a prosaic thought twisted a smile from her, for it would serve him right if she caught a cold and died of it.

Oh, Lord, what am I to do, she prayed, and traced a pattern on the windowpane with a fingertip until the chill of it sank into her skin.

What am I to do?

Thoughts whirled in confusion in her head. If she could not have her mother's advice, she needed someone's. And there had been but one lady who had provided guidance to her. True enough, Lady Albers had betrayed her trust. But perhaps there was a good reason. Yes, that must be it. Lady Albers might not have been at fault. Someone else must have said something and the blame had been mistakenly mislaid.

That could be true. That must be true.

Suddenly, she knew that she had to speak with Lady Albers. She had to find out her side of it. Then she would be able to go to Duncastle and tell him how wrong he had been, and he would be sorry for being so harsh and she could apologize wholeheartedly, and they would make it up, and all would be as it had been before.

With her heart lifting, Olivia went at once to her writing desk, which stood in the salon that connected to her bedchamber. Rummaging through the stack of invitations, she found the one she sought for Lady Albers's musical evening. She had not expected to go, for she hated opera singing and disliked that she felt compelled to praise it anyway. With a shock, she realized that she had learned to tell untruths about such things.

Well, that did not matter. Uttering such small falsehoods was part of being in Society. Still, it troubled her that she actually had learned to be dishonest.

She pushed aside the notion. The issue of honesty over musical preference was not at stake. Something far more important mattered.

Going back to her bedroom, she went to her wardrobe and pulled out evening gloves and a black velvet cloak. Then she glanced into her mirror. She had worn only a plain silver necklace, quite ancient in design, made up of dozens of intricate links. It had been given her by Layton on their wedding day. On St. Valentine's. She had hoped to please him by wearing it tonight. Only she seemed unable to please him, or even interest him of late, and now the necklace lay around her neck like an iron band.

With shaking fingers, she struggled with the clasp to remove it. Stubbornly, it refused to unlatch. She tugged at it, her patience worn thin, and then tugged again.

The necklace came loose in her hands.

Glancing down at it, she saw that she had broken the link that held the clasp of the necklace.

I am breaking everything tonight, she thought, miserable. And then fear coiled inside her, sliding into her like a fog creeping in from the Thames.

What if Layton saw it and took it as an intentional slight that she could destroy the token he had given her when they had wed on St. Valentine's?

TWO

For an instant, Olivia glanced around her, uncertain what to do. Then she went to her wardrobe and pulled open a drawer at random. Stuffing the silver necklace into the back, she pushed it under the fine lawn undergarments that her maid had folded so neatly. Then she shut the drawer. She would take the necklace to be mended tomorrow. Duncastle need never know she had snapped one of the links. No, she would not have him thinking that she did not care for his gifts. She cared far too much for that.

Still shaking inside, she took up her cloak and gloves and fled her room without donning any other jewelry.

Downstairs in the main hall, she asked the porter to summon the town coach. Then she waited, fretful, struggling with her gloves. She glimpsed herself in the hall mirror—pale-faced, a worried furrow dug between her eyebrows, eyes glistening wet with unshed tears—and she knew that she must calm herself or her distraught appearance would create even more gossip.

That was the last thing she wanted.

Taking deep breaths, she pinched color into her cheeks. Then she brushed at the curls around her face, trying to coax them into order. Her mother would hardly recognize her, she knew, with her hair cut so short, and her gown so stylish and revealing. As of late, she had sometimes looked into the mirror and had seen this strange society lady staring back at her.

Had she lost herself even as she was now losing Layton?

Disturbed by such dark thoughts, she pushed them away. Now was not the time for doubts and soul-searching. Tonight, she had to act. She had to mend things between herself and Duncastle before it was too late.

At last, the porter announced that the coach stood at the front steps, awaiting her. For a moment she hesitated, thinking that she would leave word she had gone to Lady Albers's in case Duncastle should ask for her. However, after what had transpired between them, that seemed too much like inviting more disagreements. Better he should know only that she had gone out.

So she swept out to the waiting coach, her head up and determined that this whole wretched mess would be sorted out, even if she had to drag Lady Albers back with her to explain it all to Duncastle.

Her courage lasted until she was shown into the hallway, with its towering Grecian pillars and overwhelming statues, at Lady Albers's town house on Brook Street.

The laughter from the upstairs drawing room, the clinking of glasses, and the hum of conversation, informed her at once that she had arrived during an interval in the evening's performance. She realized then that she had not the nerve at that moment to deal with large numbers of people.

Aware that two footmen, in white wigs and formal black satin knee breeches, stood in the hall with her, waiting for her to relinquish her cloak, she turned to one of them. "Please tell Lady Albers that I must speak with her in private."

The servant's expression soured, as if this request was not to be tolerated on an evening when her ladyship entertained. But he merely bowed, said he would inquire, and directed his fellow footman to show Olivia into a small salon.

Nervous and pacing, Olivia waited as the servant lit the candles and the fire and then shut the doors behind him. The room, painted Wedgwood blue and dainty in size, was sparsely furnished in low Roman-style couches. Olivia could not sit, so she took a deep breath and rehearsed in her mind what she would say.

She wanted to phrase her question as a polite and friendly inquiry. But when Lady Albers bustled in—all glowing smiles and happiness—resentment welled in Olivia and the words burst out in a rush. "How could you betray my confidence?"

Lady Albers's eyes widened and she paused on the threshold. Her striking black hair was curled and pulled into a knot at the back. Black eyes dominated a narrow face, made plain by sallow skin and a too-sharp nose. Ruthlessly slender, she wore her burgundy satin gown with an innate sense of style, and her jewels were the envy of many. Tonight, diamonds and rubies glittered around her neck and dangled from her ears.

Her lips thinned as she fixed her smile in place and entered, shutting the door behind her. "My dear, whatever has distressed you? You look utterly ghastly."

"I feel ghastly. Oh, Agatha, you vowed not to tell anyone what I revealed to you about Guillium!"

Lady Albers sat on one of the Roman couches, with its side arms and no back, and arranged her skirt as she spoke. "But, my dear, I only spoke of it to Lord Albers. You knew I would. I had to. And of course he was not included in my promise."

"Then you did not tell the Comte?"

Lady Albers fussed with the arrangement of the gold-and-black embroidered shawl that draped from her elbows in artful curves. "Of course not. I did no more than drop a hint that I did not like my husband losing to him, intentionally or otherwise. Your name did not even come into the matter."

With a groan, Olivia sank onto one of the low couches. "That is not what you promised. How could you betray me?"

Her ringed hands stilled and Lady Albers stiffened. "Betray? I think you are being overly dramatic, my dear. Besides, how else was I to put a stop to Albers's losses? And as for the comte, he did not know from whence I had my information, so it hardly matters, now does it?"

Irritation fired in Olivia. "I did not confide in you so that you could tell others. I thought—"

"You thought you had a bit of news that I had not, and I grant you it was vastly clever of you to come up with it first. And you know very well that it pleased you to impress me. But I should have heard it eventually from someone, you know. So I do not see what all this fuss is about."

"The fuss is that Duncastle believes I broke his trust. And I did, more fool that I was!"

Lady Albers lifted one hand, palm upward. "Men! They are always upset at some little thing, are they not? But honestly, you must learn not to care about these little contretemps of theirs. It was a silly notion, anyways, that Guillium's taking the guineas from my husband's pockets might make these talks of theirs drag on. Leave it to the gentlemen to think that their schemes are so much more important than anything else."

Putting a hand to her temples, Olivia could only shake her head. Of course. By playing on Guillium's passion for gaming, the hope had been to have him lingering in London, keeping the peace talks continuing. Now, if anything should go wrong, the temperamental Frenchman might easily decide to have done with negotiations and quit England.

Thanks to her indiscretion—and to Lady Albers's—England had one less trump to play in this high-stakes game.

Oh, why had she not kept quiet?

Lowering her hand, she looked up at the woman she had believed to be her friend. She had thought she was doing Lady Albers such a service. She had not spared a thought to the damage that could be done.

"You do not see any harm then, in what you have done?" she said, struggling to believe that she might yet make her friend see the truth.

Lady Albers lifted her eyebrows. "I have done? To whom? To you? Olivia, I am very sorry if you and Duncastle have fought over this trifle, but that is not my fault."

"We did not fight!"

"Then why are you here now? Really, Olivia. Do not be so tiresome. Of course you fought. He is upset, but you only acted as a good friend to me. Now, he shall be excessively cold to you. So you shall have to flirt with some very dashing fellow to make him suffer until he comes crawling back to you. I have been married far longer than you, and I know exactly how these little situations always work out, my dear."

Olivia rose. "You do not understand. It is I who suffer—and who deserve to do so for having said things I should not have."

"Nonsense. You did as you saw right. And you should not allow Duncastle to be awful to you for doing so. I told you that I should have heard it from someone else. So you should stop making yourself so miserable." She gave Olivia a warm smile and patted the seat beside her. "Now, come and tell me all about how horrible Duncastle was to you, for you shall feel so much better for telling me all about it. You know you shall."

The urge to unburden herself, to have sympathy and comfort to lessen her guilt, tempted Olivia like the heat of a fire on a cold night. She ached for a friend just now. She wanted someone to assure her that she was not really wicked. But a flicker of honesty warned her that she had been in the wrong.

It would be even more wrong to condemn Duncastle for being upset with her. And she knew with all her heart that if she started to justify her bad actions now, it would be so much easier next time to repeat her folly and still feel righteous about her acts.

For a moment, she wanted to rage at Lady Albers. To give her such a scathing lecture that the woman would regret this as well. And then she realized the folly of such a thing. She had admired this lady, and she had indeed wanted to impress her. That, as much as anything, had led her into telling Lady Albers things she should not have. Lady Albers was indeed at fault, but the fault was far greater on her part for betraying her husband's trust in the first place.

She loathed herself then. And she looked back with shame at how she had once sat in ballrooms with Lady Albers, cattily discussing other ladies' poor taste, and casually swapping bits of scandal as if they were delicious treats.

She was well served for her hurtful words and thoughts. And she saw that if she gave in to the temptation to confide in Lady Albers again, that woman would quite happily tell the world all about Olivia's problems with Duncastle.

This had to end. And it had to end with her now.

Stiffly, she pulled at her gloves. "I think I had best go home. I owe my husband an apology."

Lady Albers rose, her eyebrows arched and a speculative gleam in her black eyes. "It is your affair how you handle Duncastle, but I do warn you that if you ever admit any fault to them, they never let you forget it. And they always make you pay for it."

The warning struck a raw nerve inside Olivia. She had married late in life, at twenty-four, after waiting for a love that she had believed would be true. She had thought—had hoped—that love could prevent a marriage such as her parents had had. They had married for convenience, and as a child Olivia had watched her father's indiscretions and her mother's tears. Her parents had somehow managed a truce between them, but Olivia had vowed to have a different marriage. One of love. One of trust.

Had she ruined her chance at such a thing? Would Duncastle punish her by turning away, or by turning to other women? Would he find a way to make her pay?

Struggling not to believe such a thing, she tried to remember that she could not trust Lady Albers. But as she bid her ladyship a good evening and swept from the room, the insidious thought remained.

What if she had forever damaged Layton's trust in her?

The maid brought the broken necklace to the butler the next morning. She had found it while she was tidying up after helping Lady Duncastle rise for an early ride in Hyde Park. New at her position and worried over doing things proper in a lord's house, the maid had handed over the strand of silver links with a trembling hand and a hasty vow that she never broke it and did not want to be accused of stealing.

The butler, Henderson, fixed a stern eye on the maid, decided he would have to watch the girl to ensure she did not break anything else, and then acted in the proper interest of the house.

He took the necklace to Lord Duncastle.

Layton accepted the chain, with its broken link, into his hand without so much as a quiver in his cheek or a flicker of emotion in his eyes. Or at least he hoped there was none. He had learned early to school his emotions, to hide them. That training served him well in his diplomatic career. It felt, at times, as if it crippled him in life's other matters, but just now he was grateful for such a skill.

"Thank you, Henderson," he said. "I shall have it repaired."

Henderson bowed and left the room, his features as schooled and impassive as Layton's. *Quite a pair we make,* Layton thought. *An unfeeling master and an unfeeling servant.*

Only while Layton could hide his emotions, he could not bury them so deep that they did not scratch at him like a cat struggling to get loose.

So he sat in his study and stared at the necklace in his hand.

It was an odd necklace, made of individual silver links chained together. Crafted three hundred years ago by some past Carlisle, it had been given to each bride that came into the family. He could recall no story of it having been broken before, and for a moment foreboding filled him. He did not like to think of himself as a superstitious man, but he had seen enough of life in his twenty-nine years to know that whims of fate could favor or frown on endeavors.

Was this a sign of things to come?

He had been too harsh on Olivia last night, and that harshness sat ill with him now, like the aching aftermath of having indulged in too much drink. He ought to have had more patience. He should have been with her more this past year to guide her in society and help her make better friends than Lady Albers and her lot.

Why had he not waited until his temper cooled before he spoke to her?

But he had not been able to wait. He had not been able to control himself well enough. He had only known that he needed to confront her. He had prayed that Lord Albers had gotten the story wrong, and that it had not been Olivia who had let the secret out. Only she had been at fault.

With a weary sigh he went to his desk and sat, toying with the ends of the chain, ignoring his paperwork—the estate business, the foreign dispatches, the letters—which ought to command his attention.

At least she had been honest. He had to give her that. He twisted the chain so that it glimmered in the pale winter sunlight. She must have been upset afterward to break this chain, and he was sorry he had made her so. But how did they go forward from here? He dared not trust her again, not with so much in the balance. And how did he live with a wife he could not trust?

His brain spun in circles until he realized that this path led nowhere. Sitting up, he put the chain into his waistcoat pocket. He would have it mended. And he would wait for her to tell him how it came to be broken. That would be a sign for him. A sign that he had not ruined everything between them.

And he shut out the thought of what he would do if she did not ask about the necklace, or that he might have hurt her far deeper than he had ever intended.

Olivia came back from her ride still uneasy. For the first time since they had wed, Duncastle had not come to her chamber. She had been glad at first, and then relief turned to worry. No difficulty between them had ever spread before to their marriage bed. And she tried to tell herself that it would pass, that it did not matter. But she woke still disturbed by what had passed between them. So she had summoned her maid, slipped into a riding habit, and had had her bay gelding brought round from the stables before the sun had barely risen to warm London's streets.

Thankfully, it dawned with clouds scudding over the city, but without rain. She had the park to herself and her groom, and she made the most of it, enjoying a long canter down the hard dirt, with the wind in her face to blow away her thoughts.

By the time she dismounted before Carlisle House again, and dug in her pocket for a slice of carrot for her gelding, Tor, she felt almost normal. Almost cheerful. Pale sunlight warmed her skin and there was something enormously comforting about the large, solid presence and elemental aroma of Tor. She allowed the gelding to nose the pockets of her riding habit for more carrot, then scratched just under Tor's jaw—his weakness. Giving the reins back to her groom, she turned and mounted the white stone steps.

The house seemed dreadfully quiet, even though a footman opened the tall walnut front door for her and a maid paused in her dusting of a vase that stood on the hall table to bob a curtsy.

Olivia went upstairs at once to change. She had so much to do today. A necklace to mend, a marriage to patch, trust to repair. For a moment it swamped her, leaving her almost unable to move.

Start with what you can do, she told herself. And she went to pull the necklace from its hiding place.

But her hand closed only on soft fabric.

THREE

Olivia's stomach knotted with sick dread and she tried not to panic. The maid must have found it. Oh, why had she not locked it away? But she knew the answer. Duncastle kept the most valuable jewels locked in his study, and the rest of her trinkets lay in a cedar box that had been given her by her mother and which stood on her dresser.

That was it. The maid must have put it away, perhaps thinking that it had caught on a garment. Yes, that was all that had happened.

She hurried to her dresser and flipped open the lid to her jewel box. The cameo from her mother lay there, as well as a favorite necklace of lapis, and two pairs of gold hoop earrings. But no silver chain.

Oh, Lord, if only she had not allowed fear and guilt to drive her, she would not be in this agony now. Moving to the bell pull, she tugged on it. *Please let the girl only have tidied it away,* she prayed.

Her maid arrived, cheerful and ready to please, but her smile faded as Olivia asked about the necklace. The girl's eyes widened, and from her stammered explanation it soon became clear that she feared her own neglect might have caused the damage.

"It must have caught on sommat, my lady," she said, her country accent rising as her agitation grew. "I took it to Mr. Henderson and he said his lordship should best have it mended. Was I wrong, milady?"

Olivia forced a smile and rubbed at the furrow between

her eyebrows. Fear. It seemed to drive them all to do such stupid things. She let out a tired, shaking breath. Ah, well, what would come of this would come. She could not hold this poor girl at fault for a disaster she had caused herself. Not when she seemed to excel at that.

"No. No, of course not," she said. "I am certain it does not matter in the least, actually."

And she only wished she believed her words.

Olivia did not see Duncastle that evening. He dined with friends, Henderson informed her. The next day Duncastle rose early to breakfast at his club and Olivia did not see him that day, either. Twice each day she almost knocked on his study door to confess her guilt over breaking the necklace. But he already thought so badly of her that she could not bring herself to make him feel even worse.

Perhaps he, too, blamed the maid for being careless. She knew she should not saddle that poor girl with the responsibility of it, but she could not bring herself to claim fault, either. Not just now. And she did not wish to go into Duncastle's study again. The pain of her last interview lay too raw in her. She feared making a fool of herself with tears that would only repel Duncastle.

Thankfully, she had her own set of parties to attend, as well as a breakfast given by Lady Jersey, and morning calls to pay upon other ladies. She saw Lady Albers twice, but did no more than offer a civil greeting, although it cost her a good deal not to say more. She longed to talk to someone. Anyone. Only the greatest force of will kept her from going to Lady Albers and leaning on her for that comfort she had offered.

But she did not. And she realized now that those she knew in London were acquaintances really, not friends.

She knew people, but she could not name one whom she held dear. Back home in Devon she could have talked to her mother, or to Vicar Ainston, or to Julia Fustham, who lived but one house away. Or even to ancient and deaf Mrs. Hammersmith-Fellows, who always held one's hand and said in such a comforting and sympathetic voice, "But it will be all right eventually."

Olivia would have given much for such reassurance. From anyone.

Instead, she had to listen to the avid gossip from those she had once called friends, and she saw reflected what she had been on her way to becoming. Fear of saying anything, of saying too much, and loathing for their malicious criticism, held her silent. But was it perhaps already too late for her? She so desperately wished for that feeling she had once had of belonging in their circles.

That night, she lay in her bed, miserable, tears leaking from her eyes. She tried not to give in to the horrible emptiness that lay in the darkness with her. She tried to believe that this estrangement between her and her husband could not last forever. She prayed that it would not.

Turning her face into her pillow, she prayed for some sign that he might be able to forgive her. That he still loved her. She ached to go to him, to knock on his door, to beg his forgiveness.

But what if he could not?

And the dread crept into her heart and whispered to her that he must be turning already to other women, and that was why he no longer sought her or her bed.

"Good heavens, man, who died in your family?"

Layton glanced up from his brandy. He had taken refuge in his club after an awkward meal that evening with Lady Duncastle.

Disappointment curled in him, as harsh and smoldering as his brandy. For days now he had waited for Olivia to make some mention of her silver necklace. Or to say something of what had occurred between them. But she had not sought him out. So, finally, thinking that perhaps she felt too ashamed by what she had done, he had taken the effort to dine with her.

He ought to have spared them both.

She had not even wanted to converse with him. For every

topic he offered, she gave a brief reply. And then said nothing more.

When he casually mentioned the necklace and that he had sent it off for repair, she had held still a moment, and then uttered a polite thank you, as if she had not even known that it was broken. As if it was of no importance.

Well, such a trifle should hardly matter to him, if it mattered not to her. So he had stamped down on the wound left by her lack of concern, and told himself not to be a fool about it. After a quarter hour more with her being unable or unwilling to speak to him, he fled the dining room, giving the excuse of needing to meet someone.

Thank heavens he had met someone. He hated to be made a liar.

Without waiting for an invitation, Lord Albers sank his bulky frame into the armchair next to Layton. He gestured to a waiter to fetch him his usual bottle of burgundy, then he turned back to Layton. "What's bedeviling you, Duncastle? Trouble still with your good lady?"

Layton stiffened. He had known Albers for six years, and had been drawn to the man by the fact that Albers had suffered a similar fate to his father—that of being married to a gossip. Unlike Layton's father, however, Lord Albers seemed to have learned how to live with his wife, and to deal with her. Layton had to admire such skill and fortitude.

But though he considered Albers one of his closest friends, Layton still disliked discussing his private life. And he wondered now how Albers knew of any trouble between him and Olivia.

"It is just this mess with Guillium," Layton said. "He is threatening to break off negotiations, you know. Though I think it a pose on his part to try and force us to yield on the issue of the lands that France wishes to retain."

"Quite possibly. But he will make trouble for us, if he can. He is a man who enjoys making difficulties."

Layton frowned. "Do any of the French negotiate in good faith, or do they buy time to build an invasion fleet?"

"Well, let us just say that that Corsican fellow has more ambition than is good for anyone. But now we've beaten them back in Egypt, we could use the breather as much as they, don't you know."

"I do. At times, I am tempted to take just such a breather myself from this whole mess called politics. The entire campaign in Egypt would have taken half the time, if not for interference from London."

Albers gave a dry chuckle. "Spoken like a young man— with impatience. But you would miss it, if you quit. The frustrations, and the gains. That feeling of doing some good, despite the world's attempts to do bad. And do not underestimate the lure of power. A man who does not recognize that seduction can too easily fall victim to its siren's call."

Layton gave a snort. He had had no need to make politics a career, and it held no magic for him. He had enough work to occupy him, what with five estates to manage. However, the need to compensate for his father's legacy, to repair the past, had driven him hard. And now he felt himself at a critical point at which he must tread careful lest he duplicate his father's errors in judgment.

"You are too quiet tonight, Duncastle. And that tells me there is more than Guillium troubling you. What is this difficulty with your lady wife that I've heard mentioned. Is that what has you drinking alone in dark corners?"

Glancing up, Layton scowled. Silver-haired and thick-set, Lord Albers seemed a jovial fellow without much sense or guile. He had the appearance, in fact, of an elderly, sad-eyed hunting dog, long past his prime. Layton knew the opposite to be true.

Lord Albers presented to the world the face he wished them to see. But he never spoke without calculation, and the brain behind those sad eyes was as shrewd as any Layton had ever watched at work.

"What have you heard?" Layton asked.

Albers's wine arrived. The waiter poured it and left the bottle, and Albers held his glass to the firelight as if to study the deep red hue. "Nothing too worrisome. Not yet. But your wife seems to have told mine that you had an argument. Something to do with Lady Duncastle not being able to keep any confidences to herself."

Layton let out a curse. How long had it been before Olivia

had run to her friend to tell her everything? And what story would she spread next—that he no longer sought her bed? Had she no discretion?

"Don't look so thunderous, my lad. Everyone has also seen that your wife and mine are also casting sharp glances in each other's directions. There are those who think the rumor little more than my wife's being out to sharpen her tongue. However, it might be wise just now to be seen a bit with your lady wife. No need to overdo such familiarity, of course. The opera, or a ball perhaps, would quiet what talk there is."

Layton tossed back his brandy. It stung his throat and burned his stomach. Then he met Lord Albers's interested stare. "Is that the worst of it?"

"At present. But the world knows you married for love. And the only thing the world enjoys more than a deliriously happy wedding is for it to turn bitterly unhappy. Ugly words such as divorce begin to bubble. And while the talk is not yet that progressed, the foundations are being laid. That, of course, is not a problem for most men. But it is certain death to political careers.

"And the Prime Minister would take it amiss if he thought you preoccupied with other matters. You know how Pitt is. Nothing distracts him, so he cannot see why lesser mortals should think of women, family, or anything else but work. So it might be best to nip this tattle before it grows roots."

Jaw set, Layton gave a grim nod. He knew the wisdom in that far better than most.

Albers sipped his burgundy, and then added, "You might also consider buying her some trinket. Do you not have an anniversary upcoming? St. Valentine's even—a most apt day to celebrate. Agatha always becomes most amenable when I give her diamonds, though she does have rather a soft spot for emeralds."

Layton's frown deepened, and he could not keep the distaste from his voice. "Buy her silence you mean?"

"Ah, if only we could. No, just buy a fleeting happiness. It is an odd thing, but a happy woman talks less to others and more to you. I have no idea why that should be, but if I were a richer man, my Agatha would have lips only for me. However, a woman who talks can have her uses. There are compensations in life, and you may find your lady's too-free tongue may help you place those words that you would have widely known."

Drawing back, Layton studied his friend, even more appalled. "I did not marry her to use her as a . . . a political tool."

Albers lifted his glass again to the firelight. "I know. We marry for passion. Or for money. Or because we must. And then we have to live with such a bargain for a lifetime. That is no easy thing; let me tell you that from the distance of twenty years wed. Time is what you must master. And you might want to remember one thing. You may use your father's path as a guide, or you may use mine. The choice is yours. But you had best act while you do have a choice still."

For a moment, Layton wanted to fling himself from his chair and stalk out of the room. The idea of using Olivia—of encouraging her gossiping—strung tight every muscle in his body. His back ached with holding in the desire to storm away.

But he forced himself to stay and hear the sense in Albers's words. He had to. For while he had married Olivia from love—from a hot passion that still could leave him light-headed with desire—he realized now that perhaps he had been unwise to allow his heart to rule his head.

He had sense enough to know that love always carried the seeds within it to grow other strong emotions—such as hate. And he could not bear that he might come to hate her. So he stayed and listened to how Lord Albers had learned to live with his wife. And he thought with despair of how happy he and Olivia had once been.

Two days later, Olivia was ready to murder her husband. Shame and anguish had given way to bitter resentment, and she thought if he gave her one more diamond broach with that uncaring and set look upon his face she would happily open the clasp and stab him with the pin.

He smiled at her, with that wide, attractive mouth of his

set in such a fixed expression that it left her palm itching to slap his face so that she might see some real feeling from him.

He gave her presents. Bribes, really, she knew. She could not imagine him taking any time in selecting the gaudy diamond and ruby broach with the matching necklace for her. His gifts brought to mind the guilty offerings that her father had showered on her mother whenever he had strayed from her bed.

And while he gave her things, he also gave her as little time with him as humanly possible. For that, she could hate him.

Then, on the second night, he surprised her by offering her his escort to the opera.

As she dressed, she dared to hope it was the sign she had been seeking. At last, perhaps, his heart really had softened toward her. If he wished to take her someplace with him, then he must really still care, after all.

She took care with her dress, selecting the blue silk gown that he had once admired back when he still said loving words to her. Her maid took extra care in arranging her hair into shining curls, and Olivia even wore the heavy diamond necklace that she did not like, but which he had given her.

It all went wrong.

From the moment she came downstairs, he seemed unable to bring himself to touch her. He allowed the servants to put on and remove her evening cloak—something he had always held as his exclusive right. He moved his hand away from hers when she had lain hers over his in the carriage.

Then he had gone out of his way to act the smiling husband in public, and to tell her, his gray-green eyes narrowing in hard speculation, "We must put on a good appearance, you know. We hardly want everyone to think that Lady Albers's story of us having fought is anything more than the normal tiff between married folk, now do we?"

She had stared at him, then, shocked and cold.

The urge to turn on her heel and walk out on him rose inside her. Almost, she gave into that blazing, hurt anger. But then she took a breath and decided that she would show him instead that if what he wanted was the perfect wife in public, she would give him that.

And nothing more.

The rest of the evening passed in a painful torment that left her unable to remember anything except that he kept anything he might be feeling locked behind an impossible wall. He would not even look directly at her to meet her gaze.

On the carriage ride home, she did not attempt to touch him, but sat in her own corner of the swaying coach. Only once a rut in the road jostled the carriage, sending her up against him. His hands closed on her arms, and she looked up into his eyes, trying to see his expression in the dark, all the feelings she had ever had for him—the love, the desire, the yearning—stark and desperate inside her.

Then the coach rocked to a halt before their house, and the door opened, and the footmen let down the steps.

"Dreadful roads," Duncastle said, his tone unruffled. "We shall have to see what Parliament can do."

Numb exhaustion settled over Olivia as she climbed from the carriage. She went up the stairs and to her room without a backward glance. She no longer knew this man she had married. All she knew was that the fault lay at her door for having become something he did not want.

He accepted nothing from her now. It seemed that one mistake forever tainted her. And what if he was right to so distrust her? What if she had become a gossip? For she ached to go back to her old friends. She longed to confide her troubles to them. She certainly could not talk to her husband.

The man who had held her, who had made passionate love to her, who had declared undying devotion, no longer came to her bed. Not for his comfort. And not for hers.

That decided her at last.

The next morning she gathered the last scraps of her courage and her sense for survival. This could not go on. She could not go on. Something or someone had to change. And she was wretched enough for it to be her.

With her heart in her throat and her palms damp, she went and knocked on her husband's study. And when he bade her to enter, she did so, determined to have it out with him.

FOUR

Layton glanced up from his desk, saw that it was Olivia and put down his papers. A fragile surprise and delight stirred in him, but the tension in her slender figure and the glitter in her eyes set off warnings inside him. She looked ready for battle.

On guard, he rose and came around his desk.

He had been cautious last night in taking her to the opera. Everything inside him had been far too receptive to her mood, and his body had been far too aware that it had been days since he had sought the comfort of her arms. When she had touched him, he had fought the urge to forgive her everything, to undo all his words, to relent on his disapproval.

It had been agony—and heaven—to hold her for that brief moment in the carriage when that blessed rut had thrown her against him. She had smelled of jasmine and had lain as soft in his arms as he ever recalled, and the desire for her had nearly undone him.

His reactions had set off alarms.

He knew now exactly how his father had fallen into the fatal trap of not being strong enough. He could see how tempting it was to be too forgiving, too adoring, too needing of a woman's caresses. The desire to hold on to his integrity, to his path, made him draw away from everything soft inside himself. Things were too critical just now for him to risk any other information slipping out. He must be guarded.

But the sight of her now tore at the wall he had put between them.

She looked pale in her green gown, and her cheeks seemed hollow as if she had lost weight of late. Dark smudges under her eyes told him that she had had as little sleep as he last night.

Before he could ask what brought her to his study, her words burst out in a rush. "You are never going to forgive me, are you?"

Her aggressive tone grated against every fiber inside him. With his eyes narrowing, he studied her. She looked not the least sorry for what she had done. It stung him raw that she should be so callous over the damage she had caused.

He hardened his feelings of a moment ago. "When you prove you can be trusted—"

"How can I prove anything when you will not even allow me the chance?"

"The chance for what, Olivia? To spread more tales about us? What else about our private lives do you intend to share with your friends? Do you want me to come to your bed so that you can tell everyone that I do so?"

She drew in a sharp breath. Her eyes glittered. And his face burned for what he had just said to her. Now she had him descending to her own level of indiscreet disclosures.

"I wish to go home," she said. "To Devon."

Frowning, he folded his hands behind his back. Of course she would say this now. Her timing could not be worse. Leave now and start up talk that she had perhaps left him.

"Do you not think it rather awkward? We have engagements to keep. Portland and Marlborough both mentioned how they looked forward to dinner here Tuesday next, and you would not care to disappoint two dukes, now would you?"

Olivia winced at his hard tone. She had come here expecting, wishing, that he would soften even just a little toward her. But he protested her going away only from the standpoint of social obligations. Not from any desire to have her with him.

When he had lashed out at her, the words of her desire to leave had pushed themselves out. She had not meant to say them, but when they had been said, she knew that she had to go.

A raw ache opened inside her at the thought of not seeing him for days, and of his hardly missing her. She blinked back the tears, and let them chill inside her into icy determination. She wanted to batter at this barrier he had put between them, and since she could not do so with her fist, she would do so with words.

"Your sister could act as hostess," she said. "And my absence, after all, ensures you no more embarrassing gossip, which is what you wish, is it not? That seems to be all you wish from me now."

She waited for him to deny it. She longed for some feeling to leap into his eyes. She wanted to hear him say that he did not wish her to go, for him to stride across the room and take hold of her arms and kiss her and tell her that what he wished for was a reconciliation.

He did none of that. Instead, he fussed with his pocket watch, pulling it out, glancing at the time as if he could hardly spare another instant, and then he strode back to his desk to busy himself with his papers.

"You shall return, of course, for our anniversary?"

Hope flickered again inside, desperate and brief. His next words crushed it like a carriage wheel rolling over a budding daisy.

"It would look odd to the world, you know, if you were not here for that occasion at least."

She turned away, the pain of his words driving so deep into her heart that it hurt even to look at him.

It would look odd to the world.

He cared for the appearance he wished her to present, but not that she might be far from his side on the day marked for lovers.

Oh, where was the man she had once known and loved? The man who made for her a Valentine's card from shells he had gathered. The man who had once walked through a downpour because he had to see her. The man who had once read poetry to her beside the fireside, with her curled up upon velvet cushions and his head pillowed on her lap.

Had that gentleman been a fraud? An illusion? What had

happened to the man who once had been unable to keep from touching her?

Pulling in a deep breath, she glanced back at him. He still stood beside his desk, his head bent over his papers. For an instant, hate seared her senses. She almost strode over to his desk to sweep her arm across it, scattering his papers and making him notice her.

She fought for control. She fought to remember this was a man whom she loved more than anything. She fought to keep her dignity. And she knew if there was to be any hope for them, she had to get away.

"I shall leave tomorrow," she said, her voice strangled, and then she strode out, determined to go someplace where she was wanted. Uncertain if she would ever return.

"Will there be anything else, my lord?" Henderson inquired after setting down the silver tray that held a dusty bottle of cognac and a single glass. His expression remained unperturbed, but Layton could not help but feel he had shocked his butler by asking that brandy be brought to his rooms. He had never done so before. But, since he had married Olivia, he had never had to spend the night without her near to him.

"Thank you, no," he said. He waited until Henderson left, and then he poured himself a liberal glass of the amber liquid. He intended to drink himself to sleep, for he could see no other way to get any rest this night.

She had left that morning. He had almost gone to her. He had wanted to stop her from going. To run downstairs and out to the coach and drag the door open and tell her that she could not go. Not with matters so strained between them.

He knew that he wanted it too desperately.

So he forced himself to remain in control. As he had learned to as a boy, he stamped down on his feelings, and he stayed where he was, one hand gripping the drapery. He had watched as her slim figure disappeared into the heavy traveling chaise, as the steps were put up, as the coachman cracked his whip, as the footman jumped up behind, as the horses clattered down the street, and as she disappeared from view.

Gone.

It is not for bloody ever, you fool.

He had wondered then if he had been wise to allow her to go, and not just for the sake of appearances, but because of his own needs. That doubt haunted him still and made him pace his room, brandy glass in hand, its strong fumes filling his senses.

He stopped beside his dresser and took up the miniature he kept there, the one she had had painted for him as a wedding present last Valentine's.

In the oval portrait, she smiled, her face radiant, a laugh in her blue eyes and the corners of her mouth curving with tempting delight. A band tightened around his chest. He brushed the pad of his thumb across the painted lips, wishing their softness lay within his touch.

Should he have demanded that she remain in London? Should he have attempted to trust her again?

But how could he? These damnable, delicate negotiations dragged on and men died while they did so. He must learn to keep his distance from her. And he was doing a bloody awful job of it just now. Lord help him, but how did he learn to give up the person who had become his closest friend—his dearest love?

Perhaps this separation was for the best. Perhaps time would ease the strain and heal them both. Perhaps she would return with some understanding of his predicament, or at least able to accept the distance he must put between them just now.

He had never been a believer that absence made any heart grow fonder, however. He thought the opposite true. And he wondered now if he had just added to his mistake of trusting her too much by not trusting her at all.

"Olivia, my love!"

With an exhaled breath that was half relief and half sob, Olivia leapt from the coach and ran up the steps of her home to her mother's plump, outstretched arms.

"Oh, Mother, I have made such a wretched wreck of things," she said, and then clasped her mother in a hard hug.

Lady Russell held on to her daughter for a moment, clutching her tightly, wondering what had gone wrong. And then she held her daughter away. "Whatever it is, it can wait for a cup of tea. Nothing ever looks so bad over hot tea, my love. Now, come and shake off you dust and then we shall be cozy."

Half an hour later, Olivia sat before a blazing fire in her mother's sewing room, a room that had always been a sanctuary. Decorated in rose hues and cream satins, the room held a feminine grace and comfort with thick Aubusson rugs, comfortable chairs, and velvet pillows. Olivia's tea grew cold in its rose-patterned china cup as her story spilled out in a jangled telling.

She knew that she jumped about as she told it, and she wished she could paint her own role as less in the wrong than she had been. But she confessed her guilt in gossiping, and in betraying Duncastle's trust.

With eyes glittering with tears, she looked up at her mother. "I fear I have acted so very badly."

Lady Russell sat in silence a moment. Silver touched the brown curls that peeked out from under a fetching, lace-trimmed white cap. Her figure had thickened, giving her a comfortable, matronly appearance, but her brown eyes were still clear and alert and her smile was still quick and soft.

She sipped her tea, and then gave her daughter a level look. "My dear, if Duncastle's love can so easily be broken, it is not much of a love, now is it?"

Picking up her cold tea, Olivia stared into the milky liquid. She had expected understanding, at the least. A pale, plump hand covered hers and Olivia looked up.

"Oh, my dear, I do not mean to cast your spirits even lower. You must try to remember that it always looks dark at the bottom of a well, but that is because we are looking down into the pit and not up at the sky. What you need most at this moment is to rest, and you need time to put everything back into perspective."

"But what if I have ruined everything?"

Lady Russell took Olivia's cup and set it aside, and then

she took Olivia's hands in hers. She could remember all too well the difficulty of marriage, of adjusting to another person. It had seemed impossible that first year. And there had been other years it had seemed even more impossible.

"You have admitted that you wronged him, and I must say he sounds as if he is making much too much out of this. But, my dearest, marriage is a living thing. It has to be remade constantly, which is both a great trial and a blessing in that it means there is always another day to deal with things. But you are not in any frame of mind to know anything at this instant. You are exhausted from your travels and your troubles. So, for tonight, there is to be no more talk—or thought. Tonight, you are at home and so you must enjoy my company. Now, let me tell you all the news you have missed."

Frowning, Olivia wanted to demand instead that they talk of her marriage. It seemed critical that she sort through the confusion in her head. But as her mother spoke of inconsequential things—of how Squire Merritt's favorite mare had foaled twins, how Mrs. Hammersmith-Fellows had finally had to bring a relative to live with her, and how the formal gardens had been done over into a meadowland—Olivia did begin to feel better.

The soothing bits of conversation flowed over her, connecting her again to a world where things ran in orderly patterns. She could smile even at her mother's small jokes, and she knew that she had done the right thing in coming home.

With a smile and a warm hug, her mother sent Olivia to her old room to rest and then change for dinner. And Olivia found herself able to do so without the hot tears that had cooled on her cheeks on the journey from London.

At dinner, her father came in with a thunderous scowl and demanded to know what was amiss with her and Duncastle that she should arrive without warning to them. However, a short exchange of hushed whispers between Lady Russell and her husband left him still frowning, but saying he would leave it to the ladies to deal with. He then gave Olivia a gruff hug, and spent the rest of dinner complaining of the economy, the war, and local politics.

Lady Russell tolerated these condemnations with detached comments, and guided the conversation back to safer topics of Lord Russell's upcoming trip north to buy new livestock, and when they might plan to visit London that spring.

For the first time, Olivia saw her parents not from the view of a child, but from that of a woman who had her own life and problems. She marveled at how they seemed so different, and yet had found common ground between them. And she wondered if this was what came from having to struggle for a marriage? Perhaps marrying for love had given her too high an expectation of what her life would be? Perhaps she would have done better to settle for someone whom she liked, and with whom she might have built something stronger than an infatuation?

However, after dinner her mother would hear no questions from her, but sent her to bed with a kiss and a sleeping draft should Olivia have need of it. In her old room, tucked into her bed, Olivia found that sleep came easily and deeply for her.

The following morning she dressed and came downstairs, grateful for her mother's wisdom in delaying any discussion. Sleep had given her more than rest. She had woken to sunshine and the feeling that perhaps she had made too large an issue out of what should have been a small matter. However, she could not forget that in London it had felt as if her world was coming apart at the seams. She could not forget the ice in Duncastle's stare.

That memory—and the swamp of feelings that came with it—sent her to find her mother at once.

Her mother always took her breakfast in her rooms. So Olivia made her way down the hall and knocked on the door. She heard her mother's voice and entered to find that lady still in bed, with a tray beside her and toast crumbs scattered across bed linens and a ruffled dressing gown.

She also found her father standing beside the bed, his wife's hand in his and a warm smile on his face. After kissing her hand, Lord Russell turned from his wife and strode toward the entrance. He stopped to give Olivia a kiss on the cheek, and whispered in her ear, "Just tell me if you want me to shoot the fool for you."

With a flick of his finger upon her cheek, he was gone.

Olivia turned to her mother, a little surprised. She had always thought that her parents had married by arrangement only, but she could not mistake the affection she had just witnessed in her mother's eyes and in her father's touch. What else had she missed seeing as a child? How was it that she never realized that her parents held deep affection for each other?

Sitting up in her bed, Lady Russell waved away her fussing maid, and then patted the bed beside her. "Come and give me a kiss, darling girl. Have you eaten? Fisher, bring another pot of hot chocolate and toast for Olivia, please. No, do not shake your head and tell me you cannot eat, Olivia. We all must eat. And you are too thin. Now, come and sit beside me."

Olivia did as she was bid and when the maid had left, Lady Russell took her daughter's hands and then said, "Now, tell me, how important is it that you love Layton?"

FIVE

Blank of mind, Olivia stared at her mother, then stammered out, "Of course it is important that I love him."

"And is it also important that he loves you in return? Do you demand that of him?"

Olivia frowned. "Well, yes. I mean . . . is that not what is supposed to happen?"

Lady Russell smiled. "In a perfect world, it would follow that love begets love. Unfortunately, it is often those things we most insist upon happening, and which do not, that bring us the most grief."

Straightening as she sat across from her mother, Olivia sank deeper into the soft feathers of the mattress. "Do you mean I am expecting too much of my husband to desire his love?"

"Oh, I know it sounds confusing. But, my dear, all I am trying to say is that you must decide what is most important to you—to love, or to be loved. It is something we all seem to have to decide at one point in our lives."

Olivia dropped her stare to the fine linen upon the bed. She pulled her hands from her mother's grasp and smoothed the creases left by sleep and dreams. Her thoughts spun and she knew only that this seemed a decision she did not want to make. One she felt incapable of making. Her mother's touch, the brush of lace across her skin, drew Olivia's gaze up again.

With a soft smile of sympathy, Lady Russell took her daughter's hand. "I was younger than you when I married, you know. Only eighteen. And I had so many dreams. So many ideas of things I thought were supposed to happen." She gave a small sigh and shook her head. "My wedding day—the day that was supposed to be so happy—was miserable. While the day that you were born—a day that had terrified me in advance—surprised me by being one of the happiest of my life."

Olivia glanced down at the hand that clasped hers, a hand that had held her and offered her comfort since before she could remember. "So I am expecting too much?"

"Oh, my dear, you can expect happiness. You should. But you must also search within yourself for where your happiness is best found. It was after you were born that I had my most unhappy times, for along with all the things I thought should happen, something quite unexpected occurred. I fell in love with my husband."

"But . . . was that not wonderful?"

Lady Russell's maid returned with a black, lacquered tray that held a silver pot of hot chocolate, a rack of toast, and two china cups. She set the tray on the bed, gave a small curtsy, and then took the old tray and herself away again.

Sitting up to pour the steaming chocolate, Lady Russell said, "Loving someone is wonderful. But feeling unloved is not. However, I am deeply grateful that I had to learn to love without asking anything in return. For I found, my dear, that far more came to me when I expected nothing than ever did when I demanded everything. I found my happiness in giving—not just to Russell, but to you, and to others. And I found that any time I began to feel sorry for myself, I could instead do something for someone else and receive such joy. But I know this is not a path for everyone—it can be as rocky as the shore cliffs, and just as difficult to tread."

Sipping her chocolate, Olivia thought about this. The frothy liquid teased her nose with its sweet aroma and went down with a comforting warmth. She wished that she was a child still and sitting here with her mother with the untried confidence of youth, instead of a very confused twenty-five with a heart torn by doubt and fear.

"So I ought to love Layton no matter how he treats me— even if he now no longer cares for me?" she asked, still struggling with her mother's words and wishing for simple advice to fix everything instead of these riddles.

Lady Russell's smile deepened so that the lines around her eyes creased. "Let us not talk of things you ought to do, or even what you feel is supposed to be, but why not look at what choices you have. It is always a choice to love. That is why I asked you how important it was to you. I had to decide which mattered most—loving my husband, or finding love from someone else. Even my own parents told me that if I found my husband's behavior to be intolerable, I should leave him and go to them."

"And you chose not to? Because you loved him?"

"Oh, at times I felt so hurt, so abandoned, that I almost could have murdered him. Other times, I felt a pitiful, sorry wretch. But he had never been dishonest about who he was. Nor was he unkind. However, I loved him, and it tore me apart that I could not seem to make him love me in return.

"And then one night, when you were ten, I finally decided that I could bear his indifference no longer. I swore I would leave. I would take you and go to my parents. I knew it would be a scandal to separate, but I no longer cared about that. But then you came to me."

Lady Russell's eyes softened with memory. "You had a toothache and were horribly cross that night, and you wanted me to hold you and yet could not bear to be touched. It took your nurse, myself, and two maids to finally coax you back to your bed. Then I went to my room to fetch my softest shawl for you—you always loved to have something with my scent upon it. And when I returned, your father was standing over your bed, your hand in his, looking down at you with such love in his eyes . . ."

Her voice faded with a sigh.

Olivia swallowed the lump that had risen to her throat. She could not recall the incident, but she could picture a younger copy of her mother—her brown hair untouched by gray, her figure not so plump, her face unlined—and she could imagine how she must have felt to see the man and child she loved in the candlelight. It was a sight for which her heart ached.

Straightening, Lady Russell sniffed and went on. "It is

odd that life seems to become so clear and certain in moments such as that. In that instant, I knew if I chose to shut my heart, to protect it, I should rob not only myself but you as well. And I knew with certainty that what I wanted most was to love my husband." Her smile widened. "Just as I loved you, even when you were impatient and demanding and upset that your tooth hurt."

Olivia pushed off the bed and paced a distracted step away. "But how do you love someone who will not allow it? How do you break down a wall, such as that which Duncastle has put up against me?"

Setting aside her cup, Lady Russell rose and came to her daughter. She took away Olivia's cup and set it on the dresser, then put an arm around her daughter's waist.

"My dear, I wish I could give you every answer you crave. But I can only tell you what I learned, and that is that love—real love—asks nothing in return. Not even to be accepted. It simply exists. But such a love works its own miracles, if you believe in it and allow it to nourish your heart. It is not always easy, particularly when someone does nothing but push away your offerings. But I found the rewards of a loving heart in the giving, more so than in any taking."

Staring at the warmth and happiness shining in her mother's eyes, hope flared in Olivia, only to be shadowed an instant later by doubt. Could she give such love without expecting its return? She had fallen in love with Layton almost from the first moment she had seen him, and he had seemed to return her sentiment. Could she now love him, even if his feelings had cooled? Or had she fallen in love with him because he adored her?

She did not want to think of herself as being so shallow that she could only love those who most loved her, but she knew that she had to be very, very honest with herself. And she did not know if she had her mother's inner strength or compassion.

Her mother's arm tightened about Olivia again, and Olivia leaned into that contact and warmth, letting it soothe the hurt inside her.

Then Lady Russell said, her voice cheerful, "But do not think that you must decide your whole life in this instant.

You have come home for a visit, and I intend to be greedy about taking up your time. I can love you with a free heart, my dear, but I can also ask to enjoy your company. So help me choose a dress to wear and then I shall show you about the new gardens. And I must take you for a visit to the Fusthams'. Julia would take it badly if you did not pay a call upon her, you know."

And so it was that Olivia's day filled with things to do and people to see. She had no time for her own thoughts, and not a moment, until she fell into bed that night, to think of her husband or her problems with him. But as her head sank against the soft down pillow, she stared up at the shadowed canopy overhead and wondered what Layton was doing. And if he missed her as much as she missed him.

The next day Olivia rose and found more visits planned, and a shopping expedition to Teignmouth, the nearest town, which also lay on the main road to London.

She had no time to ponder her mother's words, and when she protested this, Lady Russell only patted her hand and said, "You will know what is right for you to do when you need to know it."

Her father was even less helpful, for he acted as if nothing had ever happened—not her marriage, and not her sudden return. He went out shooting with his dogs, or to walk his estate, and invited Olivia to ride with him as if she still were a girl, living at home.

All of it left Olivia half wishing she could cling to this illusion that she was still unmarried and untroubled, and half desperate to sort out the turmoil inside her.

She had thought she would find comfort at home, and she had. But she found also a growing sense of loss, of missing Layton, of wishing a dozen times a day that she could share some little moment with him.

The Fusthams' spaniel had a new litter of pups, black and white jesters with floppy ears, eager tongues, and white needle teeth that they tried upon anything. As they tumbled over Olivia's lap and each other, her heart tightened with the wish that Layton could see them, and that he might want to pick one from the litter to be their dog.

At Squire Merritt's, the sight of the twin colts struggling

to handle their long legs and managing to look ridiculous instead of like the elegant creatures they would one day become, made her laugh. And then she glanced around her, thinking that it would be so wonderful to meet Layton's eyes and see her own delight mirrored there.

Would she ever do so again? Had this fracture between them started them on a path to grow apart? Had some link been broken that could never again be mended, only lived with?

On her fifth day home, after a restless night, she rose early, dressed in a high-necked green woolen gown, threw a gray cloak over her shoulders, and took herself down to the beach. The cliff footpath, narrow and steep, led from the house down to Meadfoot Beach—as difficult as her mother had mentioned, but Olivia knew it so well that she scrambled over the rocky track as surefooted as a smuggler's pony.

Since the war with France had begun, the Channel Fleet that blockaded the French ports sometimes anchored in the wide harbor of Torbay, within easy sight. In fact, it was diplomatic matters with the fleet that had drawn Duncastle here last year, and which had led to Olivia meeting him. But today, other than for a plaintive, crying seagull, she had the sea and sand to herself.

Waves hushed up to the shore, quiet and low, as if the sea had not yet woken. A cool fog hugged the bay, turning the sky as gray as the water, hiding the sun, and making it impossible to see any white sails upon the horizon, or even to glimpse the high cliffs that sheltered this scallop of sand and rocks.

Olivia had worn walking boots, but now she sat down and took them off. Undoing her garters, she pulled off her stockings and walked barefoot on the sand, letting the coarse, chilled grains squish between her toes. A soft breeze ruffled her curls, weaving into them the sting of salt and the sharp smell of sea.

Lifting her face to the breeze, she closed her eyes.

Her mind emptied at last. She let go of the confusion, the hurt, the dark fears that she had held so close for the past few days. Her thoughts drifted, and she looked past them and into her heart for her answers.

Slowly, like the mist clearing before the warmth of sunlight, a glimmering of her deepest desires stirred.

Yes, she wanted Layton's arms around her. She wanted to share his life. But even more, she wanted to love him. She wanted *her* arms around him. And she saw with a flush of shame how badly she must have wounded him for him to wish to shut her out.

She did not yet know if she could undo what had been done. And she wondered still if, each time he turned from her, it might chip away at the love that she held for him. But perhaps she could grow stronger in her love? More accepting. More giving.

At least she knew one thing clearly. She needed to give of herself. And she wanted to give to Layton so much that it filled her heart with an aching joy.

Only how? How did she offer up a bridge between them?

Opening her eyes again, she wiggled her toes into the sand and listened to the hushed waves. As difficult as the cliff path, her mother had called this choice to love. Yet, she did not find that path so difficult. Perhaps she could do this.

A flash of white in the sand caught her eye and she bent down to pull loose a shell. Water and time had worn it smooth, and into the shape of a heart.

Closing her hand around it, she took it as a sign. An omen. An inspiration.

Valentine's Day was less than a fortnight away. She could be back in London within two days, and then she would need every moment after that to put her plan into action. She would show Layton just how much she did love him. She would make him realize the truth. And then all would be well.

With a skip, she hurried back toward the cliff path, eager to get home, her heart beating fast and determined that she would at least put up a fight for her husband's love.

Olivia arrived back in London far later in the day than she had hoped, exhausted from traveling, and her temper worn to the snapping point by not one but two delays. First a wheel had come loose. Thankfully, the coachman had noted its wobble at a stop in Crewkerne, and a blacksmith had been found to repair the axle. But the delay cost three hours. And then, just outside Sherborne, one of the wheelers had gone lame, and the coachman had had to slow the team to a walk until the village where a change of horses could be made.

So it was well into the evening on the second day of travel that she arrived and found that Duncastle was not even at home.

Disappointment pulled at her, under fatigue and hunger, and she tried to keep to her thoughts of love and not to mind that he was not here to be loved. She had not written him of her plan to return, after all. So why should he be waiting by the fire for her? No doubt he had more important things to which to attend.

She tried not to wish that she was the most important thing to which he could attend.

At once she chided herself for already expecting things to be as she wanted them. To atone for her lapse, she busied herself with directing her maid to unpack, and then after a hasty tray in her room, with tea and cold chicken and a sliver of pigeon pie, she summoned Henderson to her in the drawing room.

She paced nervously as she waited for the butler, twisting her wedding ring, butterflies tumbling in her stomach as if it were spring already.

When the butler came into the room, his face impassive, Olivia turned to him. "Henderson, there is something I need for you to do for me, but first you must swear yourself and the staff to utter secrecy. Can you do that? Even from his lordship?"

Surprise and hesitancy showed on Henderson's long face, and Olivia could well imagine that he must be weighing his loyalty to his master against his allegiance to her.

"Oh, please, do say you will help, Henderson. It is nothing bad, I assure you. And I very much hope it shall be something wonderful with your aid."

He glanced at her again, worry shadowing his eyes. Then he fixed his stare on a point above Olivia's right shoulder.

"I live to serve this house and to make it a happy home, my lady."

Olivia let out a deep breath. "Oh, thank you. Thank you, Henderson. And now, do you know how to procure a large quantity of sand?"

Layton trudged up the steps to his home, his soul weary and his head aching. It had been another too-long meeting with the Prime Minister, Lord Albers, Lord Cornwallis, and Lord Grenville of the Foreign Office, as well as others, to discuss the continuing negotiations with France.

Rumors had reached London that Bonaparte was sending his own brother, Joseph, to continue hammering out the treaty work that had begun last October. Layton could not help but feel this meant, at last, that the French honestly intended peace. But others argued that too many concessions were being asked for, and that Joseph Bonaparte would be even more difficult to deal with than Guillium.

There had been times this past week that Layton had wanted to consign the entire lot of arguing, arrogant idiots to the devil. He had no patience when consideration of national pride was put ahead of men's lives, and he felt as if there was little he could do to influence the situation for the better.

He tried not to think of the empty home that waited for him. That he could not even reach for Olivia, to tell her of his troubles, to hold her, to ease his soul in her arms.

He knew that her presence—or the lack of it—should not matter so much. He had lived before he had met her. He was a man of the world, a peer of the realm, and if he wanted a woman badly enough he could find a hundred in London.

But he did not want a woman. He wanted Olivia.

And he could not trust himself with her. Heaven help him, but how had he become such a dull fellow that he could only think of politics, and only wish to talk of them? Why could he not have taken more interest in Olivia, and in her life?

The porter let him into his house, and then took his hat, gloves, cane, and coat. He started up the stairs, the carpet soft and silent under his black evening slippers, but Henderson's discreet cough made him hesitate and turn.

"Good evening, my lord. I thought you would wish to know that her ladyship has returned."

Excitement sparked inside Layton like the flare of fire from a half-dead ember. He crushed it at once. His head was too full of state secrets and the urge to talk to someone, to unburden his mind, lay too strong inside him. If he saw her, he might let something slip, and he would not do that to her or to himself. What a tangle he had made of his life.

Offering up a polite, false smile, he said, "Thank you, Henderson." He started up the stairs again, then stopped and turned back. "Is she . . . does she look well, Henderson?"

The butler hesitated a moment, indecision strong on his features, then said, "She seemed very well, my lord."

Layton's heart tightened. What had that hesitation meant? There was something that the man was not saying. Layton was too much the diplomat not to sense unspoken thoughts. But the words conveyed struck him even harder.

She looked well.

She must not have missed him.

He was happy that she had enjoyed her trip, but now he saw what an idiot he had been. He had pushed her away, and she seemed content with that state between them. *So this is how a marriage becomes a counterfeit of love,* he thought.

Rousing himself, he bade Henderson a good night and went to his room. He had to force himself not to look at the door that connected to Olivia's room, not to think how soft and warm she would feel in his arms, not to ache for her touch, not to desire her kisses.

It would become easier over time to put her from his thoughts if he could first put her even farther from his arms.

SIX

Selecting an invitation at random from the pile beside her breakfast plate, Olivia slid her thumb under the red seal, snapped it open, and then spread open the sheet of paper to stare at the writing without interest. Then she set it aside on the stack that awaited replies.

Pale sunlight drifted into the breakfast room through the large windows that overlooked the back garden. She had dressed with care in a gown that Layton had once complimented her on, a long-sleeved gown with a pattern of flowers and leaves on cream cotton. It looked well, she thought, against the cream of the room and the pale, winter greenery of the garden. But would Layton even come downstairs to glimpse her?

He had not come to her last night. And she had struggled not to fall into that well of self-pity again. Why should he come to her, after all? Simply because she had come home? Because he missed her? But, of course, he had not.

And she caught her thoughts before they spiraled down, and tried again to empty her mind.

She must stop trying to think his thoughts for him. It would drive her insane if she kept guessing at his intentions. She must focus instead on her own. On her love for him. On the invitations that had been left unopened in her absence. And on her plans for Valentine's.

But what if it does not work out?

No, she would not think that, she corrected herself. She was doing this to express her love, and not to expect things from him. But the desire for him kept slipping back into her heart as a dull, aching longing.

The soft click of the door latch startled Olivia from her thoughts and into dropping a letter into her tea. As she fished the letter from the tan liquid, Layton came in, and then hesitated.

He looked more handsome than she had remembered, his shoulders broader, his features even more arresting. That sense of masculine grace and power inherent in him swept into the room with him, and her heart skipped a beat. She had missed having that near to her. But she saw other things that tugged at her heart even more.

He wore a teal coat that brought out the green in his eyes, only those eyes seemed dulled with worry, and the thumbprint of fatigue smudged his eyes.

"Do I intrude?" he asked, his tone revealing only a cautious neutrality.

She fixed a determined smile in place. "Don't be silly—of course you do not," she said, and then bit her lip for how critical and sharp she sounded to herself. She tried again with a softer tone. "Shall I ring for hot coffee? The kippers are rather nice this morning, and Cook would do up fresh eggs for you, if you like."

He glanced at her, one eyebrow lifted, looking as wary as a wild animal, then he sat down and took up his paper. "Coffee is all I require, but thank you."

She busied herself with sorting invitations, for it gave her something for her hands to do, and she racked her brains for something else to say. Something safe. Something that was not a desperate, "Why do you not love me any longer?"

"Were you busy while I was away?" she asked.

He glanced at her over his paper. "The usual."

When he said nothing further, her own stare fell and her cheeks warmed. Of course. He did not trust her. Her heart beat faster and the pain washed over her again like a wave breaking over her, pulling her under.

Pressing her lips tight, she pushed away the hurt. *I will love him no matter how horrid he is,* she vowed, back teeth clenched.

Then she pulled in a deep breath, and began to chatter.

She told him of the puppies she had seen. And how good it had been to go home. About the twin foals—so unusual for a mare to give birth to twins and have both live. She spoke of things and people which could not possibly interest him, but which filled the strained silence in the room.

He sat behind his paper, and gradually her words dried up. He must think her a woman whose tongue ran on wheels.

So she stopped talking and sat in silence, going over the invitations again with blank eyes. She was not doing this well, so far, she feared.

He rose at last and she dared not look up, but then he asked, "There is to be a party tonight to bid the Comte Guillium farewell. May I count on your attendance?"

She glanced up at him. There was no interest in his voice. Only duty. Still, he had at least asked something of her, and she wanted to do something for him. So she put on a smile. "But of course, my lord."

Turning, he started for the door. Halfway across the rose-patterned carpet, he hesitated and turned back. "Olivia, I—"

She looked up, hope lifting inside her. "Yes?"

For an instant some feeling flashed across his eyes, and then vanished. Olivia glimpsed the man she loved in that moment, and then he disappeared again behind walls.

"I have state matters that will require my attention all of today, and I shall be dining at my club tonight. But I shall be home by nine to escort you out."

She struggled to prop her smile back into place, to maintain her composure. She was not going to make a scene that would leave her feeling horrible about herself, and which would only drive him further from her side.

"Oh, that is no matter to me. I have plenty to occupy myself with. La, how these affairs do stack up when one is gone but a short time."

She took up another invitation and pretended to give it her entire attention, even though the hurt pounded inside as if he had sliced open her heart. He wanted her to go with him for public affairs, but he had just made it clear to her that their private lives were to be quite separate.

Oh, Mother, how did you ever learn to do this? she thought.

After a moment of silence, she heard the door latch click open and close. She looked up then to stare at the empty room.

She loved this man. More than anything, she loved him. But how did love survive with only itself to nourish it?

Within the week, Olivia discovered part of her answer. Keeping busy helped. Plans for their anniversary on Valentine's distracted her from that horrible pity for herself she was so tired of indulging. She had occupation. She had purpose. And she had already started to think what she might plan to do next for Layton, for she liked this feeling that she was doing something to please him. And it was something she enjoyed, as well.

However, she had found it a struggle to go anywhere with him. It felt so odd to force a cheerful, smiling face. It felt even worse to have to meet Lady Albers again, and to turn away from that lady's attempt to make friends with her.

It was bad enough to have to endure the distance between herself and Layton, and to have to endure the whispers she heard around herself. But when Lady Albers came to her, to pat her shoulder and sympathize for how horrid men were, and to offer to listen to everything, all Olivia's troubles nearly tumbled out.

She caught herself only at the last instant, and forced herself to smile and remark that everything was as it should be between herself and her husband. And then she had turned and walked away.

That action cost her dearly, for she felt as if she had stranded herself in an ocean of strangers. But she had proven to herself that Layton could trust her. Now, if only she could make *him* see that.

And so she thought back to her mother's words, searching for some clue in them for a guide on this path, and she recalled how her mother had talked of doing something for others. Only Olivia had no idea what she even had to offer.

She looked first to the other ladies for examples, and found herself repelled by their avid consumption of scandal and their preoccupation with themselves, their positions, and their jewels. So she looked instead to the young ladies. Not to the confident beauties who left Olivia feeling inadequate and as unattractive as a maypole, but to the shy ones, the unpopular ones, the ones who reminded her of herself when she had first come to London.

Slowly, she found that she could talk to them and to their mothers, and she discovered she had learned a surprising amount about Society in her time within it. She could offer the advice to use the tailor Stultz for the making of the most fashionable riding habits. She could warn against those gentlemen who were seeking a fortune rather than a wife, and she could recommend the dancing instructor who had taught her. She found a real delight in trying to put these girls at their ease.

She realized then that she would like a daughter of her own someday. But, for that, she was going to have to find a way to coax her husband back to her bed. Back to being her husband. So she redoubled her efforts at loving him, and she put all her hopes with the thought that the day set aside for love would prove to him that she cared for him more than anything.

Layton watched his wife as if observing a stranger. She had become one. She smiled. She treated him with respect. And yet he could not help but feel the growing chasm between them. She went her own way, and he went his. And every day he began to hate his path even more.

It made it no better to realize that this situation was of his own making. He did not know how to unmake it. He had failed in so much it seemed, and now he felt himself failing even worse in his duties to Olivia.

Perhaps he should simply go to her and take his rights as her husband, and demand the obedience she had promised in her vows. But she already did what he asked of her, and the thought of going to her bed, of using her body as if she meant no more to him than a common strumpet, repelled him. He loved her. Only he did not know how to trust her— nor himself. If he went to her now, with his need for her so raw, he might end up just as his father had—a man who loved too much, too unwisely. How did he give of himself without giving his soul away?

And so he watched her.

She moved so confidently now in this world, seeking out the younger girls just come to London, showing them kindness and smiles. He ached to have those smiles—real smiles—turned toward him. But she did smile at him. A stiff, practiced smile that she seemed to keep just for his use.

And she seemed always to have something to do.

He had arranged on several nights to dine at home, thinking that would offer a chance to talk, to be together, only to find that she had gone out. He had taken her to the theater, only to have her leave his side as soon as the interval arrived so that she could talk to someone else.

She never complained that he did not seek out her bed. And it began to eat at him that since coming back to London, she seemed to be wearing a mask. That was when the suggestions crawled into his mind that perhaps this happiness of hers came from her having an affair.

He could find no real evidence. No one gentleman to suspect. But he did suspect. He knew it was madness to do so, but still the jealousy crept into him.

He had seen her go through the morning post, pulling out letters before he glimpsed them. When he had asked her about them one morning, she had said at once that they were simply bills. Then she smiled and fled. He had frowned over that. He had made her a generous allowance, so why should she be secretive about mere duns from tradesmen?

And there was an air in the house that disturbed him. The servants whispered in hushed tones that stopped whenever he entered a room. Something was going on. Something was being kept from him. He could only imagine one thing that could be.

An affair.

Pacing his room in his breeches and shirtsleeves late one night, the awareness of Olivia's bedchamber, empty and silent, ate into him. She rarely came home these days earlier than dawn. Whom did she smile at and dance with tonight?

Whom did she talk to now that he had made it impossible for her to talk with him?

And then he stopped and stared at his own reflection in his mirror. Dear God, how had this gone from a rift between them to a gulf? He had started this all with his too-strong accusations, and now he was making it worse by choosing to believe the worst of her. How could he believe that she would play him false?

He recognized the madness then, the distortion in his own thinking. He had made Olivia into a woman like his mother, rather than looking at her as a unique person in her own right. He had judged her by unfair standards and they both had suffered for it.

Well, he could change that.

He could make amends for such terrible doubts as he had had of her. And with their anniversary a scant two days away, he had a good enough idea of how he could do that.

Still pacing, he began to lay out his strategy for how he would surprise his wife, and sweep her off her feet as he had once before. After all, if he had won her heart once, there had to be a chance that he could do so again.

SEVEN

"A list of invitations to go out, my lord?" Henderson asked, his expression startled.

Layton continued holding out the sheet of vellum with the guest list. "Yes. Invitations. And they must go out today. It's short enough notice, but I daresay most will attend." He gave a small smile. His political connections had proved useful in one respect—the Duchess of Devonshire herself had offered her support when he had told her his plan. His notion for a ball on St. Valentine's Day had appealed to her romantic nature, as he thought it would. She had offered at once to dragoon her friends into attending, ensuring the evening's success.

And how could any woman not be flattered and put into a forgiving mood when such a fete was being held in her honor?

Henderson glanced at the list, his long face pulled into a tight frown as if his smallclothes had suddenly shrunk to half their size. He opened his mouth as if to say something, then seemed to think better of it and stiffened like a corpse. "Very good, my lord."

"Oh, and, Henderson, not a word about this to her ladyship. It is to be a surprise for her."

"A surprise, my lord?" Henderson's narrow face took on an even more pained expression.

"Henderson, is there something you wish to say about this?" Layton asked. It surprised him that his butler—a paragon of self-effacing servitude—should act so odd. Was the fellow sickening with something? He looked more than a little ill.

After clearing his throat, Henderson seemed to recover. His expression resumed its normal lack of emotion, although spots of color stung his pale cheeks, and distress haunted his pale eyes.

"My lord, it is not my place to comment on your lordship's actions. However, I should be derelict in my duty if I failed to mention to you that her ladyship . . . she, well, allow me to phrase it this way, I believe there has been some mention of other plans she might have for that night. I certainly do not wish to put myself forward, my lord, but might I perhaps recommend that a brief discussion of this between yourself and her ladyship might not be such a very bad thing?"

Layton stared at the fellow, astonished that his servant should presume to urge any action upon him. In his past year of service, Henderson had hardly ever uttered more than a civil, "yes, my lord," or at most a, "very good, my lord." However, the man had an excellent point. It would do no good to make plans if Olivia failed to keep her part in them. And Henderson certainly had gone out of his way to be diplomatic about this.

Rising from his desk, Layton folded his hands behind his back. "Thank you, Henderson. Your recommendation is noted, and appreciated. Now, you will please carry out my instructions?"

Face wooden, but with an air of relief about him, like a man who had just seen a deep hole open before him and had been able to recover his balance and step away from it, Henderson bowed. "But of course, my lord."

The butler left the room with his expression controlled, his feelings concealed, and leaving Layton with the oddest sense that the fellow had just done his best to drop a most discreet word of warning about something.

Layton pondered this a moment longer, and then went in search of Olivia.

He found her in her sitting room, working on a watercolor. The scene was of the bay near her home, and brought back to him memories of walking along that beach in the moonlight, her laughing as the surf chased them, and of stealing a breathless, salt-tinged kiss just before he asked her to marry him.

As he entered, she looked up and put her brush down, then stood to block his view of the painting.

"Layton . . . my lord, I did not expect you." She fussed with her paint-stained hands. "I fear I am not presentable."

He wanted to take her hands and wipe the blue smudges from her fingers, but he did not know if she would welcome such attentions. So he merely stood there like a schoolboy, wondering how was it that she could look so lovely. So desirable.

"Is there something you wish?" she asked.

He heard the anxiety in her tone and shook himself from his thoughts. "I . . . I wanted to ask if you dine at home the night after tomorrow? On our anniversary."

She glanced away and busied herself with washing her brushes in a glass jar half filled with water. "Yes, I suppose I shall."

Layton watched as the water turned a muddy brown from the mix of too many colors.

Shyly, Olivia glanced up. "Will you dine at home as well, my lord? I mean, that is to say, not that I am demanding your attendance, but perhaps it would be nice to have an evening just for the two of us. If you wish it, that is."

He relaxed into a tentative prayer that things would get better between them, and then he gave a silent thanks to his butler that the fellow had urged him to talk to Olivia. Tomorrow he would stop by the jeweler's to pick up the repaired necklace, and perhaps some other gift for Olivia. She would enjoy the ball. She would be surprised, and she would understand that he did care for her in his own fashion. And they could at last start to mend matters between them.

"Of course I wish it," Layton said.

Olivia's smile widened with the first real delight she had allowed herself to feel in days. Now, all she had to do was keep Layton unaware of what was happening in the ballroom for the next day, and then they would have a perfect evening together. A time for just the two of them. And she would

have a chance at last to lure him back into her arms and
show him how much she truly loved him.

Cupid's day dawned with the threat of rain, but the skies
changed their mind and a sharp wind chased the banks of
gray clouds into scattered puffs of white. Layton had always
left the matter of balls—and what went into them—to
Olivia, and now he found just why he had done so before
this. He tried to leave all to Henderson, but the fellow kept
asking what food should be served, what drink must be purchased, and the whole affair seemed to be taking its toll on
the butler, who looked positively haggard.

Layton made a note to himself to give the staff an extra
holiday. Perhaps he would even take Olivia away for a few
days, when and if this blasted treaty was ever signed. The
talks were due to continue in London for some time, although the French had proposed that better progress would
be made on neutral soil, such as in the Low Countries.

But while Layton did not want to think of treaties and
diplomacy on his anniversary, the foreign minister had other
ideas. Layton found himself kept from home far more than
he would have liked, and unable to spare even a moment to
supervise preparations for his own anniversary ball. He
would have to trust that Henderson could manage.

He did have time to wonder what Olivia was doing that
day, and if she would be pleased. And he made time enough
to stop at Rundell and Bridges to get the silver necklace
they had mended. It glinted in its velvet box, the links once
again whole and locked together. Layton was pleased
enough to select a sapphire broach for Olivia, but at the last
moment he changed his mind and chose instead pearl earrings set in silver that would match the silver necklace. The
earrings were not as costly, but he could picture Olivia wearing them, and the thought of her seaside watercolor made
him choose the gems from the ocean for her.

Olivia herself spent the day fretting over everything. She
had not wanted Layton to see the watercolor before she gave
it to him today as her anniversary present to him. Now she

wondered if she ought to buy him something instead, only she could think of nothing else to give him.

He had four pocket watches already, he did not take snuff, and he did not collect anything. He liked books, she knew, but he bought them to read, not to sit upon the shelf. She went out shopping to see if any new editions could be had, but she found nothing that might please his taste, which left her only with her watercolor to present to him.

Tired from shopping and not buying, she came home to find Henderson waiting for her. All seemed to be in order for the evening. The butler asked discreetly, and with a worried frown, if his lordship had spoken to her, and she smiled at Henderson and assured him that he had and all seemed to be well for this evening. Henderson said that he very much hoped so and bowed himself out.

There was nothing more to do other than to dress, and then to wait, with her watercolor done and hung in the ballroom for tonight, and to hope that Layton would not be too late getting home that night.

In fact, Layton did arrive home late, but in time to change for dinner. He dressed quickly in formal black silk breeches, a black coat, and a richly embroidered waistcoat, done up in a flowered pattern in colored threads. With his palms damp, his pulse quick, he felt as if he were ten years younger and courting his first sweetheart, instead of dressing for dinner with his wife.

The silver necklace lay in its box, given over to Henderson's care, along with the pearls, so that they could be produced for Olivia at a suitable moment tonight.

With a last glance in the mirror at his reflection, and a last hope that Olivia might be pleased with him, Layton went downstairs.

Dinner passed all too slowly, and all too quickly, Olivia thought.

They dined formally, with the footmen carrying in each course and arranging it on the table, and then carrying the dishes out again. Neither she nor Layton ate very much, she noted. And Olivia's throat ached with the desire to ask Layton about his day, only she feared that her questions might return that shuttered look to his eyes. So she spoke of trivialities, of dresses she had seen, of shops, of items she had read in the newspaper.

At last, the puddings came and left the table, and Olivia rose, shaking out her skirts. She had worn a white muslin gown, heavily embroidered with silver around the hem and the bodice. Cut enticingly low, she knew that it revealed a good deal when she stood with the light of a fire behind her, and so now she moved around the dining table and stood before the fireplace that occupied the middle of one wall.

Holding out her hand to Layton, she said, "Come. I have a surprise for you."

For an instant, Layton seemed distracted, but then he rose and took her hand. "For me? Well, I shall have one for you in"—he glanced at the clock on the mantel—"in a quarter hour."

"My surprise first," she told him.

She led him up one flight of stairs and to the ballroom that lay in the adjacent wing at the back of the house.

For a moment as they stood before the wide double doors that led into the ballroom, Layton wondered if she had somehow guessed his surprise. He had intentionally not ordered any decorations, for he had not wanted a parade of flowers and such nonsense to rouse Olivia's suspicions. But had she guessed that others would be arriving within minutes?

"Close your eyes," she ordered, her hands upon the brass doorknobs.

He complied. Perhaps she had his gift in the ballroom, he thought, and then he recalled her watercolor painting. Had she done that for him? And perhaps had it hung here for him to view? Yes, that must be it, he decided, smiling as he heard the doors open. Then he felt her gloved hand slip into his and tug.

She led him forward two steps. Something crunched under his feet and a sharp, salty tang filled the air.

"Open your eyes," she said, her voice low and breathless.

He did so, and his eyes widened in shock.

The ballroom, long and narrow, had been transformed. White sand covered half the floor, and the other half seemed to be a pond. No, he corrected, his eyes narrowing as he studied the scene—it seemed meant to be taken as an ocean.

In fact, he glimpsed the watercolor that Olivia had painted, now hanging near the entrance, and realized that she had had the room made over in its likeness.

Painted waves, like those found upon a stage production rose up against the far wall. A round moon made up of muslin with a reflective candle behind it, hung from the ceiling. The tang in the air came from the smell of kelp and salt, he realized.

He turned to Olivia, who stared up at him, her eyes bright in the dimly lit room. "What on earth have you done? How will our guests ever manage with half the space taken up by water, and the rest only sand to trudge upon?"

Her smile faded. "Guests? What guests?"

He could not keep the impatience from his voice. "Olivia, I invited half of London to a ball for you tonight. Lord, where did Henderson put the musicians?"

"Here, my lord," piped up a voice from the dim reaches of the beachlike room.

Startled, Layton swung around, then glimpsed a fellow with a fiddle stand at the far end of the room to wave his bow. "Shall we begin to play, my lord?"

Layton scowled and started to answer, but Henderson arrived, his face pale, to announce, "My lord, the first guests have arrived. Do you receive them here?"

With a frustrated oath, Layton glanced around him. He took in Olivia's bowed head, he took in the ballroom with its floor of sand and water and dim lighting, and he took in Henderson's nervous fidgeting. For an instant, he thought of sacking the fellow for allowing this to happen. But the man had tried to warn him, had he not, as best as could a servant without giving offense.

Layton threw up his hands. "Well, we cannot very well show them into the library. Bring them on, Henderson. And pour the champagne liberally. It may be the only thing that can get us through this night without utter disaster."

EIGHT

It was an utter disaster, Olivia thought half an hour later. She stood next to her husband, her smile stiff as she welcomed people to her home, when she would much rather wish them to perdition. She watched eyes widen as others saw the room she had meant only for herself and Layton. She listened to nervous titters and huffs of disapproval, and to muttered oaths as gentlemen and ladies trod into a room she had decorated for an intimate evening, not for the comfort of dozens.

It was supposed to be a romantic cove, not an uncomfortable curiosity. And while a few praised such original décor, most stumbled over the sand, looked in desperation for a chair to sit upon and seemed to recall within a quarter hour another event that beckoned their attendance. The footmen tried to serve the champagne and to carry trays of cold food around the room, but they struggled over the sand, tripping and unbalancing trays, sending champagne and delicacies equally into the sand and water.

The room emptied almost as rapidly as it filled, for there was no place to dance, no card table rooms set aside, and the death knell for the evening seemed to come when the dowager Lady Malcolm wandered too close to the pool, created from wood and canvas, and fell in. Two gentlemen fished her out again, and assisted her, dripping and sobbing, from the room. That seemed the signal for one and all to flee, before they, too, suffered a similar fate.

Olivia watched it all, and watched the closed look stiffen

on Layton's face. Embarrassment and irritation with him swirled inside her in a volatile mixture.

She tried to tell herself that she did not care that he had thought to fill their house with his political friends on the one night she had hoped to have his whole attention. But she did care. Only her ill will at his not telling her about this, about ruining her plans, sputtered out when she overheard him tell a guest, "Well, of course it is a unique setting. There is no one in this world quite like my wife."

She could not mistake the glow of pride in his voice, and it brought a sharp reminder to her that Layton was not the only one who had built walls of late.

Yes, he had pulled away from her. In turn—from hurt and fear—she, too, had turned from him. He had stopped talking to her, and rather than reach out to him, rather than act with love and kindness, she had stopped talking to him as well. Tonight would not have happened if she had not attempted to manipulate and manage him. Surprise. Oh, yes, she had wanted to give him a surprise. For her own benefit. Not for his, she realized.

She watched him now as their guests—people of note, of political power, of influence—forced their smiles and departed. She had ruined this evening for him by trying to force her ideas for how they should be together. Her surprise had cost him dearly and had probably put back his career any number of years.

Oh, why had he not at least even dropped a hint to her that this was what he wanted?

At last the nightmare ended. The last guest, Lord Albers, departed, taking Layton with him to see him to his carriage.

Olivia walked around the empty room.

Champagne glasses stuck out from the sand or floated within the platform and canvas that encased the lapping water. She dismissed the servants who remained to sort through the debris, saying tomorrow would be good enough to cart everything away. She thanked the musicians for their efforts, though no one had seemed to notice their music.

And then she tugged off her long white gloves and sat down in the sand to stare up at the candle that flickered behind the muslin moon.

It was not even ten of the clock. It was a time when most successful events had just got under way. It was the most awful disaster of an anniversary, and she did not know how she was ever going to make it up to Layton that she had made his ball into such a mess.

Hearing the scrunch of sand underfoot, she straightened, and then rose as Layton came across the sand toward her.

She could not look up to meet his gaze, and so she stood there, mute, uncertain. Oh, bother, this was how she had got into such trouble, with this fear of saying the wrong thing, and this worry of how he must hate her.

Gathering her courage, she looked up and met his shadowed stare. Her mouth dried. She swallowed, and then said, "I wanted it all to be perfect. I wanted it to remind you of Torbay, and of the night you proposed to me, and I am so very, very sorry. But I seem always to be sorry for something, do I not?"

He stood with his hands behind his back, staring down at her. Then, bringing his hands around from behind him, he thrust two small boxes at her. "Here. This was to be the rest of your surprise, but I hardly think anything can top the earlier shocks."

She winced at his comment, but she took the boxes and opened the longest one. The silver necklace, now whole again, glinted in the artificial moonlight, reminding her of other guilts.

"I . . . I . . ." She looked up at him, at his shadowed face, at those features she loved too well. "I might as well just say it all and have done. I broke your necklace. I am sorry for that, as well. I am sorry for everything, in fact. That I betrayed your confidence. That I am such a horrible wife."

"You are not a horrible wife."

"Am I not? I feel like one. In fact, I do not feel a very good person at this moment. I thought that I was doing all this to show that I loved you, but I think, really, what I wanted was to make you remember that you loved me. I was not looking for what I could do that would be of help to you. If I had, I should have thought of a ball myself, and would have done something splendid to add to your consequence and influence."

He stared at her a moment, his jaw tense, then said, his voice harsh, "Do you think I held this . . . this debacle for myself. For my consequence? I hate these rubbishing affairs. I hate all this maneuvering. All this pleasing of people who must be pleased because they do hold influence. I hate the whole lot of it. But I thought you . . . well, you seemed to have time only for such grand affairs these days. I thought it would please you. That it would—"

He bit off the rest of his words.

She stared up at him, astonished at the raw emotion in his voice. "But I thought you loved your diplomatic work. That you lived for it."

"I live with it. I struggle to make good upon the things my father never could do, and I wish I had been born a farmer." He glanced around at the scenery. "Or even a sailor."

Glancing down at the other box in her hands, she tried to reshape the image of her husband. And then it occurred to her that perhaps that had been part of the problem. Perhaps the image she had of him—and that which he held of her—were only illusions they had shaped and formed, but which did not really matter. Perhaps the art of a good marriage came in letting go of such illusions, and in learning instead of the person underneath the masks.

Suddenly curious, she asked, "Layton, why did you want to give a ball for me?"

He shifted on the sand, as if uncomfortable, and then he gestured to the other box she held. "Are you not going to open it?"

Frowning, she tugged off the ribbon. Her eyes widened as she glimpsed the twin pearl drops. "Oh, Layton, they're lovely. How did you know I have always wanted such a pair?"

He took the box from her. Lifting her chin, he put the pearls on her. His fingers brushed her chin, and then caressed her ears. Liquid heat pooled in her stomach and her pulse fluttered in her throat.

Without a word he took the necklace from its box and tossed the box aside. She started to protest, but he told her to leave it.

When the silver links lay around her neck, he rested his hands on her shoulders, his thumbs lightly stroking the hollow of her throat.

Staring up into his face, she asked again, "Why did you hold this ball? Was it because you love me still? For if you do, I need to hear you say that. I need to hear that you can forgive me, if you can?"

He stared down at her, old fears tightening in his chest. Was he a fool to forgive her, as his father had forgiven his mother for every indiscretion? And then he glanced around the room.

For him, she had brought a beach from Devon to London. And she had done so without letting slip a word about it. His mother never could have carried off such a thing.

Yes, it had been a surprise. A bloody great shock. But suddenly, he no longer cared if such a fiasco cost him anything. If his political career was such a fragile thing, better to let it die now than to forever be nursing it along and struggling to make it thrive.

Glancing back at Olivia, he touched a finger to her cheek. "I thought a ball would please you. I thought—" He broke off, finding it hard to admit his fears. But then he took a breath and said, "I thought I could win back your heart. I think I shall love you forever, Olivia, but can we ever mend the trust between us? Can we?"

She took his face between her hands. "If you can mend my necklace, why can we not also mend our love? Those links are but silver. What links us is far more than that."

He kissed her then, a tentative touch of his lips to hers that fired desire in him. God, he did love her. He would always love her. And faith stirred inside him with the glow of dawn that the fires in their love could heal anything.

Pulling back from her, he went to the ballroom door and closed it. Then he strode back to her side. "My Lady Duncastle, would you care to walk with me upon the beach on this moonlit night?"

He leaned closer to her then, pulling her into his arms, so that he could whisper into her ear, "And would you care, my love, to find out what it is like to make love in moonlight upon a sandy beach?"

Smiling, she wrapped her arms around her husband's neck. "Oh, there are a hundred things I want to discover with you. A lifetime's worth, in fact. But for tonight, let us do whatever you wish, my lord. For I want my giving to be a present of my heart—and my Valentine's gift to you."

THE VALENTINE HUSBAND

Alice Holden

ONE

Lord Markham roared, "What do you mean when you say that Tristan Darius made love to you? Answer me, damn it! Answer me!"

Jenny was too stunned to speak, for her usually indifferent father was pushing his angry face precariously close to hers.

Lady Markham thrust herself between her husband and her daughter and cried, "For pity's sake, Jarvis, stop!"

His wife's entreaty got through to the baron, who backed off, shocked by his own loss of control. Never had he cursed his only child, or sworn at any woman for that matter. But Jenny had admitted to being ruined. Ruined! All his dreams for an advantageous marriage for her and the hopes for a grandson whom he planned to make his heir had been shattered. No decent man would have his daughter now!

Lady Markham led Jenny to the sofa that was situated in an alcove beneath the library's stained-glass clerestory windowpanes. The plump lady eased herself down beside her taller, slimmer daughter.

Still agitated, Lord Markham prowled back and forth across the Persian rug in front of the shelves stacked with leather-bound volumes. He had spent his entire life protecting his family name against any hint of impropriety or scandal. And now Jenny had confessed that five years ago she had been debauched by the most unlikely of seducers, Tristan Darius. The baron's orderly world had suffered a serious chink.

Lord Markham stopped pacing and reached for a walnut

chair with molded saber legs and positioned it before the sofa. He sat down on the red tapestry seat and faced Jenny, whose pretty features mirrored his own handsome masculine ones in a much softer form. She had his dark brown hair and golden brown eyes. Resting his hands on the knees of his broadcloth breeches, he reminded himself that anger simply impaired one's judgment. Recovering as much as was possible under the circumstances of his august dignity, he said in an intentionally reasonable tone, "Jenny, do you know the difference between passionate kisses and improper fumblings and actually being deflowered?" He waited to hear that the daughter he had thought of as an intelligent being was, in fact, a secret peagoose who knew nothing of the mechanics of becoming pregnant.

"Yes, Mama explained the process of getting with child years ago," Jenny said with lowered eyes.

His lordship's tentative hopes that she might, after all, be one of those muddle-headed chits who had no idea from where babies came plummeted.

"You are saying, unequivocally, that Tristan stole your virginity?"

Jenny bit her lower lip. "Yes."

"Why did you not speak up at the time? You could have been married to Tristan Darius these five years. I would have seen to it," the baron said plaintively.

Jenny stared down at the knots of green ribbons that trimmed the bodice of her pale yellow cambric gown. Pulling an excuse from the air, she claimed, "Tristan left for America immediately afterward."

"I never would have expected such perfidious conduct from him," Lord Markham said, addressing his wife. "Tristan Darius was not some petticoat chasing nodcock who tumbled dairymaids in the hay. He was a grown man of impeccable reputation."

"Just so," Lady Markham agreed, but did not take the subject further.

The baron rubbed the ridge of his nose to ease the ache that was developing behind his eyelids. His gaze fell on the mantel clock.

"What a dilemma you have created, Jenny," he moaned.

"Lord Duson will be here within the hour to sign the marriage contract. I cannot foist damaged goods on a lord of the realm. I must find a reason to cancel our verbal agreement before putting pen to paper without divulging that you are sullied."

Jenny felt a stone lift from her heart. Whatever happened now did not matter. She would not have to marry the loathsome Lord Duson.

"You must fall back on the truth, Jarvis," Lady Markham counseled. "Jenny dislikes the marquess. Take on the role of an indulgent father and say you did not realize how set Jenny was against the marriage and will not force her to wed where her heart is not engaged."

Lord Markham gave his wife a dark, incredulous stare. "Never! Duson will think this house is run by petticoat rule."

Lady Markham shrugged. "The only alternative is to confess that Jenny is compromised and hope that the marquess will overlook her youthful indiscretion."

The baron experienced a ray of hope. "Perhaps that would work. Lord Duson is under the hatches and is counting on Jenny's dowry to shore up his property, which frankly is worth saving. It is the reason I accepted his suit."

Jenny's heart dropped. "No!" She had kept her mutinous emotions under wraps until now and had forced herself to be contrite for her sins. But the danger of being forced into an odious marriage had surfaced again. "I can't marry him."

Lady Markham said, "Hush, child," and turned back to her husband. "Of course, Jarvis, you would be taking a risk. Suppose Lord Duson refuses to have her. He is just the sort of man to spread her shame to the world at large. Right now we are the only three people aware that Jenny is blemished. Do you really want to give his lordship the power to bring disgrace upon your good name?" She paused to let her words take root.

Feeling ill-used, Lord Markham stared into space. He was not a care-for-nothing father. Jenny had the best clothes, vouchers to Almack's, and private boxes at Drury Lane and Covent Gardens. He had done his duty and paraded a number of suitors before her. But she had rejected every eligible gentleman. Of course, he now knew the reason. He shuddered. Suppose Jenny had held her tongue and let Duson exercise his right in the marriage bed. Now that would have created a real mare's nest. Duson would have had the union annulled and his own good name would have been dragged unrelentingly through the gossip mills.

The baron got up and carried the saber-legged chair back to its usual position against the wall. Thinking himself the most luckless of fellows, he nevertheless said, "Yes, letting the marquess believe I am nose-led by a female is preferable to unleashing a full-blown scandal against the Markham name."

In the privacy of her bedroom, Jenny was denouncing the baron for having forced her to lie. She didn't like doing it at all. She sat on a chintz-covered window seat and gazed outside toward the green hills and the clusters of trees that made up the terrain of Lindwood, her father's country estate.

The baron could have avoided his upcoming confrontation with Lord Duson if he had not been so cruelly indifferent to her complaints.

From the beginning, Jenny had argued that she did not like the marquess and that the lecherous lord has acted improperly toward her. But Lord Markham had dismissed her importunities as foolish female weaknesses.

He had scoffed, "What does like or dislike have to say to the matter? Marriages have to do with trade-offs involving wealth, land, and titles. You will become a marchioness and gain valuable property for the son you will have, my grandson, who will be my heir, as well. So Duson isn't everything you want. You and he will find a way to deal together after you have made your vows. Once you have produced the male heir and, possibly, a spare, you can lead separate lives."

Hearing the click of the latch, Jenny looked toward the door to the hall. Lady Markham stepped inside with a rustle of brown-checkered tafetta, closed the door, and leaned back against the wooden panels.

"Tristan Darius was never intimate with you, Jenny," she said. "He was in love with Serena from the time he was fourteen and even after she married his brother. It is commonly held that he fled to America because he could not bear to live at Albinore with Gerald, Serena, and their child. He was a man of twenty-two years when you were sixteen. It was not Tristan's style to dally with girls barely out of the schoolroom."

Jenny gave a resigned sigh. The tall, handsome neighbor boy who had grown into a fine young gentleman, and who had been like a hero in a Minerva novel, deserved better than to have had his reputation blackened with a lie. Yet, she could not be sorry. Tristan was dead and past being hurt while she was alive. What else could she do when her father would not budge? Her deception had been necessary to save herself from a horrible fate.

"You won't inform Father, will you, Mama?"

Lady Markham walked up the length of the room and sat down on Jenny's bed.

"I had the opportunity to tell Jarvis, and did not do so. But, Jenny, it is lunacy to deceive your father. What if you meet someone with whom you do fall in love?"

Jenny left the window seat and sat down at her mother's feet on a wooden step stool that she had used when a small child to climb into her bed. She laid a hand on the baroness's knee and said, "If I find someone to love, Father will be so glad to know that I am not truly a fallen woman that he will not be as incensed as he was today."

Perhaps, Lady Markham thought, but Jarvis would not take kindly to having been tricked. She was beginning to regret having been drawn into Jenny's hoax. But she had not realized how set against Lord Duson Jenny had been. Yet, was the child being too finicky? A thirty-four-year-old man was bound to have formed a few alliances with loose women. The marquess did have a reputation as a libertine. He was rumored to have fathered an illegitimate child. But men were judged by less moral standards than women. Producing a bastard was counted as no more than a peccadillo in a peer.

The baroness's curiosity suddenly redirected her thoughts from the marquess's failings to Tristan Darius.

"How ever did you come up with such a Banbury tale?" she asked.

"It was Tristan's cenotaph," Jenny replied.

Lady Markham raised a brow. "Cenotaph?"

"You know, Mama, a monument which is raised to memorialize a family member when the remains are not found. Gerald erected a small marble obelisk near the pond to mark his brother's drowning at sea. I sometimes ride in that direction. Last week when Father had dismissed my every argument against a marriage to Lord Duson, it occurred to me that the marquess would not accept an impure bride, nor would Father with his high sense of honor palm one off on him. I racked my brain for a logical story to convince the baron that I was no longer a virgin. I was beyond hope when fate took a hand. My eyes rested on Tristan's cenotaph and my scheme was born."

The rumble of carriage wheels sent Lady Markham to the window. She pushed aside the lace curtains. A coach with the marquess's crest prominent on the door was rolling through the open gates. "Lord Duson has arrived. I must go below stairs and give your father my moral support. It is the least I can do."

Lady Markham employed Jenny's cheval glass to pat a few stray wisps of her blond hair into place.

"I cannot like your deception, child. Yet, at times it is more prudent to do nothing than to make a move which might make matters worse. For the time being, I shall keep your secret," she said. She gave a last glance in the mirror and swept from the room.

TWO

The November sky was a cloudless blue as Jenny walked toward the woods, swinging a wicker basket on her arm. The wind ruffled the edge of her ruched bonnet, but the matching spencer she wore over her dark blue wool gown kept out the coolness of the late fall afternoon. She saw a red flash among the withered leaves on a nearby oak tree.

Jenny smiled. Amy Darius was hiding in the branches. She had befriended the precocious six-year-old when some months ago Amy's father Gerald Darius had run off with his mistress. Humiliated by her husband's abandonment and in dire straits financially, Serena Darius had fallen into a decline and left her small daughter virtually unsupervised.

Stopping under the tree, Jenny was pelted from above with acorns.

Looking up, she said, "Come down here, you little hoyden, before you break your neck."

"Oh, Jenny, I hoped you'd think I was a squirrel," the little girl lamented as she agilely climbed down.

When Amy's booted feet touched the ground, Jenny gathered her into a hug and smoothed back the child's blond hair from her forehead.

Dusting off the red skirt of Amy's long-sleeved woolen dress, Jenny said, "Climbing trees is not a fitting pastime for a young lady."

Amy screwed up her small nose. "Pooh, boys get to have all the fun. I am not going to be a lady when I grow up.

I'm going to be a knight and ride around the countryside
on a white charger slaying dragons."

"Well, Sir Knight, you had better put on your cape before
you take a chill," Jenny said, reaching for the hooded cloak
which had been discarded on the ground.

Amy slipped her hands through the armholes, and Jenny
tied the black frayed ribbons at the neckline. The dark colored garment needed a good sponging. But Jenny knew that
Pecks and Mrs. Druback, the two old retainers with whom
the child's mother was making do in the manor house, were
overworked. Those servants who had been employable had
found new positions when Serena had failed to pay them
their quarterly wages. Only the few workers who were too
old to go elsewhere remained on the estate.

Jenny picked up her basket from the ground. "Come,"
she said to the child, "you can help me gather nuts from
beneath the big hickory tree near the sheep's meadow."

Amy fell in step beside Jenny. "I looked for you yesterday, but you didn't come for a walk," she said.

"The baron was here from London. He kept me at home
on some family business," Jenny explained.

"Did the business have to do with Lord Duson? I saw
his rig turn in at your gate. I don't like him. He comes to
visit Mama a lot since Papa left."

Jenny greeted this information in a thoughtful silence.
Gerald and Lord Duson had been friends. The marquess was
probably offering Serena comfort to assuage the heartbreak
brought on by Gerald's desertion. *Better her than me,* Jenny
thought, shivering inwardly. She never again wanted to be
in the position of having to fend off the revolting marquess's
roving hands.

"Did it?" Amy pressed.

"Hmm?" Jenny asked, having lost track of their conversation.

"Did Lord Markham's business have to do with Lord
Duson?"

"Yes," Jenny said, "but it's all settled. My father has returned to London to take up his duties with the Prince."

Walking on, they stopped beneath the hickory tree and

gathered up the few nuts they found on the ground and put them into the basket.

"I think someone has been here before us," Jenny said.

She lifted Amy onto a wall that fenced in a herd of peacefully grazing sheep and pulled herself up beside the little girl.

Amy was uncharacteristically quiet. After a while, she asked, "Jenny, remember that herb called 'grimony? The one with the tiny yellow flowers?"

"Yes, our Anglo-Saxon ancestors used it to heal wounds, but we have better medicines today. The season for agrimony is long over, Amy."

"I know. But you told me a story, Jenny, about some evil monks who put a sprig of 'grimony beneath a person's pillow."

Jenny smiled a little. "I remember. The story goes that the herb induced a deep sleep. The victim would not wake up until the agrimony was removed. But the tale is make-believe, Amy. The plant does not have magical powers; it's just a pretty weed."

"Was res'rection what happened to the people who woke up when the monks removed the herb?"

"I suppose. But resurrection can mean that someone who is already dead is brought back to life as in the Bible," Jenny said.

"Did you know my uncle Tristan who was drowned?"

Jenny's heart jumped when she heard her fictitious seducer's name on the child's lips. But she answered in reflex.

"Yes, I imagine there was never a time that I did not know Tristan Darius. We both grew up here in the country. I was younger, so we were never playmates, but I saw him everywhere . . . in church, in the village stores, and riding his horse over the countryside. Your mama and your uncle, though, were close friends, being of the same age."

"What about Papa? Wasn't he their friend?"

"No, not then. Your papa was already a man and not interested in young people still in their teens. It was not until your mama became a grown woman that your papa courted her."

"I heard Mama say to Lord Duson that Uncle Tristan might be res'rected. Could that be, Jenny?"

"Not if he drowned," she said. A sense of unease swirled through her. "What makes your mama think that your uncle was resurrected?"

Amy shrugged. "A letter came, I think, from America, but I'm not sure about that part."

Jenny jumped down from the wall. She lifted Amy to the ground and picked up her wicker basket. Taking the child's hand, she set off in the direction of the path to Albinore and Lindwood.

Amy looked up at Jenny. "Do you think he was res'rected?"

"I don't know," Jenny said, not bothering to correct the semantics. "I suppose he could have been rescued."

Amy lapsed into a silence that Jenny welcomed, for her own mind was churning. Could Tristan be alive? The dispatches had said there were no survivors when the *Sea Witch* sank during a storm. And why would he wait five years to inform his family?

Amy could be mistaken. Children often misunderstood adult conversations and misinterpreted what they heard. Yet, it did not take a giant leap to conclude that Tristan might be alive when the word *resurrection* was coupled with his name.

Amy looked up into Jenny's face when they reached the well-worn path that generations of country folk had used as a shortcut between Lindwood and Albinore.

"When is Papa coming home?" the child asked, woefully.

Jenny had no answer and lifted her shoulders a little.

"I don't like the feeling of the house since Papa and so many of the servants went away." Amy's lower lip quivered. "Mama said since Papa left there is no money to pay the servants or to buy new gowns. Why can't Papa be res'rected instead of Uncle Tristan. I don't even know my uncle."

"Oh, Amy," Jenny cried, dropping to her knees and gathering the child to her. She felt a tightness in her throat.

Amy threw her arms around Jenny's neck and clung tightly.

"You are my only friend," the child sobbed, before disengaging herself and racing toward Albinore.

Jenny set off in the opposite direction toward Lindwood. Had Amy mixed up what she heard, or had Tristan somehow miraculously survived the shipwreck? There was only one way to find out.

The next morning Jenny walked onto Albinore's grounds through the creaking wrought-iron gate, which had not been oiled anytime recently and from which the hasp dangled on a single screw.

She speculated about the letter from America that Amy had mentioned. Had it come from Tristan? If so, what reason would Serena have to keep the news that he was alive a secret?

Tristan and Serena had been sweethearts from the time boys and girls are of an age when some of them paired off. But Serena had wed Tristan's brother Gerald in a marriage arranged by their respective fathers, it was said. When Tristan did not attend the wedding, rumors had circulated that he was bitter and blamed Gerald for stealing the woman he loved.

Jenny traversed a lane lined with beech "hangers," the foliage so thick that the leaves remained on the trees all winter. She and Serena had never been friends. Jenny had no reason to believe that Tristan's sister-in-law would confide in her. Yet, she felt compelled to take some action to get to the bottom of the mystery of the letter, even if her efforts came to nothing. Her curiosity, as well as her self-interest, would not allow her to let the matter drop.

Jenny crossed the lawn to the front of the red brick house and looked up at the cracked glass in the attic window. The green paint was peeling on the shutters. Weeds crowded the foundation, one more sign that the estate had an absentee landlord.

She climbed the three brick steps, pounded the brass knocker, and waited for some time before the door was opened by Pecks, the frail butler.

"Why, Miss Jenny," he wheezed and stared at her through rheumy eyes.

"Good day, Pecks," Jenny said politely. "I would speak with Mrs. Gerald Darius, please."

Pecks stepped aside, waited for her to enter, and closed the door behind her.

Jenny sat down on the visitors' bench to wait while the elderly butler shuffled off at a snail's pace, his knees creaking.

The last time Jenny had been in this house was for a ball over two years ago, but her memory went back to a day when she had come with her parents to offer condolences to the Dariuses on Tristan's death. The villagers had always had a soft spot for Tristan, which was something Gerald had never enjoyed. That day, many had whispered that if Gerald had not stolen the woman his brother had loved, Tristan would not have run off to America and perished at sea.

Pecks reappeared rather quickly from a door down the hall and motioned for Jenny to come forward. She slipped her wool cloak from her shoulders, draped it over the arm of the oak bench, and walked to where the butler stood.

"Mrs. Darius will see you now, Miss Jenny," he said and directed her into a small parlor.

Inside the room, Serena reclined on a chaise by the fire. She wore a long-sleeved silk *peignoir,* trimmed with white ostrich feathers, and was covered from her waist to her ankles with a warm blue knit shawl. Her dark satin hair was pulled back in a simple style that set off her dramatic dark eyes and her beauteously symmetrical features.

"What a surprise, Jenny," she said. Her smile contained no hint of warmth only a cool politeness. "Is this about Amy? Mrs. Druback says the child has attached herself to you. Amy can be such a nuisance, I know."

Jenny made herself comfortable on the sofa where Serena had suggested that she sit with an imperious motion of her small white hand.

"On the contrary," Jenny said sincerely, "Amy has a way of keeping me in a good humor. We take long walks and read together the same books in the baron's library which I myself enjoyed as a child."

Serena arched her brows. "It is beyond me how you can voluntarily devote so much time to a pesky child, but I am not complaining. I was beside myself when Amy's nitwit of a governess abandoned me because I was a month or two in arrears with her wages. Today's servants have no sense of loyalty."

Jenny felt that her humane views on the treatment of servants were best left unsaid. She would only succeed in alienating Serena if she defended the governess. Instead, she said, "I came to see you because Amy said something strange to me yesterday. She has this idea that Tristan is alive."

No more than a moment or two went by before Serena spoke, but to Jenny it seemed a small eternity, for Tristan's sister-in-law was looking at her with suspicious displeasure.

"Amy must have eavesdropped on my conversation with Lord Duson," she said. "What is your interest in Tristan?"

Serena's eyes were cold. Jenny realized her mistake. She should have eased into her query. She backed up. "Amy misses her father."

Serena laughed, but it wasn't a nice laugh; it was one filled with derision.

"How idiotic! How can she miss Gerald? He was less of a father than he was a husband, if that is possible. Gerald's taste runs to low females. You must have seen the condition of the estate. Such neglect does not happen in a few months. He was always gone more than he was here. His women invariably came before his family." She waved her hand through the air as if tired of the subject. "What does Amy's alleged pining for Gerald have to do with Tristan? She can't possibly remember him."

"Amy heard you use the word *resurrected*. Once I explained the meaning to her, she said that she wished that her father was resurrected, as she put it, instead of her uncle," Jenny said, fudging her answer. "She mentioned a letter."

Jenny let her statement hang and waited nervously for Serena to make the next move.

Serena gave a sigh of exasperation. "Oh, Lord, I suppose there is no harm in giving you the particulars. It is not some enormous secret, just a bit of an enigma."

Jenny sat up straighter in anticipation.

"Some months ago a letter did come from America for Gerald from a Mr. Peregrine Jones, an acquaintance of his," Serena said. "Since I have no earthly idea of my husband's direction, I opened the correspondence. Mr. Jones claimed that he saw Tristan walking along a street in Philadelphia. But before he could get his cabbie to pull over, Tristan had vanished. Unfortunately, Mr. Jones could not investigate further since he was on his way to the docks to take passage to Jamaica, where he has a plantation. But he took the time to write Gerald a letter and put it in the hands of a ship captain who was leaving for England that very night."

Jenny sat forward on the sofa, her fingers tensed around the edge of the cushion.

"But why would Tristan himself not have written to Gerald if he is alive?"

Serena shrugged. "Therein lies the mystery. In the message Tristan left for Gerald when he emigrated from England, he wrote that he was taking passage on the *Sea Witch* out of Portsmouth. But, as you know, we learned he was lost in a shipwreck off the American coast during a severe storm."

"Shouldn't you send someone to Philadelphia to see if Mr. Jones's sighting is true?"

Serena said bluntly, "I have little enough money for my own needs without spending precious coins on a wild-goose chase. However, Gerald's former man of business has already helped. He wrote to the authorities in Philadelphia a while ago and enclosed a letter to be given to Tristan which explains that Gerald has left me destitute and that Albinore has fallen on hard times." Serena's voice became harsher. "Even if the man that Mr. Jones saw turns out to be Tristan, my brother-in-law will be useless to me unless he has a very fat purse. Tristan has a generous nature. He will be appalled to see me impoverished and will want to jump in to help. But I do not need his sympathy; I need his money. If Tristan does not have deep pockets, he might as well stay where he is."

THREE

Resting a hand on the sill, Jenny stared from the library window at the persistent drizzle, which had turned the morning as gray as her thoughts. For weeks now she had been unable to shake the recurrent feeling that Tristan Darius was alive and sailing toward England.

She had derived no comfort from her mother's insistence that if Tristan were living in America he would have let Gerald know. "As for Mr. Jones," the baroness had said, "I discount his sighting. He only saw the man he believed to be Tristan briefly and never made contact with him."

Jenny turned from the window when a commotion in the hall interrupted her reflections.

Amy's cry, "Jenny, Jenny, where are you?" was followed by the child hurling herself through the library door and breathlessly declaring, "Uncle Tristan is alive! He didn't drown! I ran all the way from home to tell you. He landed in Portsmouth and is now in Lun'on."

"Your uncle is in London?" Jenny's voice came out in a high squeak.

Amy nodded vigorously. "Mama got the letter this morning. Written in his own hand, she said."

Lady Markham came bustling into the room. "What is all the shouting? Lud, Amy, your hair is wet. Where is your bonnet?"

"I forgot it," Amy said indifferently. "Lady Markham, aren't you 'mazed?"

"Amazed at what, child?"

But it was Jenny who answered. "Tristan Darius is alive and has come back to England."

Lady Markham sank into a chair. "Oh, my," she gasped. "He is at Albinore?"

"London," Jenny said.

Amy looked from one woman to the other with a puzzled expression. "Aren't you happy? Isn't it the best news?"

"Yes, dear," Lady Markham said. "We are in shock since we believed that the dear man had drowned."

Jenny removed Amy's cloak from her thin shoulders and had draped the garment over a drying rack near the fire when the butler's appearance at the door had all three females turning in his direction. He walked to where Lady Markham sat and proffered a letter on a silver tray.

"This message from Lord Markham arrived from London, my lady."

The baroness picked up the envelope and thanked him. "Please take Miss Amy to the kitchen, Clarke," she said. "Have Cook fix her a hot drink and ask one of the maids to towel the child's hair dry."

"But, Jenny," Amy protested, "I want to tell you more. Mama did a little dance because Uncle Tristan has assured her that he would see to the bills. We are going to have money again."

"We will talk about it later, Amy. Do as Lady Markham said. Go with Mr. Clarke and get dried off and warmed up."

Amy grumbled something incoherent, but placed her hand into the butler's and left with him.

Jenny carried an ivory letter opener from the baron's desk to her mother, who slit open the wax seal and handed the instrument back to her daughter.

Lady Markham read the message, raised her head, and turned a stricken look on Jenny.

"Jarvis is arriving in time for supper this evening."

Aware there was more, Jenny said, "And?"

"He has met with Tristan Darius, but prefers to relate the results of the interview to us in person."

* * *

By the time Lord Markham arrived from London and summoned Jenny to the drawing room, she was expecting a fine trimming and was growing impatient to face the music and get the baron's tongue-lashing behind her.

Her father stood by the fireplace with his back to the blaze and waited for Jenny to sit down in an armchair.

Anticipating an explosion, Jenny was surprised when the baron said, "My talk with Tristan Darius went more smoothly than I expected." He sounded almost cheery. "In truth, I thought he would deny the whole affair."

Lady Markham, ensconced on a green silk sofa, looked somewhat benumbed.

Jenny's eyes grew wide. "Tristan did not dispute the seduction?" she said.

"No. Our encounter early this morning was necessarily of a short duration as I had to be at an appointment with the Prince, and Tristan had to see Gerald's man of business before coming on to Albinore tomorrow. Although he seemed bowled over that I knew of his misstep, overall, he assumed a rather reasonable mien."

Her mind boggled, Jenny asked, "What exactly did Tristan say?" She had been certain that he would be furious when he heard about her lies.

"He wants to talk with you. Straighten things out, he said, before he puts matters right." Lord Markham's smug expression worried Jenny, especially when he said, "That is exactly what he said, my girl. Put matters right. Obviously, the man is agreeing to marry you."

"No, no, Father, you are wrong. He couldn't mean to wed me. It is not necessary. You see . . ."

But before Jenny could complete her sentence, the baron jumped in, indignant. "On the contrary, it is very necessary. He has a duty to rectify his shameful behavior, even if he is five years late. He violated you, leaving you in a state that will forever keep you from making a suitable match."

The baron reached a taper into the fire to ignite it and lit the cigar in his hand. He breathed life into his smoke, inhaled, and proceeded to blow a cloud into the air just as Jenny said, "But Tristan never ruined me. I made up the sordid tale out of whole cloth to keep from marrying Lord Duson."

Lord Markham nearly choked on the smoke, coughing and sputtering before he regained his breath. He turned to his wife. "What kind of May game is she playing?"

Lady Markham twisted the handkerchief she held in her hands. "It's as Jenny said. She believed herself safe from exposure because she thought Tristan was dead."

The baron glared at his wife. "You knew?"

Avoiding her irate husband's accusing eyes, Lady Markham looked down at her lap and nodded almost imperceptively.

"Vipers in my bosom," Lord Markham muttered. He pointed his glowing cigar at Jenny. "Why would Tristan want to speak with you? Did a tryst of some sort take place between you? Was there a modicum of veracity in your tale?"

"No, not even a vestige of truth. Tristan loved Serena. He looked upon me as a child," Jenny said with feeling. "I'm as bewildered as you are."

The baron took on a pensive air. "Tristan did not seem too prosperous," he mused aloud. "With Gerald off with that hussy, it is possible that he may see a union with you as a heaven-sent opportunity to secure your dowry in order to shore up the estate, which is sorely rundown. I still think he means to offer for you, for whatever reason. And why look a gift horse in the mouth? I intend to accept him."

Jenny was confused. She had never thought of Tristan as being mercenary, but what did she really know of him? She remembered the amiable boy and the golden youth, but not much of the grown man.

The baron engaged in some more useless speculation before Jenny could make her escape. Thankfully, he left the following morning for the City on some business for the Prince, which could not be put off.

Jenny stood behind Amy's chair, her hands resting lightly on the child's shoulders. With her index finger, the little girl pointed out the parts of a castle on the illustration in a history book open before her on the library table.

"That's the turret and that's the moat," she was reciting when Tristan appeared unannounced in the doorway.

Amy had said earlier that her uncle was expected to come home sometime before the day was out, but Jenny had not foreseen that Tristan would call in at Lindwood so soon.

Her heart hammered when her brown eyes locked onto his hard blue ones. He was taller than she remembered. His unruly hair the color of old gold hung past his shoulders. His dark coat and homespun breeches, the attire of a workingman, were rumpled. Yet he was devilishly handsome and a compelling presence.

Even the simplest greeting stuck in Jenny's throat. Paralyzed, she could only stare.

Not so Amy, who asked, "Are you my uncle Tristan?"

Tristan's lips curved ever so slightly. In a deep voice that had a natural huskiness to it, he said, "I am your uncle if you are Amy Darius."

"I'm Amy," the child replied.

"Yes, I can see that you must be. You have inherited the Darius family's corn-colored hair and deep blue eyes. Is that your pony and cart I saw parked out front?"

Amy nodded. "His name is Sylvester."

"Uh," Tristan grunted. "I want you to go home now, Amy. I wish to speak privately with Miss Markham."

"That's Jenny," Amy said artlessly.

"I know," he replied. "Now do as I ask."

Amy looked at Jenny for confirming approval. She nodded her assent.

"I am not to leave books scattered about," Amy said, pushing back her chair and taking the history book and replacing it on a lower shelf.

While Jenny helped Amy into her cape and bonnet, Tristan leaned against the door frame and studied his neighbor. She was changed from the likeness of the girl-child he had carried in his brain for the past five years. Oh, she still had the same lustrous brown curls and expressive golden brown eyes. Tristan allowed himself a small smile. However, he had no recollection of the deliciously rounded hips or the enticing breasts. He could find no fault with Jenny's slender figure in a ruby high-waisted gown which followed her feminine curves. No doubt about it, she had grown into a beautiful young woman.

When Jenny had finally bundled Amy into her outer garments, the child walked to the door, where Tristan stopped her. He braced his hands on his knees and bent down to her eye level.

"Later you and I shall have a long talk, Amy," he said, "and you can tell me all about yourself."

"And you can tell me all about yourself, Uncle," she replied.

Amused by her free speaking, Tristan smiled at her and let her pass into the hall before he himself walked into the room with long-legged strides. Ignoring etiquette, he left Jenny standing and sat down in Lord Markham's favorite chair.

Tristan steepled his fingers under his chin and looked around the room. The library had not changed in the years since he had come here to study when Lord Markham had allowed the vicar's students to make use of his superior book room. Jenny, who had been about Amy's age at the time, would sit cross-legged on the carpet in the corner, reading books meant for adults.

"Sit down, Jenny," Tristan invited with a sweep of a large hand, as if he were the host instead of the visitor.

Bewildered and wary despite his cordial tone, Jenny turned around the chair that Amy had abandoned and sat down facing him.

"I was recalling my days as a schoolboy in this room," he said, appearing perfectly at ease. "You read books which must have been above your head. Do you remember?"

"Yes, very well. You were eleven or twelve, one of the vicar's boys. And the books were not above my head. Just think, I might never have learned how to go on in society had I not read Fanny Burney's novel *Evelina*," she said drolly.

When Tristan smiled, Jenny relaxed and let down her guard. "I recall the vicar placing Gibbon's *Decline and Fall of the Roman Empire* into your hands. As soon as he left the room, you sneaked over to the bookshelf and substituted Fielding's *Tom Jones.*" She grinned at the memory.

"Myths and legends were your favorites, though," he recalled. "I can still picture you standing there with your hands on your hips and a fierce scowl on your little face when I disputed the origin of Valentine's Day. You kept insisting the day was in honor of St. Valentine, who married lovers, despite some ruler's edict against the practice. Julius was it?"

"Claudius," Jenny said. Her mouth widened into another smile and her eyes sparkled. "You asserted in a disdainfully superior tone that the day had nothing to do with the saint but was connected to fertility rites and the mating season of birds."

He chuckled. "You asked me what fertility and mating meant."

"And you blushed as red as a paper heart."

Tristan's smile faded; the kinship vanished like smoke, and his tone became sharp. "I trust that at your more advanced age you have learned the meaning of mating; so refresh my memory, Jenny. I am not in the habit of seducing innocents. Just when did I compromise you?"

"Never." Jenny's voice was low. She found speaking directly to the victim of her injustice embarrassed her. Yet she wanted him to understand her desperation.

Tristan let her tell her story without interruption.

"I could not bear the thought of being wed to Lord Duson. He is not an honorable man," she finished gloomily.

He showed no signs of being shocked, but asked rather mildly, "What did you think Lord Markham would do if you refused to marry? Drag you kicking and screaming to the church?"

A flash of resentment flared in Jenny's breast. "Of all the absurdities. A signed marriage contract is as good as a ceremony in the eyes of society. I would have had no choice; you of all people should know that. Isn't that what happened to Serena? Didn't her father and old Mr. Darius pledge her to Gerald when it was you she loved? Why did she not resist?"

"Serena's marriage to my brother is immaterial. My quarrel is with your slandering my good name with lies." His tone was surprisingly lukewarm.

Yet Jenny regretted her rash outburst. She should not have brought up Tristan's unhappy love affair. "I'm sorry," she said. "You are right. This is about my sins."

"Sins may be a little strong," he said generously.

Tristan sensed that Jenny was not the sort of woman who would have used him had she not believed that he was dead. Moreover, he was relieved that the ramshackle tale had been contained within her own family.

Tristan leaned forward in his chair. "How do you intend to put things right with Lord Markham, Jenny?"

"I already made the truth known to the baron yesterday. He came to Lindwood after he spoke with you in London. He knows that I deceived him."

"You say that Lord Markham is aware that your story was all a hum?"

"Yes."

Tristan was profoundly relieved. "Then why are we having this parley? I accept that your act was not done maliciously. Since all is now resolved and no harm done, we can forget the whole matter."

Jenny squirmed. "Not exactly."

"Not exactly?" he repeated.

"From the manner in which you couched your response to the baron's accusation, he has been left with the distinct impression that you have your own reasons for wanting to marry me."

"Such as?" There was a renewed ring of metal in his voice.

Jenny shrugged. "You might want my dowry to save Albinore."

"Fustian," Tristan said tersely. "I have money. I do not need your portion."

"But did you say to the baron that you would straighten everything out and set matters right?"

"Something of the sort, I suppose. I can't remember exactly what I said. I was too dumbfounded and needed time to think."

The memory of the child Jenny had stirred the softer side

of Tristan's nature when he had spoken with Lord Markham. In a misguided moment he had decided to hear her version of the story before issuing a denial. The lady should have her say. He should have disclaimed the charges immediately and forcefully. So much for being noble.

"There is nothing I can do immediately to set Lord Markham straight," he said. "Gerald has left Albinore in a sorry state with much to be remedied. Unfortunately, I cannot hie off to London posthaste to correct Lord Markham's false perceptions. Yet, what I have to say to him is best done in person rather than entrusted to a letter. The matter will just have to wait until I can get to Town again."

He rose to go and Jenny stood up also.

"Is Lady Markham in residence?" Tristan asked out of politeness.

"She is here at Lindwood, but from home this afternoon. The ladies' group at the church are going through the poor box for clothes that can be salvaged. Many people donate unusable garments."

"Pass on my compliments to the baroness."

Jenny nodded and walked Tristan to the front porch as if his coming to Lindwood were nothing more than a routine social call. Their talk had defused most of the tension between them.

"I see you still prefer to ride Perseus," Jenny said, indicating the big dappled gray stallion tethered to the iron hitching post.

Tristan removed his leather riding gloves from his saddlebag and worked them on one finger at a time. "Fortunately, Gerald left the stables intact," he said dryly.

The gloves in place, Tristan untied the horse and sprang into the saddle. He gave Jenny a small wave, which she reciprocated, and rode off. Only when he had reached the end of the drive did it occur to her that she had not asked him about the shipwreck and how he had escaped drowning.

FOUR

Jenny sought out her mother when she learned from a maid that the baroness had returned from her charitable duties a short time before and had gone to the conservatory to tend to her indoor plants.

Lady Markham had a Holland apron tied around her plump middle and a watering can in her hand. "How does this philodendron look to you?" she asked.

"A little anemic," Jenny said, seating herself on the blue cushions of a white wicker chair. "Mama, Tristan Darius called on me."

Lady Markham set the copper can down on a tiled workbench. "I heard at church that he was back. What did he say?"

Jenny described their meeting. "Father is entirely wrong. Tristan has money and does not need my marriage portion, nor does he want to marry me."

"I am not surprised," Lady Markham said. "Tristan was never an exploiter. He would not take advantage of a situation to feather his own nest. He was the first to render aid when a villager ran into a bit of hard luck. Was he terribly angry with you?"

Jenny shook her head. "Not at all. He accepted my explanation with good grace. But of course he is determined to set things straight with Father and make clear that there was no seduction. You know, I forgot to ask him about the shipwreck."

"The *Times* Jarvis brought home from London is on the table beside your chair. It has the story."

Jenny picked up the London newspaper. "I don't see anything on the front page," she remarked.

Lady Markham looked up from snapping dead leaves from an African violet. "The article is just a half a column at the bottom of an inside page."

Jenny found what she was looking for. After reading the item, she said, "It seems the shipping company mistakenly gave out that all hands and passengers were lost when the *Sea Witch* sank while, in fact, there were four survivors. The report, though, does not mention how Tristan came to be rescued, only that the long-ago error was discovered when he was interviewed on returning to England."

Lady Markham looked up from fingering the fronds of a fern, searching for signs of blight. "Someone is sure to mention those details to you sooner or later," she said, brushing Jenny's curiosity aside and voicing a deeper concern of her own which had been preying on her mind. "I was wrong not to side with you against your father when you first objected to Lord Duson," she said. "If I had intervened promptly, all of this tangle with Tristan would never have occurred."

She pulled off her gardening gloves and sat down in a wicker chair opposite to Jenny's. "Because my own marriage was arranged and worked out satisfactorily, I lost sight of the fact that no woman should be made to marry a man against her will."

"You never regretted marrying Father?" Jenny leaned toward her mother, her expression earnest.

Lady Markham gave her a faint indulgent smile. "Never? Well, let me say, never seriously. Jarvis is neither the best of men, nor the worst. But he has been a faithful husband, is not at all tight-fisted, and, most times, he behaves reasonably. Perhaps, he longs overmuch for a grandson, not having been blessed with a boy of his own. It's a shame that you do not have a *tendre* for a man whom you could bring up to scratch, Jenny. I am certain, your father would stop arranging your life if you found a husband on your own."

Jenny had discouraged qualified admirers because she believed that she could not marry without being in love. But perhaps love was not necessary for a successful marriage. Generosity and faithfulness might be enough to achieve wedded bliss.

It's a shame that you do not have a tendre for a man whom you could bring up to scratch. Lady Markham's words echoed in Jenny's mind as she rode over Lindwood's fields on Benjy in welcome sunshine. Cold December rains had pelted their area of southern England for days. Her horse was restive and wanted his head after being cooped up overlong in the stables without exercise.

Influenced by her mother's marital contentment, Jenny had put aside her rose-colored dreams of a passionate romance. She had decided that she would settle for a suitor whom she could at least like and respect, if not love.

She reached the woods at the edge of the fields, slowed her horse's gait, and, abstracted, loped along the forest fence. She needed a plan to forestall the baron from making another heinous match once Tristan made clear that he had no intention of taking her to wife. Finding a man who would be faithful and generous and willing to marry her would take time.

Jenny became conscious of the galloping hoofbeats racing down the dark shadows of the woodland path directly in front of her. Before she could take evasive action, Tristan Darius cannonaded from the woods. Benjy reared up onto his hind legs and unseated Jenny, who landed on the soft meadowland, her dignity more bruised than her person. Her horse ran off and stopped a short distance from her, lowered his head, and unconcernedly began to crop the green turf.

"Silly creature," Jenny muttered. She sat with her arms dangling over her knees and watched Tristan canter back toward her. He snatched Benjy's reins in transit and led her horse to where she fumed on the ground. His long blond hair was pulled back into a queue and tied with a black ribbon in the old-fashioned way.

"You idiot!" Jenny cried, gnashing her teeth. She jumped to her feet and remounted.

Tristan was relieved to see that she was not hurt; his initial stab of guilt at being responsible for unseating her vanished.

"Took a toss, did you, Jenny?" he said, his blue eyes twinkling. "Calling your horse an idiot won't help. You are the one in charge."

"I was not castigating Benjy, but you, you idiot," she repeated heatedly. "You burst from the woods like a bat out of hell without looking."

"Why were you hugging the trees? If you had been farther out in the field, I would have seen you," he replied unapologetically.

"And if you rode with some caution, you would not endanger other riders who may be in the vicinity. How can you justify leaping from a hidden path without looking both ways?"

Tristan cocked a brow. "I have come this way a thousand times and, frankly, you are the first human I have ever knocked over."

Jenny simmered wordlessly. He tried to stare her down, but his chest began to heave with laughter until he could not contain his mirth.

Jenny found herself laughing with him.

"Ride with me to the pond," Tristan invited. Jenny set her mount in motion, copying the sedate pace he had set which made conversation possible.

"The rain has kept Amy from going to see you," Tristan said. "She will, no doubt, show up on your doorstep today since the sun is shining. She misses you, but I kept her awestruck with some embellished tales of the shipwreck."

"How *did* you come to be saved?" Jenny asked, curious.

"I clung to a bit of flotsam until I drifted close to the shore. Being a strong swimmer, I made it to the beach, where I was eventually found by a rescue party who were searching the shoreline for survivors."

"Why did you not write to Gerald to let him know you were not lost at sea?"

"The Philadelphia papers published the names of those of us who survived. I had no notion that the London *Times* had not followed suit. I assumed, wrongly as it turned out, that my brother knew that I did not drown. Besides, at that time, I was not in charity with Gerald."

Tristan spurred Perseus and rode ahead. When he reached the pond, he looked back over his shoulder and called, "What is that stone structure on the hill? Something new?"

Jenny rode up abreast of him. "It is your commemorative stone," she said. "Gerald had it raised when he learned that the *Sea Witch* had no survivors."

She remained beside the reed-fringed pond while Tristan rode up to the top of the small hill.

From high in his saddle, he read the sentiment on the cenotaph. IN MEMORIAM, and below it, BELOVED BROTHER LOST AT SEA. Withered morning glory vines twined around the sides of the obelisk. Weeds grew tall against the base, partially obscuring his name and the dates of his birth and his supposed death.

Tristan felt a catch in his throat. He and Gerald had enjoyed a companionable relationship before Serena had come between them.

Yet Tristan's bitterness had vanished long ago once he had faced the truth. Serena's indulgent father would never have forced her to marry against her will. Gerald had been the one pressured to take his father's choice. The old gentleman had a serious heart condition and wanted to see his older son settled before he died. Serena had found the heir more desirable as a husband than a lovesick younger son with few expectations. In time the pain of betrayal had run its course and had brought Tristan a return to sanity, but by then he was penniless and across the ocean in a new land.

Tristan joined Jenny at the edge of the pond. In the warmer months, lily pads floated in the black water and iridescent blue and green dragonflies flitted among the cattails, their wings flashing brightly in the sunlight.

Tristan chuckled. "One summer," he said, "I shoved Rolfe Kittredge into the pond during an argument. He pulled me in after him and the two of us ended up thrashing among the cattails. We might have done some damage to each other if we had not been laughing so hard."

Jenny knew Rolfe Kittredge well. "Rolfe is an army captain now, you know," she said.

"Yes, we shared a brief conversation at a coffee house in London," Tristan replied.

"Rolfe is back in Town? I thought he was stationed in France." Rolfe had been a serious suitor during Jenny's first Season. She remembered the lacy valentine with amorous sentiments he had sent her a few days before she had rejected his proposal.

"Rolfe is on leave and staying with his cousin Anne and her husband Lord Coombs," Tristan said. "Lady Coombs is a particular friend of yours, isn't she?"

"Yes, we came out together, but Anne took at once and married Lord Coombs. Speaking of marriage, I would ask a boon of you, Tristan." The idea had been forming in her mind.

"What manner of boon?"

Her heartbeat accelerated.

"I know it is a lot to ask," she hedged.

"Let us have plain speaking, Jenny. Say what is on your mind without trying to turn me up sweet."

"Would you consider putting off telling the baron that you never seduced me and have no intention of marrying me?"

Tristan frowned. "What the devil are you up to?"

"As long as the baron believes that you may yet take me to wife, he will not act to find me a husband. I need time to select my own spouse."

Tristan shook his head slowly from side to side. "It would be a lie. I can't do it, Jenny."

"I don't want you to lie outright, Tristan. Just let things ride. I need to buy time to find a suitable mate."

Tristan sympathized with Jenny's desire to pick her own husband. He had never been persuaded that a woman should be forced to marry where her parents dictated. But it would be folly to be drawn into her scheme to deceive her father.

"You can't wrap it up in clean linen, Jenny. Even by omission a lie is a lie. Lord Markham deserves to know the whole truth."

Jenny gave him a wan smile. "I should not have asked."

"Jenny, it just would not be right." He removed a gold

watch from his pocket and flipped open the lid. "I have business to enact with a steward I hired."

Prudence told Jenny to drop her petition. She said, "You are employing new people at Albinore?"

"Yes," he answered. He chuckled. "Unfortunately, I am treading on shaky legal ground. Even though Gerald is an absent landowner, he is the master of Albinore, not me. I am not empowered to either hire or fire anyone."

Tristan clicked Perseus into motion. He had been shattered by Serena's marriage to Gerald, but his boyhood home had remained the haven of his dreams. He could not watch Albinore fall into ruin and do nothing. Fortunately, he commanded a fat purse for the first time in his life.

Tristan was thinking about the source of his considerable wealth when he and Jenny reached the path that led into the woods. Before they parted company, he smiled spontaneously.

"Something amuses you," she said, for the grin came out of nowhere and was not directed at her.

"I won a lottery," he said.

"A what?" Jenny's expression was so comical that Tristan threw his head back and laughed.

"A lottery," he said. "In America lotteries are a form of what they call a voluntary tax which raises money to build universities and for other public good. Tickets are sold for a nominal sum, but the prize goes to a single winner and is very large. I was eking out a living as a bookkeeper at an iron-monger's in Philadelphia when I found I was in possession of the winning ticket."

"I am astonished," Jenny said. "Your newfound wealth will be all the buzz in the *ton*."

Tristan grumbled good-naturedly. "I would much rather it not be. You will do me a service if you remain close-mouthed about my good fortune, Jenny."

"But, Tristan, it is such a delicious tidbit," she said.

"Please, Jenny," he begged. "Keep mum."

"Oh, very well. I owe you something for having vilified you."

"There is no need for you to atone on that score. I do feel badly, Jenny, that Lord Markham will renew his matrimonial search once I make him aware that I have no intention of marrying you. But it would be dishonorable for me to hoax him."

"I know," she said. "But at least I will have some elbow room. You are here at Albinore, and he is occupied in the City. You yourself said that you are not about to go off to London anytime soon."

"That was before I had assessed the situation at Albinore fully," he said. "The roof of the manor house needs to be repaired and some of the upper rooms have serious water damage. While the improvements are made, I will take Serena and Amy to London, probably the day after Christmas. My man of business has been sending me City rentals. Already, Serena has chosen a house on Curzon Street."

Jenny found his revelation alarming. Christmas was only a week away.

"Oh dear, then I will have to convince Mama to remove to the baron's Jermyn Street town house immediately, so I can begin my quest for a husband." Her soft mouth trembled slightly.

Tristan was amazed how easily Jenny could move him to sympathy. She was hard to resist. He even admired her ingenuity in getting rid of Lord Duson, even if it had been at his own expense. But while he could not in good conscience humbug Lord Markham, perhaps he could think of a way to help Jenny without compromising his own integrity.

FIVE

As Tristan had predicted, Amy was waiting in the library for Jenny when she returned to the house after her ride. The little girl was excited from the vivid images of the shipwreck with which Tristan had filled her head. She spoke with rounded eyes of the blinding rain, the powerful winds, and the huge waves that had sent the *Sea Witch* to her watery grave as she repeated to Jenny what her uncle had told her of the storm.

After Amy left, Jenny joined Lady Markham in the conservatory, where winter sunshine brightened the plant-filled room. A tea service rested on the Irish linen cloth that covered the wicker table.

Lady Markham poured the rich brew into two china cups and handed one to Jenny.

"Amy was looking through books for a picture of a shipwreck when I left her to her own devices in the library earlier," the baroness said. "Did she find one?"

"No, I promised her I would search for a book about ships at Hatchard's the next time I am in London."

Jenny wrapped her fingers around her cup and took a sip of the hot tea. The cucumber sandwiches and the iced pastries remained untouched.

"Tristan plans to remove to London with Serena and Amy," she said. "He leased a place on Curzon Street."

"I heard in the village that workers had been hired to make extensive repairs to the manor house," Lady Markham said. "Does Tristan intend to see Jarvis while in London and finally clear the air with him?"

"Yes," Jenny said, She set her cup down onto the table where the tea service had been laid and glanced at the rows of African violets on a decorative plant stand near the window. "I wish there were a way to keep Father from taking up the task of finding me a husband. I would like to have had the opportunity to try to bring a gentleman to the sticking point without the baron's interference."

Lady Markham put her cup down beside Jenny's and squared her plump shoulders. "I have an idea, child," she said. "What do you think of this? I will speak with Jarvis and ask him to give you a few weeks to make a match on your own before he renews his search. Would you like me to do that?"

"Oh, Mama, that would be splendid," Jenny said. "Do you think Father will agree?"

"I don't know, but he is not an unreasonable man when approached in a logical way."

"Can we go to London soon?" Jenny asked. The question had been on her mind since she had entered the conservatory. She had been waiting for an opportunity to broach the subject, for regardless of the baron's reply to his wife's request, Jenny was anxious to test the marital waters of the *ton*.

"I think we can leave before the end of the week," Lady Markham said, lifting Jenny's spirits. "I'll direct the maids to start packing." She smiled. "We can keep Christmas with Jarvis."

While Jenny hoped to run across Tristan in London, she doubted he would want to have anything more to do with her. There was no compelling reason for him to stay in touch, for he had already clarified his position with the baron.

Therefore, Jenny was surprised when soon after the New Year he showed up at her father's London town house in Jermyn Street for a social call.

Tristan was smartly dressed in new clothes that bore the

mark of Bond Street's best shops. His golden hair was cut short in a modern style.

Jenny greeted him wearing one of her prettiest gowns, a round dress of leaf green cambric.

She commented on how fine he looked. He thanked her for the compliment, reciprocated, and shared a smile with her.

Jenny motioned Tristan to an area of the room where comfortable chairs had been arranged into a group, which was conducive for conversation.

Once seated, Tristan said, "I am meeting a friend here later, but I wanted a private word with you before he arrives. I heard from Lord Markham during our interview that your mother persuaded him to give you a reprieve."

"Yes, I have until the end of January before he once again meddles in my life," Jenny said, but she chose not to expand on the subject, for she suspected that Tristan already knew the details. In any case, he seemed absorbed with another matter.

He rubbed his chin. "Jenny, from Amy's conversation and little bits that Mrs. Druback and Pecks have dropped, I have concluded that you have been the one warm, supportive presence in Amy's life while Serena neglected the child."

"I love Amy," Jenny said simply.

"Excellent. Then may I ask that you visit her when you are able? I think the child would be crushed if you dropped her while you are here in Town." He gave Jenny a ready smile that she found terribly appealing.

"I offer myself as an escort if you would be willing to show Amy some of the City's attractions," he said.

Jenny warmed to his request. She adored Amy and liked so many things about Tristan, particularly his understanding nature and innate kindness. Never had she been more comfortable in the presence of a man.

"I need no persuasion," she said, "for I value my friendship with Amy. As a matter a fact, I plan to see her this afternoon." Humor quirked Jenny's mouth. "Moreover, I would be honored to be escorted by such a fashionable Corinthian as yourself," she said. He laughed at her quip,

We'd Like to Invite You to Subscribe to Zebra's Regency Romance Book Club and Give You a Gift of 4 Free Books as Your Introduction! (Worth $19.96!)

If you're a Regency lover, imagine the joy of getting **4 FREE Zebra Regency Romances** and then the chance to have these lovely stories delivered to your home each month at the lowest price available! Well, that's our offer to you and here how you benefit by becoming a Regency Romance subscriber:

- **4 FREE Introductory Regency Romances are delivered to your doorstep**

- **4 BRAND NEW Regencies are then delivered each month (usually before they're available in bookstores)**

- **Subscribers save almost $4.00 every month**

- **You also receive a FREE monthly newsletter, which features author profiles, discounts, subscriber benefits, book previews and more**

- **No risks or obligations...in other words, you can cancel whenever you wish with no questions asked**

Join the thousands of readers who enjoy the savings and convenience offered to Regency Romance subscribers. After your initial introductory shipment, you receive 4 brand-new Zebra Regency Romances each month to examine for 10 days. Then, if you decide to keep the books, you'll pay the preferred subscriber's price.

It's a no-lose proposition, so return the FREE BOOK CERTIFICATE today!

Say Yes to 4 Free Books!
Complete and return the order card to receive this $19.96 value, ABSOLUTELY FREE!

If the certificate is missing below, write to:
Regency Romance Book Club
P.O. Box 5214, Clifton, New Jersey 07015-5214
or call TOLL-FREE 1-800-770-1963

Visit our website at www.kensingtonbooks.com.

FREE BOOK CERTIFICATE

YES! Please rush me 4 Zebra Regency Romances without cost or obligation. I understand that each month thereafter I will be able to preview 4 brand-new Regency Romances FREE for 10 days. Then, if I should decide to keep them, I will pay the money-saving preferred subscriber's price for all 4...that's a savings of 20% off the publisher's price. I may return any shipment within 10 days and owe nothing, and I may cancel this subscription at any time. My 4 FREE books will be mine to keep in any case.

Name _____

Address _____ Apt. _____

City _____ State _____ Zip _____

Telephone ( ) _____

Signature _____
(If under 18, parent or guardian must sign.)

RN012A

Terms and prices subject to change. Orders subject to acceptance by Regency Romance Book Club.
Offer valid in U.S. only.

Treat yourself to 4 FREE Regency Romances!

A
$19.96
VALUE...
FREE!

*No
obligation
to buy
anything,
ever!*

PLACE
STAMP
HERE

lll..l..lll....ll.l.l.l.l.l..l.l.l.l.ll.l.lll..l

REGENCY ROMANCE BOOK CLUB
Zebra Home Subscription Service, Inc.
P.O. Box 5214
Clifton NJ 07015-5214

but the sound of the butler bringing a visitor to the drawing room door cut off her mild flirtation.

A tall army officer marched into the room.

"Rolfe," Jenny cried. She jumped up and approached him with outstretched hands, her smile broad and welcoming. "What a lovely surprise." It had been three years since they had last seen each other.

The strapping soldier seized her extended hands and brought them to his lips. "When Tristan suggested we meet here before going for a meal at Watier's, I couldn't have been more delighted," he said.

Captain Rolfe Kittredge had been one of Jenny's most devoted admirers the year she had made her come-out. He had sent her a love message on Valentine's Day, but she had turned down his proposal a few days later. The rejection had pained her, for she had hated to hurt him. She had liked Rolfe, very much, but had not been in love with him.

Jenny linked her arm with the captain's and led him to where Tristan sat smiling at them, leaving no doubt that he had engineered their reunion.

Rolfe waited for Jenny to be seated and then sank into a deep chair.

A spirited exchange of shared memories of their summers in the country went on for some time. Their conversation was alive with laughter. Captain Kittredge was also a younger son. His older brother now owned the county seat where the captain's family had summered in those long-ago years.

When the allotted time for a proper social call had been exhausted, Tristan caught Rolfe's eye and motioned wordlessly to the mantel clock.

The two men rose as one and Jenny followed in their wake to the door, where Rolfe turned to her and said, "Would you do me the honor of touring London Tower with me tomorrow, Jenny?"

His gray eyes brimmed with open admiration, confirming in Jenny's mind that he still desired her. She suspected that if she gave him the slightest encouragement, he would renew his offer of marriage. She was being selfish, she knew, but she could not help but look upon Rolfe's reappearance just when she was sorely in need of a willing gallant as fortuitous.

"I would like very much to join you, Rolfe," Jenny said. "Would you mind if I brought a young friend along? It is her first sojourn in London. I had planned to show her one of the more interesting sights tomorrow. The Tower will do fine."

Rolfe was momentarily discomposed, but he quickly collected himself and agreed. "May I ask the name of your young friend?"

"Miss Amy Darius," Jenny said, turning to Tristan. "It would be all right, wouldn't it, Tris?"

"Amy will be over the moon. Suppose we make a party of it?" he said. "I can also join you."

Rolfe grimaced openly and said dryly, "Certainly, the more the merrier."

"Don't give me such a black look, Rolfe," Tristan said cheerfully. "I am doing you a service. I will keep Amy occupied while you flirt with Jenny."

Jenny laughed. "Well, if Tristan is coming, why not ask your cousin Anne and Lord Coombs? I haven't seen Anne in an age."

The captain threw up his hands. "I surrender, but only if you promise me, Jenny, if I invite you for a ride in the park, we go alone."

Jenny raised her right hand as if taking an oath. "I faithfully promise."

"I shall hold you to your word, my dear," Rolfe said, a lively gleam in his gray eyes.

"Amy and I will take up Jenny for the Tower excursion," Tristan said to Rolfe, "since you will have Lord and Lady Coombs with you."

Rolfe pulled a face. "You are a very managing fellow, Tristan. But as you will. We meet at half past two o'clock at the main gate?" Tristan and Jenny nodded their agreement.

"Until tomorrow, Jenny," Rolfe said and kissed her hand. Tristan winked at her, and the gentlemen left marching in lockstep.

* * *

The same afternoon, Jenny rang the bell at the Dariuses' leased town house in Curzon Street, carrying a package. A butler in spanking new livery opened the door. Jenny handed him her engraved calling card and asked to see Miss Amy Darius.

His face inscrutable, the butler exhibited no visible emotion at the unusual request. Jenny was following him to a visitors' waiting room off the hall when Amy came bouncing down the stairs.

"Jenny," she cried, "you have come to see me."

Amy wrapped her arms around her guest's trim waist. Jenny kissed the child on the top of her blond head.

"I shall see to Miss Markham, Manning," Amy said in a grown-up voice.

Laughing, Jenny squeezed Amy's hand as the child pulled her down the hall and into a formal drawing room.

When Jenny was seated on a love seat, she peeled off her gloves, untied the string around her package, and removed the brown paper.

"I found an excellent volume on ships at Hatchard's," she said. She made room for Amy beside her and handed her the book.

"There are several pictures of shipwrecks in one long chapter devoted to the subject."

"Oh, Jenny, you are a great gun," Amy said, pressing the oversized book to her chest. "Thank you."

Jenny had folded up the wrappings and had placed the string and the paper on a side table when Tristan entered the room.

"Manning was shaken to find Amy had an adult caller," he said. "He ran to fetch me to be sure you were not bent on kidnapping the child, Jenny."

Amy giggled. "You are making fun, Uncle Tris." She held out her new book. "Jenny brought me the handsomest of presents."

Tristan took the book from her hands and leafed through the pages. "This should answer all the questions with which you have been bombarding me concerning life aboard ship," he said, giving the book back to her.

Amy declared that she might become a sailor instead of

a knight and said, "I want to show this book to Mr. Richards. Would you entertain Jenny for me until I return, Uncle Tris?"

"My pleasure." He sat down in a wing chair.

"Mr. Richards?" Jenny asked when Amy had left them.

"My new valet," he replied. "Amy has taken a shine to him. He is surprisingly tolerant, although she confounds him. He was taken aback when she claimed she would have a valet to see to her needs when she grew up since Richards is a much more interesting companion than her mother's new lady's maid."

Jenny laughed. "Amy is going through a stage of wishing she had been born a boy. It will pass."

Tristan sat back, his arms folded across his chest. "Rolfe and I had a pleasant meal. He seemed quite pleased to have reconnected with you. In fact, he couldn't stop talking about you."

"It was good to see him again," Jenny said mildly. For some reason she did not want to discuss Rolfe with Tristan.

Jenny looked around the room. The carved wooden doors had a rich patina. Exquisite gilded moldings decorated the ceiling edges. Her eyes on the fine marble fireplace, she said, "This is a lovely room."

Tristan took the hint that she did not want to talk about Rolfe and followed her lead. "Yes, the house is quite palatial. I would have liked something with a less expensive lease, but despite her recent troubles, Serena is not adroit at practicing economies."

"It is your money," Jenny said more sharply than she had intended.

However, Tristan did not take offense. "I suppose I am overcompensating for the humiliation and suffering she has endured," he said rather blandly. His voice took on an anxious note. "I wish I knew where Gerald is holed up. Have you by any chance heard rumors of his whereabouts?"

"Not recently."

"Neither has Rolfe. Usually the *ton* is teeming with speculation, but Gerald has managed successfully to drop from sight. I hired a private investigator, but he has come up with nothing new."

Tristan's jaw tightened. "I find myself in a bind. I cannot legally touch any funds generated by the estate, so I am pouring my own money into the house and land, but I cannot keep doing that without a return, or I shall soon be as poor as when I left England."

"You want to force Gerald to come back to Albinore?"

"Not necessarily, I just want to find him. Believe me, my brother will not tremble at my displeasure. What I hope to get from him is a power of attorney which would give me full control of the finances. I could make the estate pay if I had a free hand."

"Would Gerald give you this unconditional authority?"

Tristan smiled ruefully. "I may be able to bully him into it. After all, the contract would be to his advantage. Should he decide to make Albinore his home again, a profitable estate would be far preferable to reclaim than a run-down, debt-ridden property."

Jenny put a finger to her chin. "When people want to vanish, they often steal off to the Continent."

Tristan sighed. "Yes, and Europe is such a big place."

"I will keep my ears attuned," Jenny promised.

"Attuned for what?" Amy asked, waltzing into the room.

"Nothing of consequence," Jenny said.

"You just don't want to tell me," Amy said with a small pout.

"That's right; she doesn't," Tristan agreed amiably, ignoring his niece's small show of petulance. "We will take you up tomorrow at two o'clock for our visit to the Tower, Jenny."

Her minor sulk forgotten, Amy's eyes sparkled. "Uncle says that it was your suggestion, Jenny, that I be included in the outing. You are top of the trees."

"Thank you, dear, how nice of you to say so." She turned to Tristan. "Anne has sent a note that she and her husband will definitely join the party and ride with Rolfe."

"Who are Anne and Rolfe?" Amy asked.

"Anne is Lady Coombs, and Rolfe is Captain Kittredge," Jenny said.

"An army captain?" Amy asked, her eyes big.

Jenny nodded.

"A real one?"

"As real as they come. He cuts quite a dash in a uniform of red and blue and gold," Jenny said. "He fought at Waterloo." She rose from her chair and pulled on her gloves. "You will meet Captain Kittredge tomorrow, dear. But I must go now."

Tristan got up with Jenny, but Amy said importantly, "I will show Jenny out. She came to visit me."

Tristan watched Jenny go. She and Rolfe had some sort of romantic history. When Rolfe had decried the absence of females in the Marriage Mart who interested him, Tristan had suggested Jenny as a likely prospect.

"Jenny Markham is in town? And you think she is looking to wed?" he had asked.

"I believe she is," Tristan had said. Rolfe had been remarkably eager to see her again. It had been Tristan's first inkling that Rolfe might once have been in love with her. From his observation, it shouldn't take much for Jenny to restoke his fire.

From his coat pocket, Tristan removed the worthless report from Mr. Geiger, the investigator he had hired to find his brother, which had been in the morning's post. Nothing new there.

He already knew that Gerald had succumbed completely to the wiles of one of the loose women to whom he had been invariably drawn and, beyond all reason, had run off with her.

Tristan emitted a grumble of exasperation. He tore the investigator's useless message into tiny bits and threw the pieces into a waste bin beside a Chippendale desk. Unconscionably, Gerald had abandoned his wife and child to an impecunious existence without a backward look. If Tristan ever caught up with his lunatic brother, he would have to use every ounce of willpower to keep from putting his hands around that handsome neck and squeezing hard.

SIX

Jenny beamed when she and Anne greeted each other warmly at the Tower of London's entrance the next day. The two young women had known and liked each other since their first Season on the Town. Anne Kittredge and Lord Coombs had fallen head over heels in love at first sight and married three months to the day after meeting at Almack's.

Jenny introduced Tristan and Amy to Lord and Lady Coombs and Anne's soldier cousin to the child. Amy curtsied to the lord and his lady and snappily saluted the captain to everyone's amusement while Rolfe returned her greeting with a crisp military salute of his own without missing a beat.

The Tower was a popular attraction. Both English citizens and foreign tourists put it at the top of their lists as a site not to be missed in the capital.

With atypical interest for a female, the display of armory gripped Amy's imagination. "Aren't you thankful, Captain," she said to Rolfe, "that soldiers today do not have to wear the bulky mail of knights of old?"

Secretly amused, but keeping his mien serious, Rolfe looked down into her earnest little face tipped up toward his. "Indeed, Miss Amy. If a knight was unfortunate and tumbled over in a full suit of armor, he would be hard put to rise again unless his page was nearby to assist him."

"I would have been pleased to be your page, sir," Amy said, guilelessly. She placed a small hand on the captain's dark blue uniform sleeve and looked up his very long length with slavish admiration.

Rolfe smiled indulgently. "And I would have been pleased to have you serve me, ma'am."

The captain and his unlikely martially minded acolyte discussed with great interest the breastplates, knee guards, swords and daggers, lances and pikes, and long bows and pistols.

Tristan chuckled. "I should have purchased a sword or a cannon for Amy for Christmas instead of a doll," he whispered to Jenny as Rolfe and Amy examined a curious item labeled "Henry VIII's Walking Staff" in the collection of royal weapons. Jenny eavesdropped when Rolfe explained to Amy that the strange object was a combination mace, battle club, and three-barreled pistol. Jenny was impressed with Rolfe's patience with the little girl. He rose another notch in her esteem.

She stood looking at the Tudor king's amassed weapons and armor rather disinterestedly until Tristan bent close to her ear and spoke low. "You know, in the seventeenth and eighteenth centuries women would crowd around these suits and stick pins into the padded codpiece."

"Sir," Jenny said, "you put me to the blush. Whatever for? Surely not some symbol of revenge?"

Tristan made a show of shuddering, but his blue eyes were merry. "You have an insidious turn of mind, my girl. An old wives' tale claimed that it was a well-attested method of assuring conception."

Jenny giggled. "I had never heard that before," she said and walked beside him to where Lord and Lady Coombs were inspecting the crown jewels and other royal regalia.

Amy joined Jenny and Tristan, who moved slowly from museum case to museum case. "I have never seen so many jewels," the child said breathlessly, as she eyed the crowns and scepters and the diamonds, sapphires, emeralds, rubies, and pearls.

"The jewels have been housed here since 1303, you know. More than five hundred years," Jenny said to her. "And even though several of our English kings were driven to sell off many expensive pieces to finance costly wars, the collection is still one of the most fabulous in all of Europe in both quantity and quality."

"Mama should see them," Amy said. "She loves nothing as much as pretty jewelry."

"How is Serena?" Jenny asked Tristan when Amy ran off to catch up with the captain.

Tristan's smile was droll. "Being fitted for new gowns has raised her spirits. But she longs to be back in society. I plan to make a point of securing invitations for her and escorting her to some entertainments in the days to come."

He lowered his voice confidingly. "Your former suitor Lord Duson has called and taken her for rides in his carriage numerous times. He was a friend of Gerald's, you know, but still . . . I have warned Serena that showing particular attention to one man could be ruinous to her reputation. After all, she is still a married woman."

Jenny wondered if Tristan was aware that Serena's alliance with Duson was of a long standing. But just then, Anne intertwined her arm with Jenny's, precluding further conversation with Tristan, and he moved on to join Rolfe and Amy, who were admiring the jeweled hilt of a sword.

"It is so good to see you again," Anne said.

Jenny returned her longtime friend's bright smile. "I see your marriage is rubbing along quite above the common. You and Lord Coombs are still lovebirds even after three years."

"My husband makes me happy, Jenny. And you are the first to know that our little Alex will have a brother or sister in seven months' time."

"How lovely, my dear," Jenny said sincerely, but she was envious of Anne. It must be heaven to be able to make a successful love match, instead of being forced to fight a parent's unwelcome choice.

"What of you, Jenny? When are you going to make the leap? You know, Rolfe is quite besotted with you while you seem much taken with Mr. Darius. I saw you with your heads close together."

Jenny's mouth flew open in protest. "Don't be a peagoose, Anne," she chided. "You are imagining things. Tristan and I have been neighbors since childhood. He was being informative and filling me in on the history of the Tower."

Anne hooted. "Farradiddle. You have been here any number of times and know every trivial anecdote associated with the exhibits and every story about its illustrious prisoners by heart."

Jenny became indignant. "I did not know about pins and codpieces."

Anne said, "What?"

Jenny laughed and waved a dismissive hand at her befuddled friend. "No matter," she said. "Truly, Anne, Tristan and I are nothing more than casual friends."

"Oh, Jenny, I hope that is true; I love my cousin Rolfe dearly and cannot help rooting for him. He is a wonderful man."

"I know he is, Anne." But before Jenny could say more Amy came running up to them.

"Lady Coombs, Jenny, you are falling behind. Everyone is waiting at the exit gate."

Jenny took Amy's hand.

"Let's hurry," the child said. "Uncle Tristan said we are to stop at the confectionery shop, and I can select a whole sack of candy for myself as a treat. He is buying a box of chocolates to give to Mama as a surprise."

In the courtyard before the parties boarded their carriages, Rolfe took Jenny aside. "I thought Tristan was to keep the infant Amy occupied while I courted you," he said dryly.

"Oh, Rolfe, did you find her a chore?"

He smiled good-naturedly. "No, as a matter of fact, I was flattered. It is not often that I have a pretty female of any age hanging on my every word. But will you drive with me in the park tomorrow, just the two of us, and go for ices at Gunter's afterward?"

Mindful of the promise she had once made him, Jenny agreed and settled on a time with Rolfe.

At the sweet shop, Amy could not decide which candy to choose from among the lemon and orange jujubes, licorice sticks, and chocolate drops. Tristan selected the largest, most expensive box of imported French chocolates for his sister-in-law. The box was decorated with an enormous yellow paper rose and tied with a wide silk ribbon. Jenny found the gift a little gaudy for her taste.

Tristan smiled at her, rather foolishly, she thought. "Her birthday," he said. "Serena gives her custom to this confectioner's and will feel slighted if she comes into the shop and notices that I have not bought the best box of chocolates available."

Jenny pasted an insincere smile on her face and turned from Tristan. She felt quite annoyed with his kowtowing to Serena, recalling the woman's ungracious remarks about Tristan's finances when his whereabouts were still in doubt. She figuratively tossed her shoulder. It was none of her concern if Tristan chose to indulge his self-centered, grasping sister-in-law from his lottery winnings.

Jenny was anxious to leave, bored with the proceedings, she told herself.

Tristan, too, was becoming restive. Amy still stood in front of the huge glass jars of candy, unable to make up her mind. Losing patience with the child's procrastination, Tristan said to the clerk, "Landsakes, give her a bag of each kind," which left the clerk well satisfied, and Amy tickled pink.

When Jenny entered the Jermyn Street house, Lady Markham was in the entry hall, going through the mail.

Jenny answered her mother's questions about the excursion to the Tower, but it struck Lady Markham that Jenny gave short shrift to the main event of her afternoon. She spent more time describing the stop at the sweet shop and Tristan's purchases.

"Tristan spoils Serena," she said, sounding miffed. Jenny could not possibly be jealous, could she?

Lady Markham made a *tsking* sound. "But, dear, it seems he spoils Amy, too."

Raising a willful chin, Jenny ignored the caveat and looked through the afternoon mail left on the hall table. She picked out the letters addressed to her and put the rest back.

"Captain Kittredge is taking me for a drive in the park tomorrow and for refreshments at Gunter's," Jenny said.

"How nice," her mother replied placidly. "Rolfe Kittredge is an honorable man of good family. To his credit, he drinks in moderation, gambles sparingly, and eschews females of the wrong sort. But would you be content to follow the drum?"

Jenny shrugged. "I suppose I could become accustomed to being a soldier's wife."

Lady Markham turned to leave the hall. Belatedly Jenny called to her back as the baroness mounted the stairs, "Tristan is taking Amy and me to Astley's Circus on Thursday."

Lady Markham said over her shoulder, "Tristan is a man of infinite charm," leaving Jenny to make what she would of the remark.

At Astley's, Amy squealed and clapped her hands, captivated by the high fliers on the trapeze. Reacting to the little girl's high spirits, Tristan smiled winningly at Jenny over Amy's head.

Jenny's heart quickened. Tristan was more handsome than any man had a right to be. She felt the heat rise in her cheeks. If he would give her the slightest sign that he might develop a *tendre* for her, she would drop her plans to wed Rolfe. Her sudden change of heart left her breathless. For days she had been giving Rolfe clear signals that she welcomed his addresses.

But Jenny quickly forgot Rolfe when she became awed by the skilled jugglers. She was as enthralled as Amy with the acrobatics of the trick riders on white horses. And for over an hour her fickle emotions were pushed to the back of her mind by one marvelous diversion after another.

However, her new awareness of Tristan's powerful build, his seductive voice, and his good looks that made him seem like the handsomest man in the world were rekindled when he handed her up into the carriage for the ride home.

Amy dozed off almost immediately when the coachman set the horses in motion, her head pillowed on Tristan's lap.

Not to awaken her, Jenny and Tristan talked in lowered

tones about the Duchess of Wilcox's benefit for orphaned children, which was being held at the duchess's mansion the following night. Her public rooms were being turned into a miniature Vauxhall Gardens to raise money for the foundlings.

"I shall take you up at nine, Jenny," Tristan told her. "Rolfe was most insistent that I see that you are not late for the supper Lord and Lady Coombs have arranged. He was quite annoyed that he would be tied up with army business and not able to drive you himself."

"Yes, I know. He expects to arrive late, but he promised me he will be there," Jenny said, looking out the window. She did not want Tristan to see the glow in her eyes when he smiled at her and somehow discern that she was falling in love with him. What had happened to her? Rolfe was on the point of making a declaration. For days she had been content with the prospect, even eager to have her future settled. Tristan was not romantically interested in her. Rolfe was. It she lost Rolfe, she would be at the baron's mercy with no one on the horizon to bail her out.

The coach wheeled around the corner into Jermyn Street and pulled up to the curb. Amy sat up and rubbed her eyes.

"Are we home?" she asked and yawned.

"No, dear," Jenny said, "but I am." She thanked Tristan for the pleasant afternoon, although she still did not dare to look directly at him. She alighted from the carriage with a footman's help, feeling, for some reason, as if all the sunshine had been taken out of the day.

SEVEN

Jenny walked into the library at Jermyn Street and was startled to see the baron perusing the stacks. A sudden January downpour flung freezing rain against the windows. Customarily, her father left on the Prince Regent's business before she came down for breakfast. To find him here at ten o'clock in the morning was unusual, to say the least.

He turned from the bookcase and faced her. "Nasty deluge. I decided to wait until the rain abates before setting off for Whitehall," he said and went back to running his fingers over the spines of the books on an eye-level shelf.

Observing that the fire was burning low, Jenny stoked the smoldering ashes on the grate by adding the coals from the copper bucket on the hearth and then proceeded to poke the fire into a cheerful blaze. She returned the shovel and the poker to their brass holder and looked up to find her father watching her with a steady gaze, a book he had removed from the shelf cradled in his hand.

"Lord Berkshire was widowed nine months ago and is actively seeking a wife," he said. "He requires someone to run his household and to see to his five children, who I understand are all under the age of ten. I have been considering sounding him out for you."

"Lord Berkshire is old," Jenny said stonily.

"Not yet forty, I believe. He is still a fine figure of a man. You like children. Your mother has described how you have taken little Amy Darius under your wing. If you married the earl, you would have an entire nursery full with whom to fuss."

A smile touched his lips, but Jenny stiffened and frowned. "I thought the main reason you wanted to see me married was to give you a grandson."

"It still is. The earl fathered five children in nine years. An excellent record. There is no reason to believe he will not continue to produce progeny at the same rate."

Jenny primmed and reminded her father, "You promised Mama you would give me until month's end to find a husband on my own." Her throat tightened. She was afraid he was going back on his word.

"So I did. I just thought to hurry you along with a suggestion. I could arrange a meeting between you and Lord Berkshire. No harm in your taking a look at him while he looks you over."

"I do not care to consider the earl," Jenny said coldly.

The baron uttered a "Harrumph" and left the room with his book tucked under his arm.

Jenny took a deep reviving breath when he was gone and went to the window and gazed at the rain-drenched landscape beyond. The baron's promise had not kept him from meddling. He was already preparing to push her into another match.

Fortunately, Rolfe was at the point of proposing. She did not have to remind herself that Rolfe was not Tristan. It was always at the forefront of her mind, even though pining for Tristan was futile.

Jenny leaned her forehead against the cool glass, where raindrops on the opposite side chased each other down the pane. In time she would get over yearning for Tristan, but it wasn't going to be easy. Why couldn't he have stayed in America instead of returning to England to complicate her life?

The night saw a clearing of the skies after the morning's drenching rain. Jenny's fur-lined cloak, which she wore over a blue silk gown, kept her warm in the unheated coach on the journey to the Duchess of Wilcox's charity event. Beside her, Tristan's many-caped gray overcoat protected him from the evening's chill.

The team of horses clip-clopped along the dark streets toward their destination as the two talked.

In the course of their ongoing conversation, Jenny said to Tristan, "This morning the baron suggested a possible alliance with Lord Berkshire."

"I thought Berkshire was married," Tristan said.

"His wife died some months ago and left him with five children to raise."

Tristan chuckled. "Quite a brood to take on, Jenny. Are you ready to become a mother to so many sprigs?"

"Don't be a goose. I have no intention of marrying Lord Berkshire. I am making a match with Rolfe."

"Rolfe proposed?"

"Not yet, but he will. Only the veriest ninny could misread his intentions." She sighed. "His declaration is imminent, perhaps even this evening."

Tristan peered at her shadowy profile in the darkened coach. She did not sound at all thrilled by the prospect.

"You do want to marry Rolfe, don't you? I mean if you don't, you shouldn't rush into a union that makes you unhappy."

Jenny fought tears that seemed to come from nowhere. She blessed the darkness that hid her face. "Of course, I want to marry him. Didn't I just say so?"

Countering her combative tone, Tristan said in a low, gentle voice, "I was commiserating, Jenny, not criticizing."

Jenny could not bear Tristan's pity. "I intend to accept Rolfe happily when he proposes," she said, forcing a buoyant lilt into her voice. "Really, Tristan, the subject is closed."

Tristan made no further attempt to draw her out. He felt a spurt of resentment, not toward her, but toward Lord Markham.

Jenny was a special woman. Her preference should count for something. She shouldn't have to be dashing harum-scarum into a match simply to avert the baron's threats.

The coachman turned the horses onto the long curving drive that led to the Duke and Duchess of Wilcox's mansion. When the driver reached the house, he pulled up beneath a porte cochere at a side entrance, where an efficient footman raced over and opened the carriage door almost before the coach's wheels had stopped.

Tristan ascended the narrow steps of the coach and offered Jenny a hand down, then turned and paid their fee. The duchess had set up an entrance booth similar to the one at Vauxhall, where an attendant collected for the orphans' home the same four guineas admission charged at the Gardens.

Once inside the mansion, Jenny and Tristan relinquished their coats and entered the great hall, where many gaily decorated booths lined the walls. Mock Vauxhall vendors sold spicy gingerbread, sweet biscuits, and trinkets, the money going to the needy children. At the far end of the room, an orchestra played lively music.

Jenny and Tristan joined Anne and Lord Coombs, who were seated in a supper box. Pastoral scenes were painted on the canvas walls that surrounded their table. The murals depicted brown and white cows grazing peacefully in green pastures. The scenes were duplicates of those decorating the boxes at the famous gardens.

Conversing amicably, the party waited for Rolfe, who arrived a half hour later. He made his apologies for being late and took the vacant seat left for him beside Jenny.

Thinly sliced ham and tender pieces of chicken on platters were passed around the table, along with a basket of rolls. Slices of golden cheese were cut from a large wedge of cheddar by a waiter and heaped onto the dinner plates already crowded with the meats, bread, and a variety of condiments.

Jenny's own appetite had flown. She picked at her food, but no one seemed to notice, for everyone else ate with gusto and laughed and joked and washed down the meal with a hearty Burgundy. The wine from the duke's cellar was far superior to any spirits dispensed at the actual pleasure gardens.

Replete at last, Rolfe refused the offer of a second slice of cheesecake and said, "Shall we take a turn around the hall to work off this splendid meal, Jenny?"

"An excellent idea, Kittredge," Lord Coombs seconded and pushed back his chair. "Come, my dear," he said to his wife. Anne rose to join her husband. "Darius?" Lord Coombs asked.

Tristan declined. "I will finish my wine and enjoy the music. Shall we meet at eleven-thirty at the door that leads to the balcony from which the fireworks can be viewed?"

Everyone agreed and left Tristan to his own company.

Tristan watched Jenny walk off with Rolfe. If he had been marriage-minded, Jenny would be the sort of woman he would want to wed. Before he could explore the specifics of the random thought, he was joined by a longtime friend.

He and his old classmate addressed the duke's excellent wine and laughed over their youthful transgressions, while all thoughts of Jenny passed completely from Tristan's mind.

The duke's mammoth conservatory had been turned for the evening into an unlikely approximation of the secluded garden paths that were known officially as the Italian Walk, but had been renamed by naughty Vauxhall patrons as the Lovers' Walk.

By the time Rolfe led Jenny to the glass houses, Lord and Lady Coombs had long since joined a group of friends.

Rolfe paid an attendant the one-pound charitable donation and gained entrance to the isolated retreat.

The conservatory was a green jungle of citrus trees, tropical vines, and bushes, bright with exotic blossoms. The glass walls and clear roofs gave the illusion of walking under the night sky while the winter's cold was kept at bay.

"Not exactly a match for Vauxhall's deciduous trees and English flowers, but at least it is private," Rolfe said. He chuckled, bringing Jenny into his laughter. The wooden bench where they sat was off the common path.

Jenny's insides began to twist uncomfortably when Rolfe said, "I am about to replay a scene from years past, but I have reason to believe that this time the outcome will be more to my liking."

Jenny decided that she must stop his proposal before he committed himself. She could not let him keep thinking that she cared deeply for him. She owed him the truth.

"Rolfe," she said to forestall him, but he put his forefin-

ger across her lips. "Rolfe," Jenny tried again, but he
pleaded, "Jenny, please, just listen and don't interrupt. I am
leaving the army in a few months to take over a small property which I own on the River Ouse near Bedford. Although
I shall never be wealthy, I have an adequate income to live
comfortably and support a wife. Jenny, if you consent to
marry me, I shall be walking six inches off the ground."

"Oh, Rolfe," she said, her heart warming to him. Not wanting to hurt him, she wrestled with her conscience. She could
keep the truth hidden and make him happy by accepting him
while at the same time keeping herself safe from the baron's
unwelcome choices. Rolfe need never know what was in her
heart. He would come to believe that she loved him.

But Jenny could not bring herself to hoodwink him. She
found herself pouring out how she had used Tristan's reported drowning to save herself from an odious marriage to
Lord Duson. She even told him of her pressing need to find
a husband before Lord Markham found one for her. "I cannot trust the baron's entrants."

On the bench beside her, Rolfe became perfectly still
while Jenny went on, oblivious to his altering mood.

"I respect you, Rolfe, and I *am* fond of you. Truly I am.
But I do not think I would be contemplating marriage at all
were the baron not pressuring me."

Rolfe's dark head was bent to his chest, his eyes fixed
morosely on the pebbles beneath the soles of his leather half
boots.

His head came up in an angry motion.

"How could you, Jenny? How could you slur an honest
gentleman's good name simply to contravene Lord Markham's well-intentioned wishes? I thought you were above
reproach. Lord Markham is known to be honorable and honest and trustworthy. Never did I suspect that his daughter
was completely lacking in those excellent values."

Jenny was appalled by his inflammatory words. She had
expected some mild censure from Rolfe, but not such a
harsh repudiation of her entire character. Indignation began
building in her. Good Lord, she was hardly an unprincipled
female with no redeeming qualities.

"One mistake does not make me devoid of all integrity,

Rolfe," she defended herself. "I believed Tristan Darius to be dead. The baron and my mother were the only two people who knew about my deceit. I did not go about blackening Tristan's good name to the general populace."

"What of Lord Duson?"

"Lord Duson was put off with other excuses."

"Still you would have used me abominably to circumvent a marriage to a man of Lord Markham's choice."

"Yes, I admit it was wrong for me to entertain such an idea, but I wanted to wed someone I could respect if not precisely love. You may not have had my heart, but you had my highest regard."

"Not good enough, Jenny," he said, rising from the wooden bench and hovering over her. "You led me on to get me to propose to you. Such underhanded behavior is despicable. I could never bestow my honorable name on a female with so little conscience."

Incensed, Jenny hit back. "What I did was wrong. But you have no right to impugn my honesty. I tried to forestall your proposal before you made it, but you stopped me. A minute ago I could have fallen into your arms, and you would have been none the wiser, and what was it—oh, yes, floating six inches off the ground. But I chose to be straight with you."

He sneered. "I suppose I should be beholden to you for that small mercy."

Jenny restrained herself from lashing out any further, unwilling to waste another moment on such a useless battle. She got up, pushed past him, and hurried from the conservatory.

Rolfe had caught up to Jenny by the time she joined Tristan and Lord and Lady Coombs, who were waiting to step onto the balcony that overlooked the garden where the fireworks display was to conclude the evening's festivities.

Rockets burst high in the air and spinning wheels of fireworks spun on the ground. Sparks flew from the Roman candles and Catherine wheels. Jenny and Rolfe avoided each other as if each suspected the other of having a communicable disease.

Tristan noticed the stiff chins and flinty eyes and was not surprised when he learned that he, not Rolfe, was to see Jenny home.

Inside the carriage, he said, "Rolfe proposed, and it did not go well. Have I hit the mark?"

Jenny recounted the humiliating episode. "I can understand the blow to Rolfe's sensibilities when I admitted that I encouraged him to propose to avoid the baron's machinations, but I expected him to be sympathetic to the desperation which caused me to resort to the ruse to outwit Lord Duson. You forgave me, Tristan, even though it was you I had smeared, but Rolfe took umbrage on your behalf."

"Ah, but, Jenny, I do not want to marry you. A man expects, like Caesar, for his wife to be above reproach."

His words pained her. *I do not want to marry you* mangled Jenny's heart, but somehow she managed to keep the deep hurt from her voice.

"Rolfe said the same thing, about being above reproach that is," she said wearily.

Tristan's hand found hers in the dark coach. He pressed her gloved fingers. "Rolfe is a reasonable fellow. Once he thinks things through, he will come to his senses and be sorry that he cut up at you."

But Jenny had no desire to wed Rolfe Kittredge. She knew whom she wanted for a husband, but that would take a huge, huge miracle. Done in by the inevitable tensions caused by her clash with Rolfe, she put an end to the tiresome subject.

"Has the investigator you hired learned anything of your brother's whereabouts?" she said to divert Tristan, but not really caring what his answer would be.

"Mr. Geiger has traced Gerald to France, but he and his paramour have moved around so much it is slow going following their trail."

"Yet, surely Mr. Geiger's report is promising. He is bound to find Gerald eventually," she pointed out.

"I hope it happens before it's too late," Tristan said, his

voice turning hard. "Serena is being indiscreet with Lord Duson."

"How indiscreet?" Jenny asked, her interest awakened by Tristan's blunt revelation. "You mean flirting in public?"

"Much worse," he said. "She has made unescorted visits to the marquess's town house. I shudder to think what would happen if Gerald came back without warning. He would have grounds for divorce." He made a derisive sound of scorn. "Of course, Serena denies any infidelity and claims Duson is simply a friend."

Suddenly Jenny was sick of Serena and sick of Rolfe and even sick of Tristan. Yet she knew she would go to pieces if she learned that Tristan still loved Serena.

When Jenny went quiet, Tristan made no attempt to revive their conversation and lapsed into a similar silence. He closed his eyes and leaned back against the squabs. He had felt like a hypocrite preaching propriety to Serena when it was Gerald who was in the wrong. But he knew that society would crucify Serena if Gerald came home and named Duson as her lover.

Once the very idea of Serena in bed with another man would have driven Tristan mad. In those bygone days, he had been too blinded by infatuation to have seen her true character clearly. But not now. It was hers and Duson's complete lack of discretion in conducting their affair, not the affair itself, which bothered him.

Tristan failed to notice that the coach had stopped until Jenny said, "Wake up, Tristan, we have arrived."

"I have been poor company these last miles," he said, rummaging up a penitent smile while he walked her to the door. He bent his head and bestowed a light kiss on Jenny's lips. "Forgive me?"

The chaste touch of his warm mouth to hers turned Jenny's breath shallow. Even though she knew his brotherly kiss meant nothing, she was shaken by it. Murmuring that she, too, had been less than chummy, she said good night and escaped from him through the front door, which the butler held open, and into the bastion of the town house.

EIGHT

Two days after the duchess's charity benefit, Jenny handed her wraps to a uniformed footman and walked down the hall toward Lord and Lady Coombs's ballroom in a swish of apricot silk. Anne's party was to be a smallish affair of no more than fifty guests. Rolfe would be cool toward her, she knew, but she was relying on his inbred good manners not to be openly hostile.

Therefore, she was thrown completely off balance when she saw him standing at the entrance to the ballroom, smiling warmly in her direction. "Good evening, Rolfe," she said when she reached him.

"Jenny," he replied. Without permission, he linked his arm through hers and steered her to a bower of rubber trees in a corner of the ballroom.

In the semi-privacy of the hothouse plants, he looked down at her and said, "Jenny, I know I behaved badly the other night. I lost my temper and made malicious charges that I did not mean. I beg your forgiveness for my ungentlemanly conduct. My pride was bruised when I learned that your feelings for me were less fervent than mine for you. But isn't that the way of our class? Love on both sides is not essential. I still want you to marry me, even if our union would be unequal. I am certain we have enough regard for each other to rub along famously together."

Jenny had put behind her forever any further thought of marrying Rolfe, and in truth did not welcome either the renewal of his declaration or the need to refuse him again.

She opened her mouth to respond, but before she could get a word out, Anne appeared before them in a huff and began to scold her cousin.

"Rolfe, you promised to help out tonight," she said, shaking her finger at him. "I put you in charge of greeting the guests at the door and find that you have abandoned your post."

"You are worse than my colonel, cuz. Give me a few more minutes with Jenny."

Anne all but stamped her foot. "No, you may speak to Jenny during the rest of the evening *after* everyone has arrived."

"Shrew," Rolfe muttered, but good-naturedly. "Until later, Jenny. Please think over what I said," he pleaded and went off to perform his duty.

"Men," Anne said with mock derision. "You just can't rely on them."

Jenny touched cheeks with Anne in a belated greeting. But after a few pleasantries, Anne excused herself to attend to her hostess duties, saying, "I must see how things are proceeding in the kitchen with the new chef."

Across the room Jenny saw Tristan. He was conversing with Lord Coombs. She set off in that direction, moving from group to group on the way, speaking briefly with old friends and acquaintances. When she finally reached the two men, Tristan gave her a smile that warmed her clear to her toes. His blue eyes swept her from head to toe, his admiring expression confirming her own inkling that she looked well this evening.

For his part, Tristan thought that Jenny seemed lovelier and more desirable each time he saw her. She was rather breathtaking tonight in an apricot silk dress that clung softly to her figure without flaunting it in a bold display. But Lord Coombs commanded Tristan's attention after he, too, greeted Jenny when he said, "You and Miss Markham must excuse me. My wife is waving frantically at me from across the room. I hope the chef hasn't burned the supper."

Once Tristan and Jenny were alone, he said, "You look bang up to the mark, my dear." Jenny was heartened once again by the warm approval in his voice.

"Would you mind if we promenaded a bit," he said. "I am too restless to stand and talk."

Jenny happily agreed to his request and took the arm he offered.

"Is anything wrong?" she asked as they began their progression around the ballroom.

"No, not wrong, exactly. I have had word from Mr. Geiger about my brother's whereabouts."

"Oh, Tristan, how wonderful! Is Mr. Geiger still in France?"

"No, he is back in England, but he wants to deliver his news of Gerald in person. His secrecy has made me edgy."

"Perhaps what he has to say is too long and complicated to be handled in a letter," Jenny said. "Will you see Mr. Geiger soon?"

"I expect him in Curzon Street sometime this evening or by tomorrow morning at the latest. I have left instructions that I should be summoned immediately if he arrives at the house while I am still here."

Reaching the east end of the ballroom, Tristan passed through an arch which led into a dimly lit sitting room. He moved with Jenny to the tall windows. They looked out at the back gardens where the trees strung with colored lanterns had a fairyland appearance.

"Pretty," Tristan said, his comment offhand, his mind obviously on other matters.

"Gerald will agree to let you run Albinore, Tristan," Jenny said, surmising that the welfare of the estate and the well-being of Amy and Serena were what was burdening his mind. "We shall soon be neighbors again, you and I." She put a gloved hand on the sleeve of his black evening coat.

Tristan covered her hand with his own and gave her a halfhearted smile in the semi-darkness. "At least, until you marry and go to live with your husband," he said. "I regret, on your behalf, that Rolfe disappointed you."

Jenny lifted her silk-clad shoulders nonchalantly. "Rolfe has already renewed his proposal. But he deserves a wife who is capable of loving him. Moreover, he is too decent a man to be shackled to a woman who loves another."

Tristan was taken aback. "You have fallen in love with someone else?"

She inclined her head. Tristan had a vague notion that he should not ask the next question, but it passed his lips before the warning reached his brain. "With whom?"

"You," she said. Her response was clear and unequivocal.

Tristan closed his eyes for a long moment. Jenny enchanted him, but he did not want to be enchanted. He must not allow the seeds of desire she had sown to grow. He had too much on his plate to deal successfully with a sentiment that tended to play havoc with a man's emotions. He had once closed himself off from love. While he was less cynical now, this was the wrong time to open himself up to the fickleness of passion.

"I like you, Jenny. Very much. Probably more than any other woman I know," he said honestly, his husky voice soft. "But this is the wrong time for me to be contemplating marriage."

His heart nearly broke when he saw the hurt that leapt into her brown eyes. She bit her lip to stop the tears.

"Oh, Jenny," he moaned, "don't look like that."

His hand stroked her cheek to smooth the consternation from her face. Sliding his hands down her back, he pulled her against him and pressed his lips gently to hers in a kiss meant to comfort.

Jenny's arms curled around Tristan's neck. Her lips began to move over his mouth seductively. His noble purpose thawed. Tristan took her mouth with volatile hunger. He pressed heated kisses from her eyebrows to the base of her throat. His wandering hands had been all over her before some renewed sense of honor penetrated his brain. He was using sweet Jenny as he would a woman he planned to bed. He sighed deeply, reached up, and brought her hands down from around his neck.

Breathing hard, he stepped back, putting distance between them. "Jenny, I feel the worst bounder for taking advantage of you. You have my permission to rake me over the coals."

Jenny's head was whirling, but rake him over the coals? Hardly. She had been kissed before, most recently by Rolfe, but never so deliciously. Tristan's kiss had been wonderful.

His lips had made shivers dance up and down her spine; his touch had made her want to melt into him. *Like* he had said. *I like you very much.* But his feelings went deeper. His dark blue eyes had held love as well as desire. She was sure of it.

The future suddenly seemed fraught with promise. Jenny was not about to burn her bridges by ringing a peal over Tristan's head. A smile of wonder filled her face. "It's all right, Tris. It was quite, quite marvelous."

He looked dumbfounded as if he did not know what to reply to such a blanket endorsement. He led her back to the ballroom. When they emerged through the arch, a footman approached Tristan and handed him a note. "This came for you ten minutes ago, Mr. Darius."

"Thank you," Tristan said. He unfolded the paper and read the message.

"Mr. Geiger has arrived in Curzon Street with the news of Gerald. I must go home immediately, Jenny," he said.

Tristan left her with friends and looked around for Anne to make his excuses, but came across Rolfe first. "Do you know where I might find Lady Coombs? I must leave."

"Before supper?" Rolfe sounded scandalized. "Anne has hired a French chef who has cooked the most delectable delights especially for this party. It is not often one gets to partake of such a meal."

Tristan smiled in spite of himself. "More for you, my gluttonous friend." His face became serious. "I have been called back to the house, Rolfe. The investigator with word of Gerald has arrived from the Continent."

"Then, why are you lingering, man?" Rolfe said. He gave Tristan a friendly shove on the shoulder. "I shall make your excuses to Anne."

The following afternoon while she was reading in the library, Jenny was interrupted by the butler, who informed her, "Mr. Darius to see you, miss. I have put him in the drawing room."

A ripple of joy breezed through Jenny. She smoothed the green-and-white striped skirt of her day gown, fluffed the lace at the rounded neck of the solid green bodice, and allowed herself to dream. Yesterday's passionate kiss had brought Tristan to his senses. He had come to make her an offer of marriage. She knew she was being silly. But why not a declaration of love from him? Oh, Lord, why not?

Tristan stood with one hand on the rosewood mantel, staring into the fire, when Jenny entered the room.

He looked up and turned to face her, a weary frown etched between his brows. One glance at the bleak expression on his handsome face shattered any illusion that he was a loving suitor eager for her hand.

"What is it, Tristan?" she asked, her eyes wide with concern.

"Bad news, Jenny. Gerald is dead."

Jenny sank into a chair. "Oh, no. How?"

"In a hunting accident. His bearer reported that he tripped over a tree root, the gun discharged, and the bullet lodged in his heart."

"I am so sorry, Tristan," Jenny said. "When did it happen?"

"A month ago. His mistress is still living in the country cottage in a small village near Lyons that Gerald rented for them. Mr. Geiger verified that Gerald is buried in the village cemetery."

"It is not some ghastly mistake?"

Tristan shook his head. "Mr. Geiger interviewed the bearer and the villagers, as well as Miss Tremaine, the woman with whom Gerald eloped. Mr. Geiger brought me conclusive proof, a copy of the coroner's report and a valid French death certificate. There is absolutely no doubt that Gerald is gone."

"I'm sorry," Jenny repeated, at a loss for more adequate words.

"Serena can't seem to stop weeping. I would not have thought it, but, in her own way, she must have loved Gerald." After a moment's hesitation, he continued. "I would ask a favor of you, Jenny."

"Anything, Tristan. Would you like me to go to her?"

"No, that won't be necessary. A physician has medicated Serena. Moreover, she recently hired as her maid a mature woman with excellent skills. Miss Crawford will do well enough in looking after her. What I would ask of you is much more of an imposition."

Imposition? Jenny was more curious than apprehensive by his use of the revealing word.

"I am closing the Curzon Street house and taking Serena to Albinore. Mrs. Druback and Pecks are there, but most of the servants will be new. And I do not know how long Serena will remain indisposed. The manor will be no place for a child. May I leave Amy in your care?"

Jenny's response was instantaneous. "Of course, I will be happy to look after her." She smiled a little. "I love Amy so much I would adopt her if I could."

Tristan grinned. "Thank you, my dear. I dreaded leaving the child in the custody of an unfamiliar servant. She adores you and trusts you. With you, she will be above the inevitable turmoil which will result from Gerald's death."

Jenny rose from her chair, for Tristan had moved toward her, making to leave.

"Send Amy to me," she said. "I shall make arrangements immediately to have the bedroom next to mine, which is unoccupied, prepared for her."

Tristan took Jenny's hands into his and looked down into her eyes. "You have a genuinely kind heart, Jenny," he said and leaned down and kissed her lightly on the lips. "You are a treasure, my sweet."

For the rest of his life, Tristan was to remember that tender moment as the exact second he realized that he was in love with Jenny and did not want to live without her.

NINE

Jenny and Amy went on for a while at Jermyn Street as they had when the child had been a frequent visitor at Lindwood.

Amy had shown surprisingly little curiosity about her father's death, asking only, "What is a bearer?"

"He is a servant who holds the guns and ammunition for a hunter," Jenny explained.

But while Amy took her father's accident in stride, she was troubled and confused about her own future at Albinore. She told Jenny, "Mr. Richards said that Uncle Tristan is the master of the estate and no longer a landless gentleman, but a man of property. He owns the manor house, not Mama. Does that mean I won't live there anymore?"

What the valet had said was true. Tristan had been the male relative next in line to Gerald and had inherited the entailed estate, but Jenny quickly assured Amy that her uncle was not about to evict her or her mother. "Albinore is still your home."

"I am glad," Amy said, obviously relieved and confessing the reason, "for Mama might have married Lord Duson and I do not like him by half. He has a mean face and scowls at me." The shadows in her eyes receded. "I wish, Jenny, that you could live in Uncle Tristan's house with me."

"Only married people or close relatives live together in the same house, poppet," Jenny said.

* * *

The one change that Jenny made in Amy's circumstances was to register her in a day school, Mrs. Burford's Academy for Young Ladies. She wanted to give the little girl an opportunity to interact with children her own age. The school Jenny chose was run by a genteel, kindly lady in a house two blocks from the Markhams' house.

Amy had been skeptical at first. "I have never been to school," she had said, sounding very unsure about the prospect.

But Jenny had promised her that if she did not like it, she would not have to stay enrolled.

Amy, however, settled in quickly, got along with her fellow classmates, and even acquired a best friend named Ruth.

With the end of January approaching, Jenny's own fears increased that Lord Markham would force an unwanted match on her. Therefore, her heart beat erratically when her father summoned her to the library on the last day of the month.

"Sit down, Jenny," he said. She obeyed, but looked at him warily.

Lord Markham removed a cigar from an elaborate wooden box on the top of the desk, which was spread over with official-looking documents and a creased copy of the morning's *Times*.

Holding the unlit cigar in his hand, he used it to point toward Jenny, who sat on the edge of a chair with every nerve alert.

"I am leaving tomorrow to take a temporary post in Italy until mid-April," he announced, "which I imagine is good news to you. You will also be pleased to hear that as a diplomat, I pride myself on knowing when to withdraw from a stalemate."

A small fission of hope rose in Jenny's breast.

"What that means, Jenny, is that you can marry where you choose," Lord Markham said, his tone slightly barbed.

You may marry where you choose. Never had Jenny expected to hear those words of capitulation from the baron's lips. It took a full minute for the import of his statement to sink in.

"You are serious, Father?"

"Do you require a sworn affidavit?"

Ignoring his mockery, she said simply, "I am obliged, Father, for your change of heart."

Momentarily unsettled by her mannerly reply, Lord Markham harrumphed. "Yes, well, don't drag your feet, my girl, because I decided to be generous. I would like to meet my grandson before I meet my Maker."

He seated himself behind his desk and idly thumbed through the pile of important-looking papers. "I have work to do, Jenny," he said, effectively ending the interview, but she noticed that his voice was not unkind. It was only when Jenny was back in the privacy of her bedroom that she allowed herself to celebrate with a whoop of joy.

Early in February, Amy came home from school and joined Jenny in the library, where a good blaze had been laid in the fireplace.

She sat down at Jenny's feet on a low three-legged stool near the fire. "Brr, it is freezing outside," she said, rubbing her hands together to warm them and asked, "Do you know about Valentine's Day, Jenny?"

Jenny put down the book she had been reading. "Yes, it is on the fourteenth, about a week from now. Did you hear about the holiday at school?"

Amy nodded. "Our teacher is letting us exchange valentines. Ruth is making cards for everyone in our class and for Mrs. Burford, too. Her mama is showing her how. Did you ever get a valentine, Jenny?"

"Yes, many," she said, thinking of the lacy confection of cherubs and red hearts that Rolfe had sent her before he went to serve with Wellington's forces in France. The other night at Anne's party Jenny had tried to let him down gently after Tristan left. She had confessed that she was in love with someone else.

"It's Tristan," he had guessed. When her silence confirmed his supposition, he had said graciously, "Tristan is a good man," kissed her hand and, visibly disappointed, had hurried from her side.

Amy pulled at the sleeve of Jenny's apple green wool dress, "Are you listening to me, Jenny? Would you help me to cut out hearts from red paper? Ruth says that is how to make a valentine."

"I can do even better and design a fine card for you to make for your friends."

"Oh, good," Amy said. "Can we do it tomorrow?"

"Tomorrow? Yes, I suppose we can. I will buy the bits and pieces we will need at the stationer's on Bond Street."

Amy was pleased and said as much. She looked pensively into the fire. "How did Valentine's Day come into being anyway? Do you know, Jenny?"

"The origin is uncertain," Jenny said. She recalled her talk with Tristan on the subject during their first encounter in Lindwood's library after he had returned from America. "I read a legend about St. Valentine when I was a child. I can relate it to you. But, remember, poppet, myths are simply stories not true history."

"I know," Amy said impatiently, "like the monks and agrimony. Tell me anyway. Legends are fun to hear." She propped her elbow on her knee and fisted her hand against her chin.

"Long ago in ancient Rome," Jenny said in her storytelling voice, "there lived a wicked ruler named Claudius. He decreed that no one in his kingdom should get married."

"What is *decreed?*"

"Ordered or commanded. Claudius made marriage against the law."

"Why?" Amy asked.

"Well, it seems that newly married young men did not want to leave their brides and go to war. They refused to serve in Claudius's army."

Amy cocked her head. "What does that have to do with Valentine's Day?"

Jenny laughed and tweaked the blue ribbon on one of Amy's braids. "Patience, poppet, I'm getting there. St. Valentine was a priest at a church in Claudius's kingdom. It is said that the good cleric believed strongly in love and marriage. Therefore, he defied Claudius and married young couples secretly. Eventually, I confess I don't know exactly how, a holiday came to be named after him, St. Valentine's Day."

"Because he wanted ladies and gentlemen to be married and live together in the same house," Amy said.

"Well, yes, if they loved each other. But today all kinds of people send valentine cards not just lovers. The shops sell elaborate ones, but it will be fun for you to make your own."

Jenny purchased red paper and white lace paper doilies at the stationer's the next day. When Amy came home from school, the supplies had been laid out for her on the library table. She knelt on a chair at the table and asked questions about how each item would be used until Jenny put up her hand and said, "Everything in good time. Let me show you how to proceed."

Jenny had created a simple design in keeping with the six-year-old's abilities. She gave Amy step-by-step instructions as she worked.

With a drawing pencil Jenny traced around the heart-shaped template she had made from heavy cardboard and then cut out the resulting red paper heart with her sewing scissors. She applied mucilage to one side, glued the heart onto the center of a round doily, and printed "Be My Valentine" across it.

Following Jenny's example, Amy had the fun of constructing her own valentines while Jenny kept a watchful eye on her. Finally, after ruining some cards that had stuck to the newspapers that protected the library table and having to discard others because of various flaws, Amy managed to complete a respectable valentine for each of her classmates and her teacher.

She set the cards aside to dry and said to Jenny, "Tomorrow I will make cards for Uncle Tristan and Mama."

The next day while she cut and pasted, Amy said, "You should make a valentine for Uncle Tristan, Jenny."

"I don't think so, sweetie."

"Why not?" Amy asked. "You like him don't you?"

"Of course, I do. But an unmarried lady never sends a valentine to a bachelor gentleman. It just isn't done."

"Why?"

"It would send a message that she wants him to propose to her, which is strictly a male prerogative."

"Progative?"

"Prerogative. His right, but not hers."

"St. Valentine wanted ladies to get married. It's not fair that a lady can't ask a gentleman to marry her if she likes him."

Jenny laughed. "You know, Amy, there have been times when I have had that same improper notion."

Amy giggled and picked up the valentine Jenny had made.

Preoccupied with cleaning up the scraps of red paper and depositing them in the dustbin, Jenny paid no attention when Amy stared thoughtfully at the model card. She failed to notice the devilish expression that eventually danced across the child's face or when Amy slipped the pattern into her own stack of valentines and smiled slyly to herself.

Since Valentine's Day fell on Sunday, Amy's teacher had designated Friday for the students to trade cards. Lady Markham had found the London weather dismal and had decided to return to Lindwood, but had put off the journey until Saturday, mindful that Amy had been looking forward to being able to participate in her class's valentine celebration.

Jenny had expected Amy to rebel against leaving her school and classmates. When she told the child that the family was removing to Lindwood, she found that although Amy was silent for a moment, it was not the silence of resistance, but of reflection.

"We will be in the country in time for me to deliver Uncle Tristan's valentine to him."

Jenny eyed the child with relief, for she had anticipated an argument rather than Amy's ready compliance.

Jenny said, "Although we will arrive too late on Saturday for you to go home to your mama and uncle, you can visit them on Sunday, which is Valentine's Day."

"Uncle Tristan is going to be soooo, soooo surprised

when he sees his valentine," Amy said with what seemed to Jenny an overblown enthusiasm. But children had a way of becoming excited at any unusual event. Yet, her own intense desire to see Tristan closely mirrored Amy's zeal.

After the early church service on Valentine's Day, Jenny tucked Amy into a chaise and saw the child off in the company of a maid. Amy clutched the valentines she was taking to her mother and uncle in her gloved hand.

Although Jenny yearned to see Tristan, she felt it would be best for the little girl to have some private time with the family from whom she had been separated for almost a month.

However, a short time after Amy had driven off, a note arrived at Lindwood from Tristan, asking Jenny to meet him at the pond at two o'clock. The thought of seeing him again left her giddy.

As the appointed hour for their rendezvous neared, Jenny was flipping through a ladies' magazine, willing the hands of the clock to move. Finally, too restless to concentrate, she threw down the periodical and set off for the stables.

Jenny arrived at the pond early, dismounted, and looped Benjy's reins around a bush. Excited anticipation thumped in her breast.

The golden rays of the winter sun were melting the thin ice that fringed the water's edge near her boots. She looked up the hill and saw that the cenotaph was gone.

Her head turned time and time again toward the direction from which Tristan would come as she paced and kicked the dried grass and dreamed how wonderful it would be if Tristan would tell her that he loved her. She had reason to be optimistic, for hadn't he admitted that he cared for her more than any woman he knew? Yet she could not wholly dispel his attestation that he did not want to get married.

Her mind in flux, Jenny was looking out over the pond clogged with reeds and rushes when she heard the sound of hoofbeats. She turned in the direction of the drum of hooves and saw Tristan mounted on Perseus, cantering toward her.

Jenny's heart pounded as he approached. When he reached her, Tristan kicked out of his stirrups, leapt from the saddle, and swept Jenny into his arms. He held her tightly as if he never wanted to let her go. Happiness welled up within her.

Grasping her by her shoulders, Tristan put Jenny a little away from him and looked down at her.

"Did no one ever tell you, you saucy wench, that it is the man who proposes?"

Jenny backed from his arms. Her eyebrows inched up on her forehead. "What are you talking about?" she said.

"Jenny, love, I am delighted to accept your hand in marriage, but customarily the gentleman sends the valentine with the declaration."

"Valentine? What valentine? Tristan, have your wits gone begging?" Jenny said, her scowl deepening.

Tristan laughed. "Amy delivered your card to me this morning, a lacy doily with a perfect red heart pasted in the center." He shook his head in mock criticism. "I do think, sweetheart, you must practice your letters. You printed your proposal in the most childish scrawl. Spelling the word 'marry,' 'm-e-r-r-y' in 'Will you marry me?' Strikes me as rather illiterate for an educated lady."

Jenny's cheeks flamed. "Amy! I shall wring the child's neck!"

As if he hadn't heard her, Tristan went on. "However, I must say, the card was rather well made. Better constructed than the ones she gave me and her mother."

"Stop roasting me, Tristan. You know that Amy printed that nonsense on the model I made for her to copy and gave it to you without my knowledge." Jenny looked toward the hill. "What happened to the cenotaph?" she asked irritably. She wanted to put an end to the teasing.

"I had it carted away by a stone mason from the village, who can alter it and resell it. He was glad to have the monument once I assured him I did not want compensation. It did not seem appropriate to leave the stone standing."

Perseus butted his master's shoulder with his large head. Tristan patted the horse's velvet-soft nose distractedly. His laughter was gone.

"Serena is to marry Lord Duson," he said. "The marquess has visited her a good number of times since the news of Gerald's death and has drawn her out of her misery. I cannot like him. But they seem to understand each other. Since she wants him, I will not stand in her way."

Jenny's pulse jumped, concerned for Amy. "Oh, Tris, Amy abhors Lord Duson," she said. "I hate to see her put under the marquess's thumb."

"Don't worry, Jenny. She won't be," Tristan vowed. "His lordship bargained for a handsome dowry. I, in turn, bartered to have Amy live with me. Serena has never been very maternal. You love Amy more than her own mother does. My sister-in-law was glad to have Amy off her hands and was quick to sign the papers that made me the child's legal guardian. As for Duson, he heartily approved the arrangement, for he does not want the responsibility nor the expense of rearing her."

Tristan lifted Jenny's chin with a gloved finger and looked into her eyes.

"The valentine card wasn't nonsense, even if it was Amy who printed the words. Once you said you loved me. I think you still do."

Jenny lowered her lashes. "You are being unchivalrous by reminding me of my ingloriously lax moment."

"Yes, very wicked of me," he said tenderly. "I will play by a gentleman's rules and render a proper proposal. When I said good-bye to you that last day in London, it was the very day I guessed that I was in love with you. I never thought I would want to marry, but I was wrong. I have come to know that my future will be meaningless without you in my life. You are bright and warm and wonderful. Marry me, Jenny."

"Yes," she said. "Oh, yes, yes."

Tristan pulled her close against him. "Happy Valentine's Day, love," he said. He lowered his mouth onto hers and captured her lips in a deep kiss. It was winter, but Jenny felt as if all the birds of summer had suddenly burst into song.

AT FIRST SIGHT

Joy Reed

ONE

"There, that's the last stitch. And it looks perfect, Dorothea—absolutely perfect. No bride ever had a lovelier dress to be married in."

"Do you really think so, Phoebe?" Dorothea turned to and fro, regarding her reflection in the looking glass. "I must say that for a homemade affair, it does look very well."

"It's perfect," said Phoebe again, with satisfaction. Sitting back on her heels, she looked admiringly at her sister's ethereal garb of gauze and netting. "I'm sure no London dressmaker could have made a finer job of it than the two of us together. Why, if you weren't being married, we might put up our board on the strength of this dress and make our fortunes forthwith! 'Fairchild Sisters' Millinery'—it has a nice ring to it, doesn't it? I shall have to tell Gus that marrying you will put a distinct crimp in my commercial plans."

Dorothea laughed and turned to regard her reflection once more in the glass. "I can't believe I am really marrying Gus tomorrow, Phoebe," she said. "Ever since we became engaged, it seemed as though this day would never come. And now that it has come, it doesn't seem as though it could be real."

"Well, I certainly hope it's real," said Phoebe gaily. "Otherwise, we have made a beautiful dress and a delicious bride cake and a bushel of wedding favors all for nothing."

She rose to her feet and began to untie the apron that covered her yellow muslin dress. Standing, it could be seen that she was as tall as her sister and very like her in appearance. Both girls had long-lashed dark eyes, heart-shaped faces, and brown hair with a pronounced curl to it. Dorothea's figure was a shade plumper than Phoebe's, and her face had a rounder, more gentle cast; but the chief difference between them was the sparkle of mischief in Phoebe's eyes. The sparkle was very pronounced now as she regarded her elder sister.

"Don't say you mean to cry off at the eleventh hour, Dorry!" she said. "Though it's an ill wind that blows nobody good, as they say. If you decide not to marry poor Gus after all, then I can wear your wedding dress to the village assembly tomorrow night. And in it, I shall undoubtedly be the belle of the ball!"

Dorothea looked shocked, though she could not help smiling at the same time. "Of course I shan't cry off from marrying Gus!" she said. "You are joking, of course, Phoebe. I was merely saying that it seems strange to be marrying Gus tomorrow. I have been dreaming of my wedding day for so long, and now it's really here."

"Tomorrow," agreed Phoebe, as she gathered up needle, thread, and scissors. "St. Valentine's Day. Great-Aunt Gertrude was saying last night it's a queer start to choose mid-February in which to be married. She thought you and Gus would have done better to wait until spring."

Dorothea looked mulish. "It's not a queer start! I much prefer being married now to waiting till spring. St. Valentine's Day is a special day to me. It was on St. Valentine's Day a year ago that Gus began to fall in love with me."

"You can pin it down to the exact hour, I suppose?" said Phoebe. Her voice was teasing, but Dorothea nodded solemnly, taking the words at face value.

"As a matter of fact I can, Phoebe. It was during that week I spent at the Kettlewells'. A lot of us girls were talking about its being the eve of St. Valentine's Day, and Johanna Kettlewell said that according to the old custom, the first man you see on St. Valentine's Day morning is your valentine for the coming year. Well, I already knew that I liked Gus Early better than all the other gentlemen, so I told Johanna about it, and that next morning we went downstairs together, me with my eyes closed and her leading me. She shut me into the parlor, then kept watch outside until she saw Gus coming down the hall alone. Then I just popped out of the parlor door and told him he was my valentine. And it was right then that he began to pay attention to me—really pay attention to me, I mean, in more than just a friendly way."

"Indeed?" said Phoebe. Her voice was still teasing, but there was an arrested look in her eyes as she regarded her sister.

"Indeed, yes," said Dorothea firmly. "I think there is sometimes more in these old customs than people like to believe. You will laugh at me, of course, Phoebe, but I am quite sure Gus would never have thought of falling in love with me if I hadn't made him my valentine."

Phoebe did not laugh. She went on putting away her sewing equipment with a thoughtful look on her face.

The thoughtful look was still there later that afternoon, as she was dressing for dinner. The Fairchilds were a well-off family, but far from wealthy, and Phoebe was obliged to dress herself, unless she could persuade one of her younger sisters to lend a hand. She had three younger sisters altogether, but the next eldest after her, Tina, was seventeen now and had her own toilette to think of. Accordingly, Phoebe was forced to rely on her two youngest sisters for help, and very unreliable help it tended to be. Anthea and Allegra were twins, aged eleven and still in the schoolroom. They were both aggrieved this evening because their mother had refused to let them dine downstairs. This privilege was accorded them during family dinners, but tonight was a special occasion. Owing to Dorothea's wedding on the morrow, there were to be guests, among them Mr. Augustus Early, the happy bridegroom (better known to all and sundry as Gus) and his parents. There were also a number of other friends and relatives who had come long distances to be present at the wedding and who would be partaking of the Fairchilds' hospitality for the next few days.

"It's not fair," complained Anthea, draping Phoebe's shawl over her own shoulders and admiring the effect in the looking glass. "I'm sure I don't know why we shouldn't be allowed to eat downstairs tonight like you and Tina and Dorothea."

"We never get to do *anything* fun," stated Allegra, who was busy investigating the contents of Phoebe's reticule. "Anthea and I are eleven years old now. Eleven years old is plenty old enough to eat downstairs, even if there *are* guests. Don't you think so, Phoebe?"

They looked expectantly at their older sister. But Phoebe did not appear to have heard them. She was gazing critically at her own reflection in the glass. When Allegra poked her, however, she started and turned around in a hurry. "What's that? What is it?" she asked, looking from one sister to the other. "Allegra, what are you doing? Stop rummaging through my reticule!"

"All right," said Allegra, putting down the bag, "but Anthea and I wanted to know if you didn't think we're old enough to eat with the company. Don't you think eleven years old is old enough?"

"You two? Eat downstairs?" said Phoebe with a snort. "Don't be ridiculous. You must remember what happened the last time we had guests to dinner and Mama let you eat downstairs. You ate all the cheesecakes before anyone else could have even one, and Anthea spilled her water glass on the tablecloth."

"That was an accident," said Anthea.

"And I wouldn't eat all the cheesecakes tonight," added Allegra. "I was only ten then, and I didn't know any better."

"Well, even if you do know better now, I don't think Mama will care to risk it. Besides, there really isn't room for you at the table tonight. We are almost too full as it is. With Great-Aunt Gertrude and Uncle Andrew and Aunt Lydia and Cousin Phyllis staying with us—and then there's Gus and all his family, of course. And I think—I believe—Mr. Harris is also coming tonight."

There was a faintly self-conscious note in Phoebe's voice as she added this last name. Neither of her sisters remarked it, though Anthea demanded, as a matter of form, "Who's Mr. Harris?"

"Oh, you probably don't know Mr. Harris, girls. He has never dined here before, but I have met him over at the Earlys' a few times. He is one of Gus's oldest friends and is to stand groomsman for him tomorrow."

"No, I don't know him," said Anthea. "But I saw him. He was with Gus earlier today when Gus came by to talk to Dorothea. He has side-whiskers, and his hair curls in the prettiest way, just like a girl's."

"It does not!" said Phoebe indignantly. "I thought his hair *extremely* elegant."

"He has curls like a girl's," repeated Anthea. She giggled and began to chant, "Mr. Harris has curls like a girl's. Mr. Harris has curls like a girl's."

"Anthea!" said Phoebe furiously. "If you say one more word against Mr. Harris, I'll make sure you don't eat downstairs until you're at least eighteen. Maybe not until you're twenty!"

"Phoebe's in love with Mr. Harris," said Allegra perceptively. "That's why she doesn't want you to talk against his curls."

"Phoebe *likes* men with curls like girls'," said Anthea gleefully. "She thinks they are extremely elegant."

Phoebe's cheeks were a brilliant pink, but she managed to laugh. "Now you are being silly, girls. Of course I am not in love with Mr. Harris. Why, I hardly know him." Summoning up her best elder-sister air, she added, "I must say, I agree with Mama's decision that you should eat in the nursery tonight. If you were to say those kind of childish things about Mr. Harris while we were at the table, all of us would look no-how."

As she had hoped, this speech immediately distracted her sisters' minds to their former grievance. "We wouldn't," said Allegra. "We wouldn't say things like that while we were at table."

"We're old enough to know better than that," agreed Anthea. "I must say, I don't think it's *fair*. Tina gets to eat at the table, and she's only seventeen. That's just six years older than Allegra and me."

They continued to discuss the injustice of their mother's decision while Phoebe donned her dress and put the last touches on her hair. Phoebe hardly heard them. She was busy thinking of Mr. Randoph Harris and wondering if he would be present at the dinner that night.

Of course she was not in love with him. Her sisters'

accusation was ridiculous. How could a girl be in love
with a man she had only spoken to half a dozen times?
Especially when the conversation had been limited to saying merely, "Good morning," "Good evening," and "How
do you do?" It was, as Phoebe assured herself, ridiculous.
Yet she could not deny that when she was in Mr. Harris's
company, she felt something she had never felt in the company of any other man. His every utterance seemed to
carry a significance that went far beyond the words themselves, and when he turned his brooding dark eyes on her
and inquired, "How do you do, Miss Phoebe?" in his beautiful baritone voice, it was all she could do to stammer
out a reply.

At times like these Phoebe suspected she might be falling in love with Mr. Harris, even in spite of it being a
ridiculous thing to do. What else besides love could make
her so shy and stupid? She had no difficulty conversing
with any of the other gentlemen of her acquaintance. Indeed, she was commonly held to be a clever girl capable
of holding her own in any company. But she was certainly
unable to hold her own where Mr. Harris was concerned.
Such had been proven any number of times during the
past few years.

As a result, it was no wonder that Mr. Harris had, up till
now, hardly looked at her. He had been polite enough whenever they had met, of course, but he had also made it clear
that he considered her a mere child unworthy of any distin-
guishing attention. And perhaps this was not strange, for Mr.
Harris was at least twenty-three and a man of sophistication
and elegance. He wore the most exciting clothes—not plain
neckcloths and stodgy greatcoats like the other gentlemen,
but sweeping cloaks, cravats of fabulous complexity, and
topcoats with peaked lapels and huge, ornate buttons.

Nor were his clothes his only outstanding feature. He was,
beyond comparison, the handsomest man Phoebe had ever
seen. He was tall and dark, with side-whiskers and chiseled
features and eyes that seemed to hold a melancholy knowledge of the world. His dark hair did indeed have a curl to
it, but it was not at all "like a girl's," Phoebe assured herself

indignantly. Instead, it waved over his brow in a manner she thought too romantic for words.

Indeed, it was the air of romance about him that set Mr. Harris apart from the other gentlemen she knew, even more than his appearance. One could tell at a glance that he was nothing so prosaic as a clergyman or soldier or clerk. And in fact he was none of these things, for he had inherited a property in the north of England that enabled him to live like a gentleman of leisure. Phoebe had made inquiries, and everything she had learned had tended to strengthen her impression that Mr. Harris was the perfect man for her. The only imperfect thing about him was that he did not seem to think her perfect, too. And Phoebe did not blame him for this. Why would such a Nonpareil think her anything out of the common way? She was a mere child compared to him and had never had the benefit of travel, a university education, or a Season in London to give her Town bronze. She had no particular fortune; she was passably pretty but not an Incomparable; and it was a mortifying fact that she was not even able to use such wits as God had given her whenever he was around.

But Phoebe had vowed that all that was to change. She was nineteen now, fully as tall as Dorothea, and everyone said she looked much handsomer since she had started wearing her hair the new way. She had also been out of the schoolroom for two years now, and might be expected to have developed as much poise as she was ever likely to possess. So when she had heard from Gus that Mr. Harris was to attend the wedding as his groomsman, she had made up her mind that this time she would make an impression on the Nonpareil. Not merely an impression, as Phoebe reminded herself, but a *good* impression. A bad impression would be worse than no impression at all. So she had spent extra time with her hair and dress and studied out a few witty things to say, on the chance that she might get an opportunity to talk to Mr. Harris that evening.

Rising from her dressing table, Phoebe regarded her reflection in the cheval glass. Her short-sleeved dress of pink-flowered muslin was by no means striking, but it was pretty and becoming. The pink ribbon threaded in her brown curls matched both the pink of the muslin and the pink of her cheeks. She wished she had something more elegant to wear in the way of jewelry than her coral necklace, but there was only a limited amount of real jewelry in the Fairchild household, and the whole supply had been co-opted that evening by Dorothea and her mother. Which was as it should be, as Phoebe reminded herself. This was their occasion far more than hers. But she wished nonetheless that she might have worn the pearl necklet and earrings, or Mother's topaz set. As it was, she looked terribly young and—she feared—unsophisticated.

Well, I'll just have to show Mr. Harris that I am more sophisticated than I look, Phoebe told herself. I must win his admiration with my wit and charm. But her heart misgave her, for she had never before demonstrated much wit and charm when Mr. Harris was around. Phoebe wished there were an easier way to win his admiration. She thought of what Dorothea had told her about lying in wait for Gus on Valentine's morning. Not only had Dorothea won Gus's admiration through her stratagem, she had ended by winning a proposal of marriage from him. Of course there had been more involved than following a silly old-fashioned custom, but that was how their love affair had got started, and Phoebe was not likely to scorn anything that might get a love affair started between her and Mr. Harris.

But Dorothea was actually staying in the same house as Gus, Phoebe reminded herself. And Mr. Harris won't be staying at our house, but rather with the Earlys. I don't see how I could arrange to see him first thing in the morning unless I was staying there, too.

Seeing that this was impossible, Phoebe turned her attention back to her reflection. She tweaked a curl over her ear, smoothed her skirt, and wrested her shawl from the protesting Anthea. "I need that, you silly girl. It's chilly in the dining room, and this dress has short sleeves."

"If you don't like it in the dining room, I'll take your place," Allegra offered generously.

Phoebe laughed. "No, that cock won't fight! I'll manage to endure the dining room, no matter if it is chilly."

"She will have her admiration of Mr. Harris to keep her warm," said Anthea wickedly.

Phoebe felt her cheeks flush. "Good evening, girls," she said shortly, and swept out of the room without even bothering to draw the shawl over her shoulders.

TWO

Since it was a blustery February evening, not merely the dining room but the whole house was chilly. Before Phoebe even reached the staircase that led down to the reception rooms on the ground floor, she had to pause to arrange her shawl over her shoulders. The pause turned out to be fortuitous, for when Phoebe was halfway down the stairs, the door to the hall opened and a couple of gentlemen came in. With a leaping of joy in her heart, Phoebe recognized one of them as Mr. Harris.

He saw her almost the same moment she saw him. He stopped dead, looking up at her with an expression of surprise. He was, as Phoebe reflected, every bit as handsome as she had remembered. His whiskers were as dark and luxuriant; his eyes as deep and melancholy; and the hair falling over his forehead as romantically wavy as ever. *Not* curly, Phoebe assured herself.

But though all these things were the same, there was something different about Mr. Harris this evening. Phoebe did not have to reflect in order to decide what it was. It was the open admiration and appreciation in his eyes as he watched her descend the staircase step by step.

Phoebe felt a soaring in her heart. It was a moment such as she had always dreamed of. At last she had made an impression on Mr. Harris, and a favorable one, too, if his expression was to be believed. Now, if she could only further that favorable impression without doing anything to mar it, she might yet win her heart's desire.

The thought made Phoebe so giddy that she almost missed putting her foot on the next stair tread. Fortunately, she had hold of the banister, and the slip was an imperceptible one, but it awoke in her a sense of caution. How dreadful if she were to fall in front of Mr. Harris! She imagined herself rolling down the stairs, arms and legs flailing, to land in a disordered heap at his impeccably shod feet. The thought was such an awful one that an involuntary giggle rose in her throat. With an effort she choked it back, but it left a lingering smile on her lips as she descended the stairs and walked over to where Mr. Harris and his companion were standing.

So occupied had Phoebe been with thoughts of Mr. Harris that she only belatedly realized his companion was Mr. Augustus Early, her sister's fiancé and bridegroom-to-be. "Oh, good evening, Gus," she said, extending her hand to him.

" 'Evening, Phoebe," he said, taking her hand and bestowing a friendly salute on it. "You look mighty fine tonight—fine as fivepence." Glancing at his friend, he added, "You know Randolph here, don't you? Seems to me the two of you've met a time or two before."

"Oh, yes, we have met," said Phoebe, with what she hoped was tolerable composure. Turning to Mr. Harris, she added politely, "I am very pleased to see you tonight, sir."

"I wouldn't have missed it," said Mr. Harris. His eyes were still fixed on Phoebe—those melancholy dark eyes that seemed to pierce to her very soul. His voice was even more deep and resonant than she remembered, and she could not help putting a personal construction on his words. "I wouldn't have missed it"—that and his expression seemed to show he had been as struck by her as she was by him.

Phoebe felt another thrill course through her. But she damped it down and extended a hand to him with a regal smile. "You are too kind, sir. I am sure Gus must appreciate the support of his friends on such a memorable occasion as his wedding day."

Gus laughed. "Aye, Randolph'll see I come up to scratch tomorrow, won't you, old fellow? And he's sworn to make sure I don't drink so much wine tonight that I can't drag myself out of bed in the morning."

"Indeed," said Mr. Harris. "But I am sure such precautions will be needless. Your bride will be waiting for you, and no man fortunate enough to conquer the heart of one of the lovely Miss Fairchilds could dream of disappointing her in any way." Taking the hand Phoebe gave him, he raised it to his lips, his dark eyes fixed on hers all the while.

Phoebe was perfectly sure her own heart was conquered at that moment. She had once more to damp down the urge to laugh aloud or sing or do one of a dozen other crazy things. What she actually did was smile again and say, "Indeed," with a friendly but not effusive air.

Gus was talking again now, saying that he and Mr. Harris had driven over in his curricle, and that his parents would be coming over later in their own carriage. Phoebe tried to listen, but she was so conscious of Mr. Harris standing beside her that she was unable to concentrate on anything else. As always, he was having a powerful effect on her. Yet thus far she had held her own in spite of it, and it was obvious he had been impressed by the effort. When she roused herself to say, "But you must both come into the drawing room and meet the other guests," Mr. Harris took her arm as though he had a right to it and accompanied her and Gus into the drawing room.

Phoebe felt it to be the proudest moment of her life. Most of the guests were already in the drawing room, along with Phoebe's parents and her sisters Tina and Dorothea. All of them turned to look as she came in on Mr. Harris's arm. "Here is Gus, Dorry," said Phoebe, smiling at Dorothea. "And here"—she had to struggle hard to keep the triumph out of her voice—"here is Mr. Harris."

The next few minutes were devoted to making introductions between the two young men and the various visiting relatives. Before they were quite finished, Gus's parents came in, and they had to be introduced, too. During this time, Phoebe had no chance to exchange any more words with Mr. Harris, but she still had ample opportunity to admire his elegant bearing and polished manners as he shook hands and said, "How do you do?" to Great-Aunt Gertrude, Uncle Andrew, and the other relatives.

She was not the only one admiring him. Cousin Phyllis took the first opportunity to whisper in her ear, "Oh, Phoebe, he's charming! You lucky girl, it's plain to see he's head over heels in love with you. I do envy you, I vow and declare." This was agreeable; but much less agreeable was the moment when Great-Aunt Gertrude grasped her by the arm and inquired in a stage whisper, "That's a handsome young feller you came in with, Phoebe. One of your beaux, is he?"

Phoebe disclaimed this idea, blushing violently. She hoped with all her heart that Mr. Harris had not heard her aunt's words. As it turned out, he had, but even this embarrassment was magically transformed into triumph. For when the moment came for the guests to go into the drawing room, it was Mr. Harris who approached her, smiling down at her in a soft and intimate manner. "I may not have the honor of being your beau, but I hope I may at least have the privilege of taking you in to dinner?"

Phoebe had just presence of mind enough to stammer out, "Why, yes—yes, certainly, Mr. Harris." He smiled again, took her arm in his, and began to guide her toward the dining room.

I must take careful note of this moment, Phoebe told herself. *This is the most wonderful moment of my whole life.* But she was in such a befuddled state that she could not really savor her triumph. Before she knew it, she was seated at the table, and Mr. Harris was taking his own seat beside her.

She comforted herself with the thought that she would have the pleasure of sitting next to him for the next two hours. But that was a thought as much frightening as alluring. What would she find to say to him? It was to be an unusually long and formal meal, three full courses with removes. All the witty things she had planned to say beforehand would not fill five minutes of that time, even assuming she could remember them—an assumption that seemed now more than doubtful.

Fortunately for Phoebe, she was not solely responsible

for conversation at the table. As soon as they were all seated, Gus turned to address Dorothea and Mrs. Fairchild. "I see Alan isn't here yet," he said. "Poor fellow, I was afraid he might not make it. Let's hope he gets here by ten o'clock tomorrow, or there'll be no clergyman to marry us!"

Gus laughed, as at a very good joke, but Dorothea looked anxious and Mrs. Fairchild concerned. "Yes, we have had no word of him, Gus," she said. "I must confess I am a little worried. He knows he is to stay here rather than at Longacre Lodge?"

"Aye, I wrote and told him to come straight here, direct he got off the coach. You know I thought he'd be more comfortable here than at the Lodge, where we're already full to bursting. And of course it's more convenient for the ceremony, too. I wouldn't have asked it of you, Mrs. Fairchild, but since you were good enough to say you wouldn't mind—"

"Indeed I do not mind," said Mrs. Fairchild, smiling warmly at Gus. "I would be glad to put up any number of your friends, Gus. And of course Mr. Stanfield is a special case, as he is to officiate at the wedding. But I must say I am worried about him. You are sure he was to take the early coach?"

Gus laughed. "Oh, there's no being sure where Alan's concerned! Not that he isn't a conscientious fellow—in fact, that's half the problem. I wouldn't be a bit surprised if one of his parishioners didn't have some last-minute crisis, and he got so involved in trying to help that he lost track of time, missed the early coach, and had to take a later one instead."

Mrs. Fairchild suggested it would not hurt to send one of the servants to the Crown to make inquiries, but Gus vetoed the idea, saying that his friend was bound to get there sooner or later. "He knows I'm relying on him," said Gus. "And it's not like Alan to let a fellow down." All this gave Phoebe a perfectly good opportunity to turn to Mr. Harris and ask, "Are you acquainted with Mr. Stanfield, too, Mr. Harris?"

"Oh, yes, I know Alan Stanfield," said Mr. Harris. "He and Gus and I were all at university together."

Phoebe noted that he sounded less than enthusiastic. "What is he like?" she asked. "I have never met him myself.

Gus has spoken of him often, but so far as I know he has never visited here."

Mr. Harris nodded, looking more bored than ever. "No, you wouldn't have met him. It's as Gus said: he's a terribly conscientious fellow. A clergyman, you know—he took orders as soon as he got out of university. Alan was always a serious sort—salt of the earth, of course, but dull."

"Oh, I see," said Phoebe sympathetically. "A case of all work and no play making Jack a dull boy."

Mr. Harris received this trite comment as though it had been the highest order of wit. "That's it exactly," he said with approval. "You are exactly right, Miss Phoebe. All work and no play do make Jack a dull boy. And I think, too, that such a regimen must compromise his essential humanity. Of course there must be churches and clergymen—I don't dispute that. But I rejoice that my own circumstances do not require me to burn out my soul in writing dull sermons and helping a lot of ne'er-do-wells who aren't a particle grateful for it."

Phoebe was thrilled to be having such a deep and serious discussion with Mr. Harris. She agreed warmly that it would have been criminal for him to burn out his soul writing dull sermons and helping ungrateful ne'er-do-wells. Mr. Harris nodded solemnly. "You may well say so, Miss Phoebe," he said. "I have a spirit that will not brook the daily toil and grind of a profession. I require leisure to meditate on the world around me and the freedom to live life as the moment offers. I cannot find inspiration in such dull things as sermons and liturgies and hymns."

Phoebe agreed that there was little inspiration to be found in most of the sermons she had ever heard. "You sound like a poet, Mr. Harris," she commented. "Or a writer. That was very poetic, what you said about your spirit not brooking the daily grind of a profession."

Mr. Harris looked gratified, though he disclaimed any pretense of being a poet. "For even writing poetry requires restraint," he told Phoebe. "I began a book of verse a few years back, and most of my friends thought it showed real promise. Alas, I found I was limited by the constraints of the verse form. My spirit will not stand restraint in any form.

How can one truly express one's feelings when one is limited by considerations of rhyme and meter? It seems to me a nobler thing simply to *feel,* rather than to struggle to put that feeling into words."

Phoebe agreed enthusiastically that feeling was a much nobler thing than putting feeling into words. "You are obviously a woman of feeling yourself, Miss Phoebe," said Mr. Harris, fixing his soulful dark eyes upon her. "I felt at once we were kindred spirits when I saw you there on the stairs tonight. There is a spirituality about your face that shows you, too, have a soul above the common run of humanity."

Phoebe was much flattered by these words. Of course she could not help thinking that this spiritual cast to her features must have developed rather recently, for Mr. Harris had never hailed her as a kindred spirit at any of their previous meetings. But still she felt very flattered.

She would have liked to hear more in this vein, but Mr. Harris had gone on to discuss something else. It might have been more accurate to say that he had reverted to discussing his previous topic of discussion, his own unique and sensitive soul. "I have found, through experience, that I must be allowed to go my own gait through life," he told Phoebe. "Even the slightest constraint frets me beyond endurance. I must have absolute personal freedom, or I wither away spiritually and emotionally."

Phoebe looked sympathetic. Mr. Harris went on, warming to his theme. "What does the common man know of freedom? He rises by the clock, dines at set times, goes to work six days and reserves the seventh for worshipping his Creator. And why? Simply because it is the custom to do so. Would he not be better served if he rose when he felt like it, dined when he felt like it, worshipped when he felt like it?"

Phoebe agreed that mankind, as a whole, would be much better served by such a regimen. She was a little distracted because she badly wanted a serving of the fricassee of chicken that stood at Mr. Harris's elbow and he was too busy talking to help her to it, but she told herself that such gross considerations as food ought to be secondary to a woman of feeling like herself.

Mr. Harris, meanwhile, was going on. "This morning, for instance, I rose before dawn and climbed to the top of Beckhurst Hill to watch the sunrise. It was a magnificent spectacle, a vision of unparalleled beauty. And as I watched, I felt my soul rise within me. Was this not as much worship as sitting in a dusty church listening to some dull parson drone out the liturgy?"

Phoebe opened her mouth to agree that it was. Then a sudden inspiration struck her.

If Mr. Harris had risen early this morning to watch the sunrise, then he might be persuaded to do so again tomorrow. And if she, Phoebe, could arrange to go with him, then she could kill two birds with one stone. Not only would she get to spend an hour alone with him, she would meet him early enough that it was practically certain she would see no other man first. And that would effectually make him her valentine. And if Dorothea was by any chance right that there was something in that old custom, then she might even end up marrying him!

So what Phoebe actually said was, "Oh, Mr. Harris, how I wish I could have watched the sunrise with you this morning! It sounds positively inspirational."

"I am sure you would have appreciated it, Miss Phoebe. Like me, you have a soul that can appreciate the beauties of nature."

"Oh, yes," said Phoebe fervently. "I adore sunrises." As if struck by a passing thought, she added, "Are you by any chance going to Beckhurst Hill again tomorrow morning? I would like of all things to accompany you."

She feared this might sound a little forward, but to her relief Mr. Harris took it as a matter of course. "I can think of nothing more delightful than having you as my companion at such a moment, Miss Phoebe. The only thing that could improve upon the beauties of nature would be to view them in the company of a lovely creature like yourself."

After this, of course, Phoebe was putty in his hands. She listened raptly as Mr. Harris expounded on his philosophies of Absolute Freedom and Living by Instinct. She had ample leisure to do so, for she was not kept overly busy eating. If Mr. Harris had a fault as a dinner partner (a thing which Phoebe would by no means admit), it was a tendency to neglect little services like helping her to dishes and seeing that she had the sauces to go with them. She got soup and fish, because those were served to her by the footmen, but the roast venison and leg of lamb passed unhindered on their way down the table along with their accompanying side dishes.

She fared a little better with the second course, mainly because Gus took time out from talking with Dorothea to call out, "Here, Randolph, stop boring poor Phoebe with your crazy theories and give her a bit of the grouse." But she was quite indignant at Gus for implying that Mr. Harris was boring her. Boring her! She had never been less bored in her life, and she would have gladly refrained from eating grouse altogether if it could have removed the stain of such an insinuation.

Since she could not, however, she ate the grouse, and it was as well she did, for she got little else of any substance during the meal. When dessert came, Mr. Harris let the butter cake, cabinet pudding, and apple charlotte go by untouched, remarking tranquilly that he had no taste for sweets. Phoebe felt obliged to let them go by also, though her taste for sweets was very strong and well developed. Still, she felt repaid for her sacrifice by the approval in Mr. Harris's eyes. "I am glad to see you do not indulge in puddings, Miss Phoebe," he said. "I have often observed a certain grossness in ladies who habitually indulge in puddings, a something that is totally at odds with one of your spiritual nature."

Phoebe tried to look spiritual, while trying likewise not to look wistfully at the cabinet pudding which her Uncle Andrew was heaping on his plate.

When dinner was over, she was obliged to part from Mr. Harris and go to the drawing room with the other ladies. This should have been a wrench to Phoebe, and in fact it was a wrench to say good-bye to him and leave him to drink port with a lot of gentlemen who would not appreciate his deep and sensitive nature. Yet Phoebe also owned to herself that it was a relief to dispense with things spiritual for an hour or so. Of course being spiritual was a wonderful thing, and she was glad Mr. Harris thought she merited so flattering an adjective, but it was rather a strain to keep up for hours at a time. So she was glad to sit and drink tea with Dorothea, Tina, and Cousin Phyllis, and chatter about the wedding on the morrow.

THREE

By the time the gentlemen began to drift back into the drawing room, Phoebe was ready to resume being spiritual once more.

She looked up quickly each time the door opened, but each time she was disappointed. The entrant was never Mr. Harris, but one of the other gentlemen. She tried to be as patient as she could, but after every other man in the party had come in, including Gus and her father, she felt she had to make inquiries. "Good evening, Gus," she said gaily as he came over to sit between Tina and Dorothea. "What have you done with Mr. Harris? Don't tell me he became so enamored of Papa's port that you could not persuade him to quit the table?"

Unfortunately for her, Gus responded in what she could not but feel a sadly facetious manner. "Oh, no fear of that, Phoebe," he said. "Randolph appreciates your father's port quite as much as it merits, but he ain't one of your three-bottle men."

Having been thwarted in her first attempt, Phoebe was forced to be more direct. "But where *is* Mr. Harris?" she asked. "I did not see him come in with you and Papa."

"Oh, he didn't come in. After he'd drunk his port, he decided he'd had enough of the party, so I let him take my curricle. He's probably back at the Lodge by now, if he didn't go haring off someplace else."

"You let him take your curricle!" repeated Phoebe in a stupefied voice. "You mean he's gone?"

"Oh, aye; he left a good half hour ago. But it's no great matter, Phoebe. You know I can always ride home later with my parents."

Phoebe had to bite back an urge to say she cared nothing how Gus got home. Her concern was all for Mr. Harris, and she could hardly believe he had left without saying a word to her. Dorothea seemed similarly surprised, for she asked, "I hope Mr. Harris was not feeling unwell, Gus? I wish you had said something to Papa about it. I am sure he would have loaned Mr. Harris our chaise rather than making him drive himself back to the Lodge in an open carriage."

"Oh, Randolph wasn't ill," said Gus cheerfully. "He'd just had enough of the party, that's all. That's Randolph for you: no saying what he'll decide to do when once he gets a notion in his head. But he sent word to tell you it was a fine party, and he thanked you very much for having him."

This speech seemed to satisfy Dorothea, for she said no more. But Cousin Phyllis whispered to Phoebe, "How very odd of Mr. Harris to leave the party without saying good-bye to anyone else! Do you suppose he was foxed?"

Fortunately for Phoebe, she could speak with authority on this question. Among other things, Mr. Harris had favored her with his views on intemperance during dinner. "Certainly not," she said decisively. "Mr. Harris says that a gentleman who lets himself become the worse for wine is no gentleman at all. I daresay he was merely fatigued. He told me he was up very early this morning, and I believe he also means to rise early tomorrow."

Phoebe could not repress a secret smile as she spoke these words. She, of all the women present, was to have the singular honor of watching the sunrise with Mr. Harris—an event which would incidentally make him her valentine. The idea did a good deal to reconcile her to his abrupt and early departure. They had already arranged the hour and place of their meeting—that is to say, Phoebe had suggested they meet at the south gate at six o'clock, and Mr. Harris had said poetically that the light of her presence would bring the dawn even before the sun could show itself over the eastern horizon. So Phoebe was able to look forward to the morrow with an untroubled spirit, even if she was a trifle disappointed not to have Mr. Harris's company tonight.

Having no choice in the matter, however, she settled back to make the best of the evening. It turned out to be an enjoyable one even without Mr. Harris's presence. The guests were all in high spirits, even the normally dour Great-Aunt Gertrude. There were many jokes, much laughter, and a lively argument about whether Gus's carriage horses were better than her cousin Edwin's. When the party finally broke up around eleven o'clock, Dorothea turned to Phoebe and Tina with an appealing look.

"Girls," she said, "it was a lovely evening, but I can't help feeling badly that Anthea and Allegra were left out of it. This is the last evening I shall spend at home, and I would like to spend time with all of you. I was thinking perhaps that we might fetch the rest of that cabinet pudding we had at dinner and take it up to the nursery and have a little party of our own."

Phoebe, who was feeling half starved after her own scanty dinner, heartily approved this notion, and so did Tina. They helped Dorothea fetch the pudding from the larder and carry it upstairs to the nursery. The twins were awake and very receptive to the idea of a second, more exclusive party encompassing only them and their sisters. It was quite as successful a party in its way as the one downstairs. There was much giggling and sisterly chatter; many silly jokes and would-be witticisms; and the pudding was eaten to the last crumb. Phoebe played her own role in its destruction, though she felt a trifle guilty as she laid her fork on her empty plate. Mr. Harris had thought her superior to the common run of pudding-eating women—more sensitive and more spiritual.

Although I don't see why one can't be spiritual and *eat puddings,* Phoebe told herself. *I am sure Dr. Thurgood at the Rectory is as fond of a pudding as anybody.* But she felt in her heart that Mr. Harris would not think Dr. Thurgood a really spiritual man. Mr. Harris had a soul above conventional religion, and a spirit that could not brook restraint. Phoebe felt a thrill in her own soul as she recalled his words. How his eyes had flashed when he had said he could not bear to spend his life writing dull sermons like—what was the gentleman's name?——oh, yes, like Mr. Alan Stanfield.

It was enough to make Phoebe feel sorry for Mr. Stanfield, stranger though he was. Possibly he had a good living, with enough means to hire a curate or two to help him with the drudgery of his profession, but she thought this doubtful. Apparently he was of an age with Gus, who was only in his early twenties, and so would not likely have obtained much preferment as yet. That was quite in keeping with Mr. Harris's assertion that he existed on a regimen of all work and no play. Probably Mr. Stanfield had a living in some poor country place with a tumbledown vicarage and an ignorant congregation and not even a wife to mend his clothes and make him comfortable.

Phoebe spent a minute or two pitying Mr. Stanfield in his lonely and poverty-stricken state. But her thoughts soon reverted to Mr. Harris. She wondered how she could ever wait until six o'clock the next morning. Of course that was not really very long to wait, for she had not left the nursery till after midnight, and she and Tina and Dorothea had spent almost another full hour talking together in Dorothea's room. They had spoken of this and that, and Dorothea had been very loath to let her and Tina go, which wasn't surprising, considering that she would be leaving tomorrow to begin her new life with her new husband. Of course she would be back frequently to visit, but it wouldn't be the same as actually living in the house as one of the family.

Phoebe felt a lump rising in her throat when she thought of Dorothea's departure. But of course it was natural and normal that she should leave to marry and start a family of her own. Why, it was entirely possible that she, Phoebe, might be the next to marry! Especially if there was anything to this Valentine business. . . .

Phoebe must have fallen asleep at this point, for she awakened with a start to a rattle of bed curtains. The housemaid Betsy had come in and was bustling about, setting a can of hot water on the washstand and making up the fire. Phoebe's first resentful thought was that it was far too early for such activities. Then she recalled that she had asked Betsy to waken her at five so she might not miss her appointment with Mr. Harris. But surely it was not five already! "Oh, Betsy, is it really five o'clock?" she said, yawning and squinting toward the clock on the mantel.

"Aye, so it is," said Betsy cheerfully. "You'll be up early this morning, Miss Phoebe."

Phoebe supposed she would be, though she felt very disinclined to it. But the thought of Mr. Harris waiting for her at the south gate galvanized her into action. How dreadful if she should be late! He might suppose she had deliberately slighted him. Still worse, he might go and watch the sun rise without her. So Phoebe stifled a groan, got out of bed, and began making her toilette.

As she washed and dressed, she regretted it was February rather than May or June. In May or June she might have worn a light dress with only a shawl or lace cloak as a wrap, and a pretty summer hat. But in mid-February she was obliged to put on her warmest dress and cloak, neither of which possessed the glamour she would have liked. However, the dress was a becoming cherry color even if it was long-sleeved and high-necked, and the cluster of artificial cherries pinned to her fur toque matched it to a nicety. The cloak was less satisfactory, being a serviceable dark gray wool, and Phoebe briefly considered leaving it behind, but then sanity reasserted itself. She would hardly make a good appearance in front of Mr. Harris if she were shivering and her teeth chattering, no matter how fashionable her attire. So she threw the cloak over her arm, opened her door, and stepped out into the hall.

At this point, it occurred to Phoebe that she had overlooked certain deficiencies in her plan. In order for her to make Mr. Harris her valentine in the old tradition, it was essential that he be the first man she set eyes on that morning. Yet how was she to get downstairs and out to the south gate without seeing any man but him? Dorothea, when staying at the Kettlewells', had simply kept her eyes shut and relied on Johanna Kettlewell to guide her, but she, Phoebe, had no one but herself.

For a moment she considered going to Dorothea's room and confiding her plans to her sister. But she found herself reluctant to do this, for several reasons. For one thing, today was Dorothea's wedding day, and she doubtless had better things to do than accompany her younger sister out to the south gate. For another, Phoebe felt embarrassed at the idea of telling anyone about her partiality for Mr. Harris, even a sister as sympathetic and trustworthy as Dorothea. There was no help for it; she would simply have to manage the business by herself.

For several minutes, Phoebe stood considering ways and means. If there had been nothing but female servants in the house, she would have risked going downstairs and out the door without taking any special precautions. But as it was, the chances of meeting some groom or footman were simply too great. The only way she could be sure of not seeing a man was to go downstairs with her eyes shut, and keep them shut all the way to the south gate.

Well, if that's what I must do, then that's what I must do, Phoebe told herself resolutely. Drawing a deep breath, she shut her eyes, put out her hand, and started down the hall.

It was very strange to go down the hall with nothing but her sense of touch to guide her. But by keeping one hand on the wall, she managed fairly well, and by the time she reached the stairs she was feeling more confident. "This isn't so hard as I thought it would be," she said aloud. She descended the staircase step by cautious step, clinging to the banister with both hands and feeling her way along. She managed quite well until she reached the bottom—or what she thought was the bottom. For it proved not to be the bottom at all, as she discovered by taking a step forward and falling the remaining distance to the ground.

Fortunately, the distance was not great. Phoebe was more shaken than hurt by her fall, but in the shock of the moment she had opened her eyes. It was only luck that one of the male servants was not standing there to spoil her plans. Quickly Phoebe shut her eyes again, got to her feet, and listened. She could hear a cock crowing somewhere outside, and the murmur of voices and the clatter of pans in the kitchen, but there appeared to be no one nearer at hand. Only a little way to go, and I'll be outside, Phoebe assured herself. And I might be able to risk opening my eyes then.

I doubt there will be any of the outside men working yet, seeing that the sun isn't up.

Once more Phoebe began to move, feeling her way along the hall that led to the side door. She could tell her progress by counting the doors as she passed. "Dining room, drawing room, saloon," muttered Phoebe. "Only the parlor and the flower room, and then I will be at the side door." But as she groped her way past the door to the parlor, it swung open at her touch. Caught off balance, Phoebe reeled, and as she sought to right herself she found herself caught in a sudden embrace. "I *do* beg your pardon," said a voice in her ear.

Phoebe opened her eyes. She had no intention of doing so; she simply did it, and found herself looking into the face of a perfect stranger. He was a young gentleman with sandy hair and blue eyes and a good-humored, even attractive face. At the moment, however, his face wore a look both startled and concerned. "I do beg your pardon," he said again. "I didn't mean to startle you. Are you all right?"

Phoebe could have wept with vexation. It was the end of all her hopes, all her dreams. But she had been brought up to be mannerly, and her manners asserted themselves even in spite of her inner vexation. "I'm all right," she said politely. "*Quite* all right."

The gentleman did not immediately release her. He was looking down at her with a concentrated expression, as though he had stumbled across something startling or unexpected. But Phoebe was perfectly sure she had never seen him before in her life. She began to be exasperated by the way he was looking at her, and also by the way he continued to hold her. Of course it was not his fault that her plans were ruined, but he had nonetheless been the one to ruin them. She could not keep a slight sharpness from her voice when she addressed him again. "I am quite able to stand now, sir. If you would kindly release me . . ."

"What? Oh, yes. Yes, certainly," said the gentleman in some confusion. He let go of Phoebe, and she drew herself away, feeling awkward and embarrassed. The gentleman seemed almost as embarrassed as she was. A faint flush had risen to his cheeks, making him look a mere boy, though his age was certainly several years older than her own.

"I do beg your pardon," he said for the third time. "I don't know what you must think of me. The fact is that you caught me somewhat off guard. Are you—can you be—is it possible you are Miss Fairchild?"

In spite of her vexation, Phoebe could not help smiling. "I will be in a few hours," she said. "But until my elder sister Dorothea is actually married, it is she who holds the title of Miss Fairchild, and I am merely Miss *Phoebe* Fairchild."

"So you are Dorothea's sister!" said the gentleman. It struck Phoebe that there was strong relief in his voice. "I am very glad to hear it. And I am pleased to meet you, Miss Phoebe." He put out his hand, then drew it back with an embarrassed laugh. "What a rag-mannered fellow you must think me! I know who you are, but you don't know me, of course. How could you? Stanfield's the name—Alan Stanfield, at your service."

Enlightenment broke over Phoebe. "Of course!" she said. "You are Gus's friend, the clergyman who is to officiate at the wedding. We have been expecting you."

Alan looked, if anything, more embarrassed. "I daresay you have been. I owe you an apology for that, too. I meant to take the early coach, but at the last minute one of my parishioners required my assistance, and I ended up having to catch the night mail instead. And the night mail didn't reach the Crown until round one o'clock this morning. I would have stayed at the Crown rather than disturbing you here, but they were completely out of rooms, and Gus had told me you would be expecting me. So I decided I'd better go ahead and come here, even in spite of it being so late."

Phoebe was staring at him. "But who let you in?" she said. "You did not wake our butler, surely. He sleeps like the dead—not even a thunderclap will wake him. And I am sure I heard no knock. I am a light sleeper myself."

Alan's flush deepened. "In point of fact, I didn't knock," he said. "The house was dark, and I didn't like to wake the household at such an unearthly hour. But I found the side door on the latch and so—" He paused, giving Phoebe an embarrassed smile.

"William," said Phoebe with resignation. "Our first footman. He goes out to meet his sweetheart in the evening, and he *will* forget to lock the door when he comes back in. Fortunately, we haven't any burglars in this neighborhood."

"No, merely importunate clergymen," said Alan.

He said it so quaintly that Phoebe could not help laughing. "Oh, well, I am sure we do not begrudge you shelter, Mr. Stanfield," she said. "I am glad you were at least able to come inside out of the weather. But I am afraid you did not pass a very comfortable night. Did you get any sleep at all?"

Alan smiled, and Phoebe observed in passing that it was a very attractive smile. "A little. I took the liberty of stretching out upon your sofa there." He nodded toward the parlor. "But I felt I was an intruder, so when I heard your step in the hall, I hastened to announce myself." Again he smiled at Phoebe. "With what result, you already know! I am afraid I startled you dreadfully."

Phoebe wondered if he had noticed that her eyes had been shut when he startled her. She thought there was something faintly quizzical in the way he was looking at her, but she had no intention of explaining herself. "If only we had known you were here, Mr. Stanfield!" she said. "I wish you had knocked, even if you did wake the household. We had a room all ready for you."

"Well, I will make good use of it tonight," said Alan. "Assuming it isn't an imposition, that is. I know Gus and your sister will be leaving on their wedding trip immediately after the ceremony, but he assured me I might stay on another day or two without inconvenience to anyone."

"Oh, yes, it's no inconvenience," said Phoebe. She spoke rather absently, for she had just heard the clock in the parlor chime six o'clock. The sound reminded her of her appointment with Mr. Harris. She ought already to be at the south gate, and now she would be late. Indeed, if she did not hurry, she might miss Mr. Harris and the sunrise altogether. Mr. Stanfield had already ruined her plans to make Mr. Harris her valentine, and if she did not shake herself free of him he might well ruin the whole morning. So she said quickly, "Let me show you to your room now, Mr. Stanfield. You can get settled and perhaps even get a few hours of proper sleep before the ceremony."

Alan thanked her effusively, though he begged her to not put herself to so much trouble. Phoebe assured him it was no trouble, then led the way upstairs to the guest chamber that had been prepared for him. She wasted no time showing him its amenities, but merely threw open the door, told him to ring for anything he might require, and fled precipitately, with his thanks still ringing in her ears.

Since she did not have to keep her eyes closed anymore, she was able to make good time down the stairs and through the house to the side door. Once outside, her progress was slower, for there had been a fall of snow overnight, and the servants had not yet cleared the paths. Phoebe drew her cloak close around her as she picked her way along the drifted walk. Wading through snow was sufficient exercise to warm her a little, but she was still thoroughly chilled by the time she reached the south gate.

Phoebe mounted the stile beside the gate and stood on its topmost step to survey the landscape around her. She could see no sign of Mr. Harris. For a moment she panicked, fearing he had already been there and gone, but a glance at the unbroken snow around the gate reassured her. It was obvious no one had been along the path as yet that morning. Still, she could not help fretting, for the sky in the east was growing lighter by the minute. Perhaps Mr. Harris had forgotten their appointment to meet at the south gate. Perhaps he thought she was to meet him at the top of the hill instead. Perhaps he was there right now, wondering why she had not come. Perhaps she ought to go ahead and climb the hill, on the chance that he was.

But what if she climbed the hill and found he was *not* there? Perhaps something had delayed him as she had been delayed by Alan Stanfield. He might even now be on his way to the south gate, and it would be just her luck to leave only minutes before he arrived. It was true that in that case, he ought to be able to tell by her footprints that she had gone on up the hill, but perhaps he might not think to look for footprints. He might suppose she had forgotten their rendezvous and go sadly home, convinced that Miss Phoebe Fairchild was a heartless flirt who did not scruple to break an engagement. Phoebe felt she could not risk this awful scenario. She would simply have to wait until Mr. Harris arrived, even if she missed the sunrise as a result.

So Phoebe settled down on top of the stile to wait. The faint warmth that walking had brought to her soon seeped away, and she found herself wishing that she had worn two flannel petticoats instead of one and eschewed the elegancy of kid gloves for woolen mittens. She huddled her cloak about her and muffled her face in its folds, raising it only now and then to check for Mr. Harris. He did not come, however, and the sky grew lighter and lighter, while Phoebe's toes grew colder and colder. At last she made up her mind. Mr. Harris must have mistaken their appointment. He must have gone ahead and climbed the hill using the path on the other side, expecting her to meet him at the summit. If she wanted to see him that morning, the only thing to do was climb the hill likewise, even if she did not get there in time to watch the sunrise with him.

So Phoebe set off along the path that led to the top of Beckhurst Hill. The hill was not a particularly steep one, but the path that led to its summit had not been cleared, and the way was hard going. As Phoebe slogged along, breathing hard, the sun burst over the horizon in a glory of rose and violet color, but she had no time or breath to appreciate it. Just a little way on—just a little way on, she told herself, slipping and sliding on icy patches where previous snows had thawed and refrozen. As she approached the crest of the hill, she paused to rest a moment. It would not do to burst upon Mr. Harris red-faced and out of breath. Phoebe had by now convinced herself that she would find Mr. Harris on top of the hill, and she wanted to make a proper entrance. As soon as she had caught her breath she started on again, walking slower and with as much dignity as she could muster. She came over the crest of the hill and stopped.

The sun, by now well above the horizon, shone down dazzlingly on the hill's summit. An irregular ridge of rock protruded here and there like broken teeth, but apart from that the snow stretched smooth and glittering white, unmarred by a single footprint. There was no sign of Mr. Harris.

FOUR

"Where is he?" demanded Phoebe, staring at the smooth expanse of snow around her. She was seized with a sense of indignation. She had risen early, made her way downstairs amid great obstacles, accomplished a cold and strenuous climb at an hour she would normally have been sleeping, and now it appeared to have been all for nothing. Mr. Harris was not there, and it was easy enough to see from the unbroken surface of the snow that he never had been.

Taking it altogether, it was enough to make Phoebe feel quite aggrieved. But then her conscience awoke, and she realized she was being unjust to Mr. Harris. After all, she had no way of knowing why he had failed to keep their appointment. Perhaps something had prevented him from coming. It must have been something serious for him to disappoint her in this way, without word or warning. Perhaps he was ill or had suffered an injury. He might even now be lying sick in bed, tormented by the thought of her waiting for him in vain atop Beckhurst Hill.

Phoebe spent a moment or two morbidly enjoying this idea before its corollary struck her. If Mr. Harris were too ill to climb Beckhurst Hill, then he might also be too ill to stand at the altar as his friend's groomsman. That would be a shame, for she knew Gus had looked forward to having his support at the wedding. Dorothea, too, would be unhappy, and not merely because her soft heart would naturally pity anyone ill. A change in groomsmen would entail last-minute changes in the arrangements of the ceremony and breakfast, and Dorothea would be busy enough this morning without grappling with any last-minute changes.

It was at this point that a hideous thought struck Phoebe. Dorothea! Good heavens! I promised to help her dress this morning. Poor girl, she will be wondering where I am.

This thought served to distract Phoebe from thoughts of Mr. Harris. Clearly she must lose no time descending Beckhurst Hill. Of course this was easier said than done, but at least going down was easier than coming up, and it was less than half an hour later that Phoebe burst into her sister's room, cheeks aglow with exertion. "Dorrie! Do forgive me. Am I too late to help?"

"Phoebe!" said Dorothea, turning to her with relief. "No, you are not too late, but I was wondering where you were. Where did you go?"

Phoebe said evasively that she had gone for a walk. To her relief, Dorothea accepted this explanation without question, being intent on other matters. "We will have to hurry a bit, for I see you aren't ready, either. But then, I suppose it doesn't matter much if we get downstairs a trifle after ten o'clock."

"They can hardly begin the wedding without you," agreed Phoebe gaily.

She set at once to brushing and arranging Dorothea's hair. Johanna Kettlewell, Dorothea's best friend and other bridesmaid, came in a few minutes later to assist in the bridal toilette. Tina joined them soon after, and Anthea and Allegra came in just as Dorothea was being buttoned into her dress. "Dorrie! You look beautiful. Utterly beautiful," said Anthea, surveying her sister admiringly.

"Ravishing," agreed Allegra.

Phoebe could only agree. Dorothea, clad in a dress of misty white with silver trimmings, was a vision of bridal radiance. A point lace veil shrouded her soft brown hair, held in place with a crown of silver flowers. She looked back at her sisters, a smile trembling on her lips. "Don't cry," said Phoebe warningly. "If Gus sees tears in your eyes, he will think you are weeping over the prospect of being married to him. Of course it *is* a dreadful prospect, but you will want to conceal your dismay at least until the ceremony is over."

"Oh, Phoebe, how can you?" said Dorothea, half laughing and half crying. "I am not crying because I dread being married, only because I dread leaving all of you."

Phoebe was conscious of tears threatening in her own eyes, but she blinked them back. "Oh, if that is all! Why, then, we shall simply abuse you like a pickpocket, until you are glad to leave us behind," she said.

She kept up a stream of raillery all the while they were putting the last touches on Dorothea's toilette. So busy was she sustaining her own and everyone else's spirits that she actually forgot for a time about Mr. Harris. But she remembered him again when she went to her own room to change her woolen dress for her bridesmaid's dress of apricot gauze. If indeed he was ill, as she supposed, then she probably should have told Dorothea that he might not be present at the ceremony. Phoebe felt a pang of conscience that she had neglected to warn her sister of this prospect. But of course there was also a possibility that it was not illness at all but some other reason that had kept Mr. Harris from meeting her that morning. In that case, he would be waiting for her downstairs and would no doubt make his apologies when they met.

The thought spurred Phoebe into action. There was no time to make the leisurely and elaborate toilette she would have liked, but she resolved to do her best. "Anthea, Allegra, will you please fetch my wreath from the wardrobe?" she told the twins, who had accompanied her into her room. "And perhaps one of you could run across the hall and beg a few hairpins from Dorothea. Half of mine seem to have disappeared."

But the twins were so flown with excitement at the prospect of the wedding that they were very unreliable assistants. When Anthea, at Phoebe's repeated urging, went across the hall to fetch the hairpins, fifteen minutes passed without her returning, and Phoebe was at her wits' end. When she sent Allegra to find out what was keeping her twin, she, too, failed to return, and after fifteen more minutes of impatient waiting Phoebe made up her mind she must get the hairpins herself if she was to have them at all.

"Of all the nuisances!" she said, pushing open her door and stepping into the hall. And then she blushed, for there stood Mr. Alan Stanfield, regarding her with mild surprise.

It was an awkward moment. Phoebe was acutely conscious of the hair trailing down her back and could only be glad she had taken the time to button her dress and put on her shoes before stepping into the hall. It was bad enough to be seen with her hair in disarray without the additional humiliation of being seen barefoot and in her dressing gown!

"Good morning, Mr. Stanfield," she said, resolving to carry off the encounter with a bold face. "Did you manage to get any more sleep?"

Alan smiled. "Yes, thank you, Miss Phoebe. I feel quite refreshed, and ready to preside at the wedding now. Perhaps you will allow me to escort you downstairs?"

Phoebe gave him an amazed look. "Oh, thank you—but you see I am not quite ready to go down." With a self-conscious laugh, she put a hand to her head. "My hair, you know."

"Your hair?" said Alan, surveying her with puzzlement. "It looks very nice."

Phoebe laughed again incredulously. "You are very kind to say so! But indeed I know better, Mr. Stanfield. I look a perfect guy, and I would not have shown myself abroad in such a state if I had not been forced to run across the hall to borrow a few hairpins from my sister."

Alan bowed. "Forgive me, Miss Phoebe, but I must take exception to your modesty. You do not look at all like a guy, but on the contrary, perfectly charming."

He spoke with such sincerity that Phoebe could not doubt he meant what he said. She laughed again and said, "Well, I thank you for the compliment, Mr. Stanfield! But I flatter myself that I will look very much better once I have my hair properly arranged."

"I do not see how you could look better," said Alan gravely. "However, I am willing to reserve judgment until I have seen for myself. Good morning, Miss Phoebe." Bowing once more, he took himself off.

Small as this incident was, it left Phoebe feeling gratified as she fetched the hairpins from Dorothea's room and returned to her own room to finish her hairdressing. It was not the words Alan had spoken so much as his manner of speaking them that chiefly flattered her. It was ridiculous to suppose he really thought she looked well when half her hair was standing wildly on end and the other half trailing in lank ringlets down her back. Yet Alan had made it sound as though he really did. She wondered a little at his taste, but still she could not help thinking more kindly of him as she set hairpins here and there amid the coils of her hair and arranged the wreath of flowers on top.

The bridal party was late going downstairs, as Dorothea had predicted. At a quarter past ten Mrs. Fairchild came rushing upstairs to find what was delaying them, but was relieved to find everything in readiness. "Dorothea, child, you look lovely," she said, kissing her eldest daughter on the brow. "Come along now, and do not keep poor Gus waiting any longer. He is on pins and needles as it is!"

Johanna elected herself responsible for keeping Dorothea's immaculate skirts from trailing as they went down the stairs, and Tina proudly carried her prayer book. Phoebe devoted herself to seeing that Anthea and Allegra did not get in anyone's way, but there was little difficulty about that. With the hour of the ceremony rapidly approaching, the twins had subsided into wide-eyed silence and seemed, for a change, quite willing to behave.

Phoebe was relieved by this, for she had enough to worry about as it was. Would Mr. Harris be there or not? That was the great question in her mind, and the question was answered as soon as she came around the curve of the staircase and saw him standing in the hall below with her father, Gus, Alan Stanfield, and several other gentlemen.

There was an appreciative murmur from the gentlemen as they caught sight of the bridal party. Gus detached himself from the others and came over to take Dorothea's hand. Dorothea, smiling and blushing by turns, said something in a voice too low to hear, which prompted Gus to kiss her. "You'd better come along and be married before you do any more of that," said Mr. Fairchild, smiling, and under his direction they were all shepherded into the drawing room.

The drawing room was a veritable bower of Love and Beauty. The Fairchilds' own conservatory had been pillaged, as had those of friends and neighbors, to fill every vase in the house with flowers. More flowers hung in festoons from the cornice of the ceiling and from the mantel of the fireplace. But the crowning touch was undoubtedly Great-Aunt Gertrude's orange trees. The old lady had of her own volition offered the loan of her cherished trees, a proceeding that had involved bundling them in sacking and transporting them some fifty miles in a closed carriage warmed with hot bricks. They had survived the journey in fine style and now stood clustered at the end of the room, scenting the air with their exotic perfume.

Phoebe had helped with some of the decorations, but she had not yet had a chance to see them in place. She paused just inside the door to admire the room in all its glory. But her thoughts were soon diverted to Mr. Harris, who had entered just behind her. He had spoken no word to her as yet about missing their appointment that morning, but then there had hardly been time. Catching his eye, she gave him an encouraging smile.

Mr. Harris did not exactly smile back, but he did look at her a moment, his dark eyes serious and intent. Phoebe's heart gave a flutter. It gave another flutter as he came a step nearer. He is going to speak to me, she thought with excitement, and waited eagerly for the expected apology. What actually came, however, was not an apology but only a compliment. "Good morning, Miss Phoebe. You look like Aurora herself in that dress."

Though Phoebe had not expected a compliment, she was perfectly willing to receive one. "Thank you, Mr. Harris," she said. She expected now he would say something about their missed appointment. After all, he had just alluded to the dawn, if in a rather poetic form. But he said nothing more, and Phoebe was forced to broach the subject herself. "I was sorry not to see you this morning," she said. "I suppose you must have had other obligations that kept you from meeting me?"

Mr. Harris looked at her blankly. "Meeting you?" he repeated.

"At the south gate," said Phoebe. "To watch the sunrise."

"The sunrise?" said Mr. Harris. "Ah, yes, the sunrise. I shall never forget it. A most majestic sight."

"But you were not there!" said Phoebe. "I waited and waited, but you did not come."

Mr. Harris was looking blank again. "I beg your pardon?" he said.

"This morning," said Phoebe, trying not to sound impatient. "I waited for you at the south gate this morning. We were going to watch the sunrise together."

"This morning?" said Mr. Harris. "Ah, no, it was yesterday morning that I watched the sunrise."

Phoebe was by now really impatient. "But we were going to watch it again this morning," she said. "We were going to watch it together."

"Were we?" said Mr. Harris. He gave her a vague smile. "It may be that we spoke of some such thing, but you know I am a creature of impulse, Miss Phoebe. Yesterday I rose early to watch the sunrise, but this morning my impulse was to sleep late. It happens that I stumbled across a most interesting old volume in the Earlys' library yesterday and spent most of the night perusing it. Really a most interesting old book, and with the quaintest illustrations. If you like, I will be glad to loan it to you."

Phoebe gazed at him speechlessly. He gave her another vague smile in return. It was obvious he saw nothing amiss in all of this: nothing wrong with staying up most of the night when he had an early appointment the next day, nothing wrong about skipping that appointment because he felt like sleeping late, and nothing wrong about not letting Phoebe know of his change of plans so she would not have been kept literally cooling her heels waiting for him. Why, he did not even see anything amiss in loaning out a book that did not belong to him!

Phoebe might have voiced some or all of these thoughts if she had been given the chance. She had no chance, however, for the guests were all in the drawing room now, and Alan Stanfield was looking in her direction. Obviously he was waiting for her and Mr. Harris to join him and the others at the altar. He smiled at Phoebe as she came forward to take her place. She smiled back at him automatically, but her thoughts were definitely elsewhere.

Alan Stanfield cleared his throat, then began to speak the opening words of the marriage service. Phoebe listened rather distractedly at first, but gradually she forgot her indignation at Mr. Harris in the interest of watching the ceremony. It was moving to watch Gus and Dorothea gripping each other's hand and speaking the solemn words of their vows, moving to watch them smile at each other as they knelt together to receive the blessing, moving to hear the words pronounced that made them officially husband and wife. She wondered if she would ever stand before an altar and receive that same blessing. She watched Alan Stanfield, his face grave and intent; listened to his clear, ringing voice; and decided he was a very fine clergyman. It was strange how different his private manner was from his public one. The few times she had spoken to him, he had seemed shy, awkward, and self-deprecating, but now he seemed none of those things. Rather, there was a confidence and authority about him that she would not have expected in such a young man. He wasn't bad-looking either, though of course that had nothing to do with anything.

Phoebe awoke from these reflections just in time to see Gus bestow his first kiss on his new wife. Then it was her turn to kiss and be kissed by him, and then by Dorothea, and then by a long train of friends and relatives who came crowding up to congratulate the wedding party. There was in Phoebe's mind enough lingering resentment toward Mr. Harris to make her avoid him during these proceedings, but when she found herself face-to-face with Alan Stanfield she smiled and put out her hand to him. "Well, and so we meet again, Mr. Stanfield," she said.

"Indeed we do, Miss Phoebe," he said. Taking her hand, he bowed over it.

Phoebe was surprised to feel his lips brush the back of it, but supposed he had been infected by the free-for-all atmosphere of promiscuous kissing that was going on around them. She would have liked to say something about how well he had read the service, but at that moment Great-Aunt Gertrude came swooping down upon her with a question about Dorothea's trousseau. Phoebe was drawn back into her duties as a bridesmaid and daughter of the house, and she did not see Alan again until the time came for the party to go in to breakfast.

FIVE

FIVE

The arrangements for the wedding breakfast had been a joint effort on the part of Mrs. Fairchild, Dorothea, and the cook. The menu had been relatively easy to settle, but arrangements for seating the guests had proved a problem worthy of Pythagoras. The Fairchilds' dining room was a spacious chamber, but by no means spacious enough to contain all the people who had been invited to the wedding. Neither did the weather allow for setting up a tent and serving the breakfast *alfresco,* as might have been done during the summer months.

The problem had been eventually solved in the same way the flower question had been settled, through the generosity of friends, relatives, and neighbors. A long table had been borrowed from Uncle Andrew and Aunt Lydia and placed in the dining room parallel to the Fairchilds' own, which had been moved to one side to accommodate it. Smaller tables borrowed from other people had been set up in the adjoining saloon and parlor. This made for a crowded situation and much difficulty in serving, but judging by the lively talk and laughter issuing from all three rooms, the guests were quite willing to overlook these deficiencies.

Phoebe, as a member of the wedding party, had a place at the head table with Dorothea and Gus. By means of adroit planning and casual suggestions, she had arranged for Mr. Harris to be seated beside her. This had, of course, been done before the sunrise incident, but though Phoebe was still rather piqued at him about his nonappearance that morning, her pique had by now faded a good deal. In fact, as she waited with the rest of the wedding party to enter the dining room, she decided she was ready to let go of it altogether. After all, she reasoned, Mr. Harris was a man unlike other men. He was a wild, free spirit with a soul that chafed under restriction, and it would be necessary to make allowances for him.

Accordingly, Phoebe resolved to make the necessary allowances. She decided she would be a trifle aloof during the meal, to show Mr. Harris that he could not slight her with impunity, but she would also be friendly enough to show him that she did not mean to hold a grudge. She glanced toward him now, ready to give him an aloof but friendly smile. To her surprise, she saw he was talking to Beatrice Larson. Beatrice was a local girl, and might even be called a pretty girl if you admired red hair and freckles, but she was also a notorious flirt. It was just like her, Phoebe reflected, to throw herself at the best-looking man at the party. But of course a shallow flirt like Beatrice Larson could never engage the attention of a deep thinker like Mr. Harris. No doubt he was bored to death and merely tolerating her chatter to be polite.

So she strolled over, smiled politely at Beatrice, and said, "Hello, Miss Larson." To Mr. Harris she said, "The crowd looks as though it is clearing at last. I believe we can reach the dining room now if we make a determined push."

Mr. Harris looked blank. "Push?" he said. "Push for what?"

"For the dining room," said Phoebe patiently. "For the wedding breakfast. We are seated at the head table. You are, too, Miss Larson," she added with condescending kindness. "I believe Mr. Stanfield is your partner."

"Oh, yes, I met Mr. Stanfield before the ceremony," said Beatrice, nodding vigorously. "He's the clergyman. And I must say he's not at all bad-looking for a clergyman. Do you know if he is married, Phoebe?"

"I believe he is not," said Phoebe. She was amused by Beatrice's question, but rather nettled by it, too. Of course to a girl like Beatrice Larson, any unmarried man was fair game, but somehow she did not like to think of Beatrice flirting with Alan Stanfield. He might be shy and ordinary compared to the darkly glamorous Mr. Harris, but still he was a nice gentleman, much too nice to be caught in the toils of a cheap coquette.

So it was with mixed feelings that Phoebe took Mr. Harris's arm and watched Alan come forward to take Beatrice's. "Good morning, Mr. Stanfield," cooed Beatrice, taking his proffered arm in a possessive embrace. "And good morning, Randolph," she added, fluttering her lashes at Mr. Harris. "It was delightful talking to you. I do hope you can come to the assembly tonight. I shall certainly save a dance for you, just in case you are able to attend." Again she fluttered her lashes.

Phoebe glanced at Mr. Harris. She supposed he would be as amused as she was by this blatant attempt at allurement. But he did not seem to be amused, though his eyes were fixed intently enough on Beatrice's face. "It may be that I shall be able to attend the assembly tonight, Miss Larson," he said. "In general I do not care for provincial assemblies, but I feel inclined to make an exception in this case."

As the four of them went into the dining room together, Phoebe pondered this speech. She dismissed Beatrice's remarks about dancing with Mr. Harris. Naturally Beatrice would like to obtain Mr. Harris as a partner if she could, but he was hardly likely to respond to her sort of cheap tactics. Still, if he was to be at the assembly, Phoebe saw no reason why she should not try to engage him as a partner herself—in a more ladylike way than Beatrice had done, of course. Accordingly, as soon as they were seated at the table, she turned to Mr. Harris and said, "It would be wonderful if you *could* attend the assembly in the village this evening. My sister Tina and I are planning to go, and several of the other girls as well."

"Yes, I believe I may go," said Mr. Harris. Irrelevantly he added, "The Miss Larson to whom I was just speaking—she strikes me as a most unusual girl. There is a certain sophistication, a certain *je ne sais quoi* in her manners that one does not expect to encounter in a provincial neighborhood. I suppose she has traveled a good deal? There is nothing like travel to broaden one's outlook, particularly travel on the Continent. I would assume from Miss Larson's manners that she has spent time in the European capitals as well as London."

Beatrice looked at him in amazement. "You are talking about *Beatrice Larson?*" she said, struggling not to giggle. "Why, I know for a fact she has never been out of the county, let alone traveled abroad. If she implied otherwise, she must have misled you."

Mr. Harris said vaguely that Miss Larson had said nothing about travel; it was merely something he had assumed from her manner. He then fixed his eyes on Phoebe's face. "I believe I *shall* attend the assembly," he said. "Normally I am not given to dancing, but I feel the mood in me tonight."

Phoebe expressed pleasure at this and said she felt in the mood for dancing that night, too. She hoped this was not too brazen, but she wished strongly to get a commitment from Mr. Harris for the first set of dances. Then let Beatrice Larson do her worst! But all Mr. Harris said was, "I shall look forward to seeing you there, Miss Phoebe. I am sure you will be as much an ornament to the village assembly rooms as you are in your own home."

Phoebe persevered. "Oh, well, as to that, I wouldn't know," she said. "But I do love dancing parties, and so do many of the other people hereabouts. The village assemblies are very well attended." Trying not to sound too pointed, she added, "It would be as well if you came early to the assembly, Mr. Harris. You also ought to consider engaging your partners ahead of time. Else you may find the prettiest girls all taken and have to divert yourself in the card room."

Mr. Harris said cards held little interest to a man of his spirit, though he had been known to take a hand at whist now and then. Phoebe surveyed him with frustration. With all her heart, she longed for the distinction of leading off the first dance with Mr. Harris. But though she had dropped many hints, he did not seem inclined to pick any of them up. "I daresay you are more at home on the dance floor than in the card room," she said, adding with emphasis, "I am certain any lady would feel privileged to have you as her partner."

To her joy, Mr. Harris immediately invited her to stand

up with him at the assembly that evening. "I would count myself honored to partner one of the lovely Miss Fairchilds in the dance," he said gallantly.

Phoebe now set herself to pinning him down for the first set of dances. She said she meant to get there early, so as to be in time for the first set. She hinted that the first sets were by far the most desirable; and then, failing to get the response she desired, she asked him point-blank if he meant to be there for the first set. "Oh, I daresay," said Mr. Harris vaguely. "Will you take soup, Miss Fairchild? I see there is both thick and clear—but of course you will take clear. With your spiritual nature, you could not eat a thick soup, any more than you could eat a pudding."

Of course Phoebe was compelled to agree with this statement, though she would have preferred the thick soup, a delectable seafood bisque that was one of the cook's specialties. She did not wish to appear unspiritual, however, so made do with a helping of chicken consommé. She still hoped to get back to the subject of the assembly and the first set of dances, but Mr. Harris began telling her about the book he had been reading the night before, and so loquacious was he on this subject that she had no opportunity to do more than say, "Yes," "No," and "How interesting." His loquacity also prevented him from noticing that she got very little else to eat besides the consommé. Phoebe bore with this as well as she could, though she wondered uneasily what would happen when the bride cake was served. She badly wanted to sample the luscious dark fruit cake that had been ripening in Cook's pantry for months. Yet she feared Mr. Harris would hold similar views on women who ate fruit cakes as those who ate puddings.

As it was, however, there was enough going on that she did not feel much deprived. Owing partly to the celebratory nature of the meal and partly to the slowness of its service, many of the ordinary formalities of dining had been dispensed with. People talked casually across tables and even got up from their seats to go talk to friends at neighboring tables. There were constant comings and goings, much noise and laughter, and a gay, casual kind of confusion throughout. When Mr. Harris pushed back his chair and announced he was going to talk to a friend for a moment, Phoebe thought nothing of it. Indeed, she was relieved, for it gave her the chance to help herself to a particularly succulent-looking roast of pork which Mr. Harris had already condemned as unfit for a spiritual woman.

When Phoebe had finished her roast pork and looked around her, however, she realized Mr. Harris was nowhere to be seen. This did not unduly disturb her, for she supposed he had merely gone to one of the other rooms and would soon be back. But when the first course was cleared and he had not yet returned, she began to be alarmed. Excusing herself to her neighbors, she rose to her feet and went to the door of the dining room. He was not in the adjoining saloon, but when she crossed that room and peeped through the parlor door she spied him, seated tête-à-tête at a small table across from Beatrice Larson.

For some minutes Phoebe stood and stared at him in mounting indignation. He seemed quite oblivious to the fact that he had left her stranded without a dinner partner. Beatrice was likewise oblivious, chattering gaily and glancing up now and then at Mr. Harris with a coquettish smile. Phoebe wondered what she had done with her own dinner partner. Had she abandoned Alan Stanfield with as little ceremony as Mr. Harris had abandoned her? Just then she felt a touch on her shoulder. When Phoebe looked up, she found Mr. Stanfield himself standing at her elbow. He smiled, then gestured toward the two at the table.

"Miss Larson excused herself ten minutes ago to go speak to a friend," he said. "I came to see if she was ready to return to the table. But she looks so comfortably settled with Randolph that I hesitate to disturb her."

Phoebe said nothing, and Alan went on, rather hesitantly, "Randolph was seated by you, was he not? Would you mind very much if I took his place while he is out of the room? To speak truth, I have been wanting a chance to talk to you all evening."

This speech was balm to Phoebe's wounded feelings. Of course Mr. Harris could not be seriously engrossed by Beatrice Larson's dubious charms. That was ridiculous, Phoebe assured herself. Likely Beatrice had manipulated him into

sitting down with her, and he felt he could not leave her
without seeming rude. But in the meantime, it was embarrassing to be without a dinner partner, and she was glad to
accept Alan Stanfield's offer. Smiling graciously, she said,
"Certainly, Mr. Stanfield. I would welcome a chance to talk
to you again also."

Mr. Stanfield gave her his arm, and together they went
back into the dining room. He helped her seat herself once
more in her chair, took the empty seat beside her, then set
about helping her to the different dishes on the table. Phoebe
could not help contrasting his quiet, considerate manners
with Mr. Harris's inattention, but she reminded herself that
Mr. Harris was a wild, free spirit above such commonplaces
as table manners. Still, it was very nice to be taken care of
and have one's wishes consulted at every turn.

It was also very nice to relax and talk in a natural manner
rather than being held to an unnatural standard of spirituality. Alan seemed interested in everything about her, and
Phoebe found herself expanding under his interest. She told
him all about the wedding preparations, how she and
Dorothea had made Dorothea's wedding dress and most of
the other bride clothes. "You are obviously an accomplished
seamstress, Miss Phoebe," commented Alan, then caught
himself with a smile. "Or I suppose I should rather say Miss
Fairchild! Not only your sister but you also have changed
your title in the course of a single morning."

"Yes, that's so," agreed Phoebe, smiling. "But you may
continue to call me Phoebe if you wish, Mr. Stanfield. It
will take me time to adjust to being addressed as Miss
Fairchild. Indeed, I expect that for the first week or so I will
probably fail to answer when so addressed!"

Alan readily consented to this suggestion, though he in-
sisted that Phoebe reciprocate by calling him by his Christian name. "I should be honored to have you call me Alan,"
he said with a bow. "If you would not consider the request
presumptuous on such short acquaintance, that is."

Phoebe was amused by the formality of his manners, but
she thought them very pleasant nonetheless. She assured
Alan she would not consider his request presumptuous. "I
will gladly call you Alan," she said. "Gus has talked of you

so much that I already feel I have known you for years. He has a high opinion of your character and talents."

Alan said modestly that Gus, as a friend, was no doubt partial. He went on to talk of Gus and Dorothea's plans for the future. "It must be some consolation that they will live close enough to visit you often," he told Phoebe. "I wish I lived closer, so I might see them often, too. Of course my living is only a half day's journey from here, but that might as well be a fortnight, considering how difficult I find it to get away from my parish."

"I suppose it *is* difficult to get away, given the nature of your responsibilities," said Phoebe sympathetically. "I have always thought it must be very awkward to be a clergyman and be constantly at the beck and call of one's parishioners."

"It can be awkward at times, certainly. But it is also intensely interesting." Alan gave a self-deprecating laugh. "But of course you are not interested in anything so dull as the work of a clergyman. And in any case I would rather talk of you, Phoebe. Did you truly help make the bride's dress? I am no judge of ladies' fashions, but it seems to me as lovely as anything I have seen out of a London shop."

Phoebe smiled. "Just between you and me, I think so, too! I scandalized Dorothea earlier by suggesting I might borrow it to wear it to the village assembly tonight."

Alan laughed. "I don't wonder! To wear something so sublime merely to dance in would seem next door to heresy. Not that I hold anything against dancing, mind you. I know there are clergymen who frown on it, but to me it seems a harmless and even beneficial recreation."

"I am glad to hear it," said Phoebe gaily. "Otherwise I would be guilty of scandalizing two people in one day!"

Alan laughed again, but his expression was wistful. "Well, you have not scandalized me," he said. "On the contrary, you have made me envious. I enjoy dancing myself, on occasion."

"Then you, too, ought to attend the assembly this evening," said Phoebe, smiling. "I am sure there is no reason why you should not. My sister Tina and I plan to attend, and so do a number of the other guests who are here for the wedding."

It seemed to Phoebe the least she could do to make sure Gus's friend was not left to his own devices that evening. Besides, she had begun to like Alan for himself and thought a gentleman with such nice manners would be a useful addition to any party. She was pleased when Alan responded by saying, "Since you are so kind as to invite me, I should be very happy to attend the assembly this evening."

Phoebe was less pleased when he added, "And I would be even happier if you would do me the honor of dancing the first set with me." This by no means accorded with her plans, for she was still set on dancing the first set with Mr. Harris. But of course Alan could not know that. And as Phoebe reflected, she could easily turn him off by saying she was already engaged for the first set. She told herself that Mr. Harris had as good as agreed to dance that set with her, even if he had not actually said so in so many words. Being a gentleman, he would naturally regard himself as engaged even if the engagement had been a less than positive one.

So she smiled at Alan and said, "I'm sorry, Alan, but I believe I am engaged for the first set. However, I would be happy to dance with you later in the evening if you so desire."

"Of course," assented Alan. "I should consider dancing any dance with you a privilege, Phoebe." But Phoebe noticed that he did not talk as much after this, though he continued to be attentive to her needs and desires. Phoebe was grateful for this, for Mr. Harris did not return until the meal was almost over, and she was thus able to indulge in bride cake to her heart's content, along with the other wonderful desserts that had been prepared to celebrate Gus and Dorothea's wedding.

As soon as Mr. Harris reappeared in the dining room, Alan quickly rose and excused himself. "It has been a pleasure talking to you, Alan," said Phoebe, giving him her hand and smiling warmly. "I shall look forward to dancing with you at the assembly tonight." She spoke loudly enough so that Mr. Harris could hear, for she did not think it would hurt him to know that other gentlemen besides himself admired her and wished to dance with her.

She was pretty certain by now that Alan did admire her. It was apparent in his manner, in the attentive way he listened to her and the way he looked at her when she was speaking. All this was very flattering, but though Phoebe admitted to being flattered, she assured herself that she had no intention of really encouraging Alan. She was not a shameless flirt like Beatrice Larson. On the other hand, Mr. Harris had just spent an hour with Miss Larson, and Phoebe could not resist the urge to get some of her own back. As a result, her smile and nod to Alan might have been a shade warmer than they would have been in other circumstances.

Alan, however, merely bowed in return and said, "I, too, shall look forward to it." He then took himself back to his own seat. Phoebe, watching covertly, saw him sit down beside Beatrice (who had returned to the dining room soon after Mr. Harris, in what was probably not a coincidence).

But as Phoebe told herself, it was no surprise that Beatrice Larson should act the coquette, or that Mr. Harris should be too gentlemanly to treat her as she deserved. She accordingly settled down to get what good she could out of the rest of the meal. This was not very much as far as Mr. Harris was concerned, for he seemed in an abstracted mood, but the other guests more than made up for it. They were very noisy and hilarious, and when the last crumbs of cake and pudding had been cleared, a series of toasts were proposed in honor of the newly wedded pair.

"To Gus and Dorothea! Best wishes from all of us, and may the two of them be as happy as they deserve!"

"To the bridal couple, wishing them the best of luck!"

"To Mr. and Mrs. Early! May their way in life be smooth, and all their ventures prosperous, and the grace of God be upon all they undertake."

Phoebe, with the others, lifted her glass for each of these toasts. She could not help laughing, yet she felt a ridiculous urge to cry, too, whenever she looked at Gus and her sister. But of course she could not do that, lest Mr. Harris think her ridiculously maudlin.

Then Great-Aunt Gertrude stood up, and embarked on a long, rambling toast in which she cited various events in her own married career. "Of course I lost my good man ten

years ago, and I'm nothing but a poor widow now," she
concluded. "But I was lucky enough to have Tom while I
did, and to appreciate him while I had him. So that's what
I wish for you, my dears: may you have each other many a
long year, and appreciate each other while you do. God bless
and keep you both." She sat down abruptly, got out her handkerchief, and blew her nose loudly.

It ought to have been a comical incident, but a brief silence followed Great-Aunt Gertrude's toast before every-
body raised their glasses and drank. As Phoebe raised her
own glass, she felt tears stinging in her eyes. She had a
strange sense of revelation, as though she were suddenly
seeing life on a different and deeper level. For as long as
she could remember, she had regarded Great-Aunt Gertrude
as merely one of her many relations, a homely, sharp-
tongued old lady to be respected but certainly not taken
seriously. Now, for the first time, Phoebe saw her as a character in a romance as beautiful and tragic in its way as any
of Shakespeare's. Looking around at the other couples in
the room, she realized it was just the same. From Dorothea
and Gus, just embarking on their married life together, to
her grandmother and grandfather, who had celebrated their
fiftieth wedding anniversary the previous summer: all had
their own hopes and dreams of love and romance, and only
one mortal life in which to fulfill them.

And as Phoebe reflected on these things, she happened
to catch the eye of Alan Stanfield. She knew at once, without
knowing how she knew, that he was feeling the same sense
of solemnity that she was. There was a smile on his lips,
yet his eyes held an awareness that was as much serious as
humorous. They held Phoebe's for a long moment. When at
last she looked away, she found her emotions more than ever
in a state of turmoil. It was at this juncture that Mr. Harris
spoke in her ear.

"What a tiresome old lady," he said. "Relative of yours,
isn't she?" He tossed off his wine, then spoke again in a
lower voice. "It's my opinion that old ladies, like children,
ought to be seen but not heard. In fact, to my way of thinking
it wouldn't be a bad thing if they were put down systemati-
cally as soon as they reached the age of forty. By that time,

a woman has invariably ceased to be decorative, and a woman who is not decorative serves no function that I can see."

Having pronounced these words, he gave Phoebe a whimsical smile. Phoebe stared at him. "Indeed," she said, then deliberately turned her back on him.

SIX

By the time the guests left the table, Phoebe had relented a little toward Mr. Harris. But she still felt annoyed that he could have made such a rude remark about her Great-Aunt Gertrude. Even worse was the remark he had made about putting down women over forty.

Of course he had not meant it seriously. He had merely been joking, making light of the subject in a humorous way. Still, Phoebe could not like such humor. She might be only nineteen herself, but she trusted she would live to forty and beyond, and the idea of someone like Mr. Harris proclaiming that she would have nothing more to contribute to society at that point was more than a little irritating.

A man who thinks and feels as deeply as he does ought to know better, Phoebe told herself. Yet from the way he talked, one would suppose he was wholly superficial.

She did not dwell long on this idea, having other things to think about. As soon as the wedding breakfast was over, Dorothea had gone upstairs to change her dress and make her other last-minute preparations for her wedding trip. Phoebe, along with Tina and Johanna, had been appointed to act as her dressing maids. They had a delightful time buttoning Dorothea into the lilac kerseymere carriage dress that was her going-away costume and packing the last of her belongings into her trunk, all to the accompaniment of jokes, laughter, and a scattering of tears. Then they had to escort the bride downstairs, where the other guests were grouped around to see her and her bridegroom off in a shower of best wishes. All in all, Phoebe had little time to think of Mr. Harris or any other man until the spanking new chaise with its festoons of flowers and ribbons had turned the corner of the lane and disappeared from view.

At this point, Phoebe did begin to think about Mr. Harris. She was engaged to dance the first set with him at the assembly that evening, and it was vital that she devote the next few hours to her toilette if she were to appear a worthy partner for so notable a beau. So she wiped the tears from her eyes, gave a last wave toward the vanishing chaise, and hurried into the house.

She was not the only girl thinking about the assembly. The excitement of the wedding might be over, but a village assembly was nothing to sneeze at—especially since, as one young lady guest sagely pointed out, it might bring some lucky girl a wedding of her own. Those young ladies not staying with the Fairchilds, including Beatrice Larson, gabbled out their thanks to their host and hostess and took themselves home to begin their preparations. Those who were staying in the house, including Cousin Phyllis, Johanna, and Tina, followed Phoebe upstairs and disappeared into their separate bedrooms to dress and make themselves as fine as possible.

Soon the upper story of the old house was as hectic as it had been during the hours preceding the wedding. Maidservants rushed to and fro; there were constant cries for hot water and curling tongs, and a general lamentation from Tina, who had spilled a bottle of eau de cologne on her best petticoat while trying to scent her handkerchief.

"What shall I do, Phoebe?" she wailed, having appeared in her sister's room to describe the disaster. "I can't possibly wear it now, and my other petticoats are all plain ones."

"Take it to the laundry and have Molly wash it out. There's still time," said Phoebe, casting a glance at the clock.

"Time to wash it, but not to dry it," fretted Tina. "Even if Molly irons it, it will still be damp. I can't go out in a damp petticoat."

"To be sure you can," said Phoebe cheerfully. "You will merely be following the latest London fashion. Cousin Phyllis was telling me the other day that the society ladies often dampen their petticoats before they put on their dresses, so as to better show off their figures."

The thought of imitating the London ladies of fashion was evidently a consolation to Tina. She went off to the laundry without another word. Phoebe cast a second glance at the clock. It still lacked an hour of the time their party was to leave for the village rooms, giving her further time to refine her toilette, though a disinterested observer might have thought her already complete to a shade. Her hair was gathered into a low knot at the back of her head with a sprig of ivy tucked amid the plaits. Her dress of ivory crepe was buttoned smoothly over a slip of green silk; her long gloves were spotless. Before leaving on her wedding journey, Dorothea had turned over the pearl necklet she had worn with her bride dress, so Phoebe was able to clasp real pearls around her neck instead of a mere coral necklace. All this was a satisfaction, and after she had spent a little time fiddling with the loose curls over her forehead and surreptitiously anointing her face with the rouge and lip salve that Cousin Phyllis had brought from London, she felt she was as ready as she ever would be. Gathering up her cloak and reticule, she left her room and went downstairs to the drawing room.

Tina was already there, looking very pretty in her dress of rose-colored muslin. There was still a noticeable odor of eau de cologne about her, but Phoebe assured her it was not offensive. She also assured her sister that the fact that her dress clung a little more closely to her seventeen-year-old figure than was its wont was not noticeable to the casual observer. "If anyone looks at you as close as that, he is already smitten, and you need not regard it. Speaking of smitten, I notice Geoffrey Tabor was hanging about you a good deal after the ceremony. I believe you have already made a conquest there, Tina. And you out of the schoolroom barely six months!"

"Oh, Phoebe, don't be silly," said Tina, blushing. She added irrelevantly, "Geoff is grown a very nice-looking gentleman, isn't he? I had not seen him since he came down from Oxford."

Johanna arrived at this juncture, and soon afterward Alan

came strolling in. He had changed his clothes for a coat of black broadcloth worn with a pearl-colored waistcoat and smallclothes. Phoebe regarded him with approval. His clothes might not sport the extreme cut and exquisite tailoring that made Mr. Harris's garments so dashing, but he looked very attractive and masculine. It was evident that Tina and Johanna thought so, too, for Tina wished him good evening in the shy voice she invariably used around attractive gentlemen, and Johanna went so far as to rally him on his appearance.

"No buttons missing—no rents or darns visible—really, sir, this will never do! You must know we women expect a bachelor to show signs of neglect. Otherwise, we cannot tell each other that he is a sad creature who wants a wife to keep him in order!"

"But the fact that I don't appear shabby doesn't necessarily mean I don't want a wife," returned Alan, smiling. "Perhaps I do want one. And if I do, I might fear the lady I hope to marry would consider it less than a compliment to her if I appear this evening looking shabby and disheveled."

Johanna shook her head gravely. "You argue like a man—which is to say, logically enough, but without understanding anything of the matter at hand. Your future wife might admire you dressed as you are, but you would be much likely to win her heart if she thought you needed her. We women like to be needed."

"Is this true, Phoebe?" inquired Alan, turning to her.

Phoebe was pleased that he should appeal to her. In truth, she had been feeling rather left out while he and Johanna had been bantering back and forth. Of course she liked Johanna, but somehow it had not been agreeable to stand and listen while she flirted with Alan—for that was what her conversation had amounted to. Anytime an unmarried young woman discussed marriage with an unmarried young man, there must be some element of flirtation involved. Yet somehow it did not occur to Phoebe to carry her argument further and apply it to her own behavior as she responded to Alan's question.

"Speaking for myself, I should say that Johanna is right,"

she told him. "To be admired is flattering, but to be needed is a higher thing. I personally do not plan to marry until a man woos me as the Prince Regent did Mrs. Fitzherbert, with threats of suicide and mental derangement."

Alan said gravely that he would bear it in mind. But he was smiling as he spoke, and Phoebe found herself smiling back at him. "On second thought, I believe I would be content to marry a man merely knowing I was indispensable to his happiness," she told him. "But I would have to *know* it. For if Prinny could prove false to Mrs. Fitzherbert in spite of all his vows and promises, then it stands to reason that mere words cannot be relied on."

"Ah, but it depends who uses the words," pointed out Alan. "Men vary widely in their characters, you know, just as young ladies do. There are some few men whose promises may actually be trusted, unlike those of our noble Regent."

He said no more, but his eyes rested significantly on Phoebe. She felt her color rise. It had just occurred to her that his words might have a personal application. She tried to laugh it off, telling herself that she must be tremendously conceited to suppose she could have made a conquest of a man in a mere twelve hours or so. But still she could not rid herself of an impression that there was more in Alan's looks and voice than mere teasing. If that were so, then of course it was her duty to let him know as soon as possible that she was not interested in him as a suitor. She was interested in Mr. Harris, perhaps even in love with him, and a nice girl did not encourage two men at once.

Yet when Phoebe considered her feelings on this subject, she found them curiously ambivalent. Was it possible she was not in love with Mr. Harris after all? And was it possible she felt something—not love exactly, but *something*—for this other man whom she had met only that morning? Phoebe remembered how she had caught Alan's eye during the meal when Great-Aunt Gertrude was making her poignant speech. She had certainly felt something then, and that same something had made her recoil violently when Mr. Harris had made that slighting remark about elderly women. And she was certainly feeling something now as she glanced at Alan out of the corner of her eye. But taking it all in all, Phoebe was not prepared to say whether what she was feeling was not merely a sense of overwhelming confusion.

Whatever the case, she was very quiet as she stood waiting with Alan, Tina, and Johanna for the other party-goers to join them in the drawing room. These included Cousin Phyllis, Aunt Lydia, and several others, so that when everyone was at last assembled it proved necessary to take two carriages to get them all to the village assembly rooms. Phoebe did not know whether she was glad or sorry when she ended up in a different carriage from Alan. She wanted time to think about her feelings and put them into order, which ought theoretically to have been easier when Alan was not there, but even without him coherent thought seemed impossible to her. All she could do was imagine what was taking place in the other carriage, and how Phyllis and Johanna, both of whom had ended up sitting with Alan, were no doubt taking the opportunity to flirt with him outrageously.

When at last they reached the village assembly rooms, Phoebe took herself sharply in hand. She was not going to behave like a giddy-headed fool simply because Alan Stanfield happened to have pleasant manners and an understanding smile. After all, Mr. Harris had pleasant manners, too—or at least striking ones. He was also the best looking man she had ever seen. And what was still more to the point, he was engaged to her for the first dance. By dint of concentrating very hard on these things, Phoebe was able to work up some of her old enthusiasm at the prospect of dancing with Mr. Harris. It would be pleasant to take the floor with him and to feel herself an object of envy to the other, less fortunate young ladies in the room. She only wished she knew whom Alan meant to dance the first dance with. Probably it would be either Johanna or Cousin Phyllis, but which? Which? Phoebe could not help wondering, though of course it made no real difference to *her.*

Once inside the assembly rooms, she looked around with interest. The rooms were their usual shabby selves, decorated with tarnished mirrors and a pale green paper that had seen better days. In honor of St. Valentine's Day, there were a few bouquets of flowers scattered about, and a large banner on which someone had attempted to depict a pair of courting doves hung conspicuously over the door.

All these details Phoebe took in at a glance, but her real interest was in the groups of guests who stood about waiting for the dancing to begin. Mr. Harris was not among them, but neither was any of the rest of the party from Longacre Lodge. Having ascertained this fact, Phoebe was not inclined to worry. Mr. and Mrs. Early never missed a village assembly, being addicted respectively to the twin amusements of dancing and cards. No doubt they would soon arrive, and Mr. Harris with them.

A young gentleman approached Phoebe just then and stammered out an invitation to dance. "I am sorry, but I am engaged for the first set," Phoebe told him politely. She was surprised a few minutes later when a second young gentleman also invited her to stand up for the first set. As a rule she did not lack for partners, but never before had she had so many invitations for the same dance.

It never rains but it pours, Phoebe told herself whimsically. Even without Dorothea's bride dress, I seem likely to be popular tonight. She felt a tingling sense of excitement. All the signs pointed to being a memorable evening. If Mr. Harris would only arrive, she would be ready for anything.

But the minutes ticked by, and Mr. Harris did not appear. The fiddlers took their places and began tuning their instruments. Phoebe kept an anxious eye on the door, certain that the party from Longacre Lodge must arrive at any moment. She could not remember the last time Mr. and Mrs. Early had failed to appear in time for the first set. In fact, it was Mr. Early's custom to lead off that set, while his wife went off to the card room to play at whist. So where was Mr. Early now? And where, more importantly, was Mr. Harris?

Right up until the set actually began, Phoebe did not really believe she would be left partnerless. She watched and waited, but her watching and waiting proved all in vain. The music began, the lead couple started off, and Phoebe was forced to the realization that instead of being an object of envy to the other girls, she was destined to be a wallflower.

It was the bitterest of bitter realizations for Phoebe. She was sure nothing save some grave cataclysm could have prevented Mr. Harris and the Earlys from arriving in time for the first dance. Yet try though she might to summon up concern for them, she was unable to feel anything but mortification for her own position. Tina and Johanna and Cousin Phyllis all had partners; even Aunt Lydia had a partner and was promenading majestically down the line with a stout gentleman in a purple plush coat. Of their party, she alone was condemned to sit and watch. She, Phoebe Fairchild, who had only a short time before felt herself favored above all other women, had instead been brought low as dust.

"How are the mighty fallen," muttered Phoebe under her breath. The words brought a ghost of a smile to her lips. Just then she felt a touch at her elbow. She turned around and beheld Alan Stanfield, regarding her with an uncertain smile.

"Do forgive me, Phoebe. I know you said you were engaged for the first set, but I thought perhaps . . ." He hesitated, then went on quickly. "It occurred to me when I saw you sitting there that your partner might not yet have arrived—owing to some unavoidable delay, no doubt. And if that was the case, I thought—well, I hoped that perhaps you might not mind taking the floor with me until he does arrive?"

Phoebe felt a strong desire to kiss him. Any gentleman might have seen her sitting there looking forlorn and guessed she lacked a partner. But how many gentlemen would had broached the matter as he had, tactfully assuming that her partner had merely been delayed and phrasing his invitation so she might accept or decline it without losing face? Phoebe felt no other gentleman in the world would have been so sparing of her feelings. Looking into Alan's eyes, Phoebe felt once again that sense of *something*—the sense that they understood each other. Smiling, she gave him her hand.

"I should be very pleased to dance with you, Alan," she said. "And I don't think we need be concerned about my other partner. Now I consider it, our engagement was not a positive one, and I would rather dance with you anyway."

A smile lit up Alan's face. Taking her hand, he led her out onto the floor.

The dance was a country dance, meaning it was a strenuous romp that provided few opportunities for conversation. Phoebe did not mind. She smiled at Alan, and he smiled back at her, and they contrived to get through the dance in a most enjoyable fashion. "You dance very well," said Phoebe, as they came off the floor. "One would not expect a clergyman to comport himself so nimbly on the dance floor."

"Why not?" said Alan seriously. "I am a man as well as a clergyman. And I learned to dance long before ever I took orders."

"Of course that is true. I suppose I never considered the matter before. The truth is, there is a great deal I do not know about clergymen in general and you in particular." Phoebe looked up at him, half smiling and half serious. "Today at the wedding breakfast you encouraged me to talk about myself the whole time. Now I would like to turn the tables and talk about you."

Alan protested that there was nothing to tell, but Phoebe told him he was merely being modest. They sat down on a bench at the back of the room, and after much coaxing Phoebe brought him to describe his early life and career. He went on to tell about his living in the parish of St. Anne's and how he had happened to become a clergyman.

"Of course it's not always the easiest occupation in the world, and certainly not the most rewarding—in a worldly sense, at least. But the other rewards are very great indeed. We have just started a Sunday school at St. Anne's, after the example set by Mrs. Moore. For some of those children, this is the only education they will ever have."

Phoebe listened in absorbed silence as he described his Sunday school and the other plans and projects he had in view for his flock. He described the people of his parish, from the wealthy squire who held the parish living to the sexton who rang the bells, and made them all so vivid that Phoebe felt she knew them personally. He described the character of his parishioners, most of them sturdy country folk; the strange mixture of ignorance and shrewdness, cruelty and kindness, stinginess and unexpected generosity he had encountered in his dealings with them.

Phoebe listened, and as she listened she began to feel how trifling and superficial was her own life in comparison with his. She expressed something of this feeling when Alan had finished describing his struggles. "You are doing a noble work there, Alan. It makes me feel quite ashamed, to think I have done so little to help the less fortunate."

Alan shook his head. "You mustn't feel that way, Phoebe. It's my vocation to deal with such things. There is no reason why it should be yours. Unless . . ."

He paused, giving Phoebe a searching look. Phoebe looked back at him, a faint smile on her lips. "Unless what?" she said.

"Well, unless you were really interested, of course. But I wouldn't want to bore you."

"You aren't boring me," said Phoebe. "I *am* interested, Alan. Very interested indeed."

"Are you?" said Alan. He gave her another searching look. "I would certainly like to talk to you about it." Again he paused, then went on with sudden resolution. "But before I do, Phoebe, I think I ought to say . . ."

Here he was interrupted, however. A shadow fell over them both, and a melancholy baritone voice intoned, "Behold Miss Phoebe Fairchild! A vision of loveliness unparalleled in this provincial gathering. A man more wise than I might shrink from suing for so great a favor as the privilege of dancing with her, but I was ever more bold than wise."

Phoebe looked up. There, smiling down at her with calm assurance, stood Mr. Harris. He was wearing a blue coat, very wide in the lapels and very narrow in the waist, with buttons the size of crown pieces. His waistcoat was embroidered with a pretty design of cornflowers, and his neckcloth was a towering edifice of knots and creases that reached to his very chin. His dark hair tumbled over his brow in picturesque disorder. All in all, he ought to have been a vision to thrill any maiden's heart.

Yet Phoebe's heart was not thrilled. On the contrary, she felt distinctly irritated at him for interrupting the conversation at such an interesting moment.

"Oh, hullo, Mr. Harris," she said flatly.

Mr. Harris was not discomposed by her lack of enthusiasm. "Good evening," he said, bowing to her with a flourish. "And good evening, Stanfield," he added, sketching another bow toward Alan. "You will not mind, I hope, if I take Miss Fairchild away from you for the space of a dance or two."

Alan looked at Phoebe. She started to speak, then hesitated. "She and I were engaged to dance this set, I believe," went on Mr. Harris, sounding as calmly assured as ever. "And like any man of sense, I hasten to fulfill an engagement so agreeable."

Phoebe found her tongue at this. "I had thought, Mr. Harris, that we had spoken of dancing the *first* set together," she said.

Mr. Harris shrugged his elegant shoulders. "One hesitates to contradict a lady," he said. "Perhaps it is as you say. You must know I have not the kind of mind to deal with such minutiae." He gave her an insinuating smile. "But since circumstances prevented me from having the pleasure of dancing the first set with you, I trust you will not compound my disappointment by refusing to dance with me now."

Phoebe shook her head slowly. "No, I will dance with you if you like, Mr. Harris," she said. To Alan, she added, "I have much enjoyed talking to you, Alan. Perhaps we can continue our conversation later, if it suits you."

"To be sure," said Alan, bowing. His face was inscrutable as he watched Phoebe walk away with Mr. Harris.

Phoebe, exploring her emotions, was surprised at her own lack of enthusiasm. Here she was, standing up at last with Mr. Harris, whom she had admired for more than a year. It was obvious from the looks of the girls around her that they envied her. Yet she felt no exultation at all, only a dull resignation. She was silent as they began to dance, but Mr. Harris appeared not to notice. He prattled away as usual, telling Phoebe how he had spent the afternoon immersed in the old book he had found in the Earlys' library the evening before. Phoebe, listening to him, wondered if his conversation had always been so vapid. She also found herself wondering if his entrancement with the book had been the cause of his being late for the assembly. When he paused for breath, she decided to ask him.

"I was surprised to see you and the Earlys come in late, Mr. Harris. As a rule, Mr. and Mrs. Early live up to their name and are among the first to arrive when there is an assembly."

A frown darkened Mr. Harris's handsome face. "Indeed. I daresay you are right—in fact, I have reason to know you are, for Mr. Early himself informed me of the fact. I tried to tell him that there is no reason for a man to let his life be ruled by the clock, but he is too old, too set in his ways to entertain any but the conventional views. A great pity, isn't it? I know a woman of your sensibility will share my feeling in thinking it a pity."

"Oh, I don't know about that," said Phoebe. "It seems to me that if Mr. Early wishes to live by the clock, his wishes ought to be respected."

Mr. Harris frowned again. "I do not deny it," he said. "However, when he tries to impose his wishes on others, that is another thing. It is as I told you before: I cannot endure restrictions of any kind. My spirit chafes at confinement and conventionality. I require an atmosphere of perfect freedom in order to live and thrive."

Phoebe looked at him, and it was as though the scales had fallen from her eyes. Instead of a deep thinker and free spirit, she saw merely a selfish, lazy *bon vivant* who would not stir himself one iota for the sake of anyone else. "It is as well that everyone does not feel the way you do, Mr. Harris," she said with deceptive sweetness. "If everyone demanded perfect personal freedom in which to live and act, the world would shortly be reduced to chaos, I think."

She was amused to see that Mr. Harris took this as a compliment. "Indeed, I believe my character is a unique one, Miss Phoebe," he said modestly. "Men of my stamp seem to be a rarity in this world."

"Perhaps it is just as well," said Phoebe.

When the dance was over, Phoebe lost no time making her escape from Mr. Harris. Her intention was to find Alan again as quickly as possible. But in this she was thwarted by Mr. Early, who came up and asked her to dance. Phoebe did not like to refuse the old gentleman, who was now not only a neighbor but connected to her by marriage, so she consented with a smile. He smiled back at her, but she noted his usually good-humored face wore a faintly disgruntled look as they went out to take their places on the dance floor.

Phoebe ventured to remark on this circumstance as they began to go through the movements of the dance. "I suppose you and Mrs. Early have had a fatiguing day," she said sympathetically. "With the business of the wedding to attend to, I am sure you have been very busy."

"Not at all," said Mr. Early, shaking his head vigorously. "The wedding wasn't a particle of trouble. 'Twas your family had all the work. All Maria and I had to do was get ourselves dressed and drive over, and we do as much as that most days of the week! No, if I look a trifle out of sorts, it's nothing to do with the wedding. It's because of that fellow there." He nodded toward Mr. Harris, who had just taken his place in the set with Beatrice Larson.

Phoebe was pleased to see that the sight of Mr. Harris with Beatrice Larson gave her no emotion save gratitude that it was Beatrice who was his partner rather than her. "I think I understand you, Mr. Early," she said. "I was dancing with Mr. Harris earlier, and from something he said I rather gathered there had been a—ahem—difference between you about attending the assembly tonight."

"Difference!" said Mr. Early explosively. "I'll say there was a difference! I told the fellow we were leaving at seven o'clock sharp, and he promised he'd be ready. But when it came to the point, he kept us all waiting near an hour because he couldn't get his neckcloth tied to suit him. Of all the nonsense! The day it takes me an hour to tie my neckcloth is the day I quit wearing neckcloths altogether."

Phoebe laughed a trifle disbelievingly. "You must be funning," she said. "Mr. Harris said nothing of this to me. He said only that you and he had disagreed about living life without reference to the clock."

"Oh, aye, he did spout off some such sort of tomfoolery. I told him that as far as I'm concerned he may live his life however he pleases in his own home and I'll never say a word against him. But it's different when his crotchets inconvenience *me*. I've got as much patience as anybody, but I don't care for a man whose word can't be relied on."

"Neither do I, Mr. Early," said Phoebe, smiling to herself. "Neither do I."

"That just shows you're a sensible gel," said Mr. Early approvingly. "Too sensible to want anything to do with that Harris fellow. A man who takes an hour to tie his neckcloth is no man at all, in my opinion. And when it comes to putting his hair up in curl papers at night—"

"Curl papers?" said Phoebe. *"Curl papers?"*

Mr. Early nodded, his eyes alight with laughter. "Aye, curl papers! I saw it with my own eyes t'other morning, when he came out of his room to fetch in his boots."

Phoebe gave a gurgle of laughter. "I shall have to tell my sister Anthea," she said. "She said something yesterday about Mr. Harris's curls being rather—er—feminine, but I didn't credit it! I believe I owe her an apology."

Mr. Early said that Anthea was a clever minx, just like Phoebe herself. Having paid her this handsome compliment, he then went back to deploring the manners and morals of the present generation of young men as represented by Mr. Harris. Phoebe pointed out that not all young men of the present generation were like Mr. Harris. "Gus is not," she said. "And I don't believe his friend Mr. Stanfield is, either." Blushing slightly, she added, "I have been talking to him a good deal today. He seems a very sensible, pleasant-mannered gentleman."

Mr. Early surveyed Phoebe with a quizzical light in his eyes. "So that's the way the wind's blowing! The young parson's the man, is he? Well, well, you could do a deal worse for a husband, my dear, and that's a fact."

Phoebe, blushing deeper, said she barely knew Mr. Stanfield. Mr. Early merely laughed. "That's a thing that can be remedied easily enough," he said. "And if I'm not mistaken, here he comes to start remedying it right now!"

Surely enough, as soon as the dance was over, Alan was there at Phoebe's elbow, requesting the privilege of dancing with her again. "To speak truth, I have had enough of dancing at present," Phoebe told him. "I would much rather sit and talk with you some more, Alan. If you have no objection?"

"Of course not," said Alan. "Perhaps you would like to go to the supper room and get something to eat and drink?"

Phoebe agreed that she would, and they set off down the corridor that led to the supper room. Alan glanced at Phoebe once or twice, but he did not speak until they were nearly at the door to the supper room. He paused then, looking down at Phoebe with a grave expression.

"Phoebe," he said. *"Miss* Phoebe. Or Miss Fairchild, I should rather say—"

"Phoebe will do," said Phoebe, smiling. "I gave you permission to use my Christian name, if you remember. What is it, Alan?"

Alan smiled back at her. "I like the way you say my name," he said. "In fact, I like everything about you. Of course I haven't known you very long—"

"About sixteen hours now, by my calculation," said Phoebe.

"Is that all?" said Alan. "I feel as though I have known you much longer than that, somehow." He was silent a moment. "Look here. I daresay all this is extremely premature, and probably presumptuous as well. But I thought—I wondered—I have much enjoyed our time together today. I would like of all things to get to know you better, Phoebe. Would you have any objection if I did?"

Phoebe smiled. "No," she said. "No objection at all, Alan."

Alan let out his breath in a long sigh. "That's good! I was so afraid I was overstepping myself. What I mean to say is, I know all this is premature. I know you can't possibly have made up your mind about me yet, let alone have any—well, any *feelings* for me. But I have made up my mind about *you.* And premature though it may be, I have feelings for you, Phoebe." He looked down at her. "In fact, to speak truth, I knew the first moment I saw you that you were the girl for me. And I intend to win you if I can."

Phoebe was quiet. Alan watched her anxiously. "I know all this is premature," he said again. "I hope I'm not frightening you off, Phoebe. But I felt I ought to tell you how I feel. I didn't want to be a wolf in sheep's clothing, talking about Sunday schools and parish festivals, and all the while thinking about how much I'd like to kiss you."

Phoebe looked up at him, a smile touching her lips. "Would you?" she said. "Like to kiss me?"

"Yes, indeed," said Alan with fervor. "More than anything." He added quickly, "But I know it's far too soon, Phoebe. I know you don't feel like that about me—not yet, anyway."

Phoebe smiled. "But I do," she said. "At least, so far as the kissing is concerned! I was thinking earlier that I would like to kiss you when you invited me to dance the first dance. You were so tactful about it—so sparing of my feelings. I was feeling like a fool because I had convinced myself that I was engaged to dance with Mr. Harris, but it turns out he didn't consider it an engagement at all. And then you came and rescued me, like a knight in a fairy tale."

Alan smiled at this. "So it was Randolph who let you down?" he said. "I might have known it. He has some good qualities, but reliability isn't one of them. Unless your interests coincide with his, he's not to be depended on."

"So I have discovered," said Phoebe, with a quick inward smile.

"Well, I am glad if I could help by picking up Randolph's slack. But much as I cherish your gratitude, I must question whether it is an adequate reason for kissing me."

" 'You argue like a man,' " quoted Phoebe, smiling. " 'Logically enough, but without understanding anything of the matter at hand.' I might have been grateful to you for coming to my rescue, but gratitude was only part of the reason why I wanted to kiss you, Alan. Just as a desire to assist me had, I daresay, only partly to do with your coming to my rescue."

Alan laughed. "Touché! I admit it, Phoebe. Though I would have tried to help any woman, I hope, I was genuinely glad to do it for you." He looked down at her, smiling. "So much wit, and so much beauty, too. It makes me want to kiss you more than ever."

"Then do it," said Phoebe.

"Are you certain?" Alan surveyed her doubtfully. "I know it's very soon—and you barely know me."

"I know a good deal about you already and am looking forward to knowing more. But I have a better reason than that. Remember we are valentines, Alan. You were the first man I saw this morning, and that makes you my valentine according to the old tradition. So it is perfectly fitting that you should kiss me."

"Very well," said Alan. "A kiss between valentines." He bent and touched his lips to Phoebe's. "Ah, sweet!" he said softly. He looked down at Phoebe some more, then drew a deep sigh. "I am tempted—definitely tempted—but I shan't abuse my privileges. I shall not kiss you again unless and until you agree to marry me."

"And I shall not agree to marry you unless and until I am convinced you really need me as well as love me," said Phoebe, smiling yet serious. "That is what I told you earlier, Alan, and I meant what I said. I believe you care for me, but only time will show whether what you feel will stand the test of time."

"Then we have a problem," said Alan. "For how am I to demonstrate the full extent of my feelings for you if I do not kiss you?"

"You can't," said Phoebe, smiling. "You shall have to kiss me again and again if you intend to convince me you are serious in your feelings for me, Alan."

"So be it, then," said Alan, and proceeded to demonstrate the depth and intensity of his feelings in a most satisfactory way.

EPILOGUE

"There, that's the last stitch. And it looks perfect, Phoebe—absolutely perfect. No bride ever had a lovelier dress to be married in."

"Do you really think so, Tina?" Phoebe turned to and fro, regarding her reflection in the looking glass. "I must say that for a homemade affair, it does look very well."

"It's perfect," said Tina again, with satisfaction. "And Alan will think it perfect, too. Oh, Phoebe, I can't believe you are to be married tomorrow! And on St. Valentine's Day, too. Great-Aunt Gertrude was saying that we Fairchild girls have a regular bee in our bonnets about being married on Valentine's Day."

"Perhaps we do," said Phoebe, smiling. "It happens that Valentine's Day has a special meaning for Alan and me. It was on Valentine's Day last year that we met. I don't believe I ever told you the full story of how we met, did I, Tina?"

Tina shook her head. "No," she said. "I knew, of course, that Alan was the clergyman who married Gus and Dorothea. I had supposed you met at the wedding."

"No, we actually met before that, earlier that same morning. It's a long story, and I come off looking rather foolish in some respects, but I don't care for that. There can be no doubt that everything turned out for the best."

Phoebe then described how she had slipped downstairs early that morning, intending to meet Mr. Harris, and how she had encountered Alan instead. "It was fate, I believe," she said, smiling at the remembrance of that chance encoun-

ter. "I could never have loved Mr. Harris once I came to
know him. But Alan—oh, Tina, there's no one like Alan! I
feel myself the luckiest girl in the world to be marrying
him."

"You *are* lucky," said Tina, with a barely repressed sigh.
"I wonder if I will ever be fortunate enough to be married."

Phoebe smiled at her. "I am sure you will be. In fact, I
could even hazard a guess as to whom your bridegroom will
be! Geoffrey Tabor has been hanging about with a good deal
of persistence during this past year, I notice."

Tina's color heightened. "Geoff is very nice," she said.
She was silent a moment, then went on, with casualness.
"So you think it was because Alan was your valentine last
year that you are marrying this year?"

"Oh, I wouldn't go as far as that, Tina. That is only a
superstition, you know, and I think it's a mistake to put too
much stock in superstitions. But then one never knows. Perhaps there is more in these old customs than we believe."
Phoebe smiled to herself. "Who knows?"

"Not I," said Tina. She said nothing more, but a little
later that day, when she encountered the maidservant Betsy
in the hall, she said, "Betsy, I wish you would wake me at
six o'clock tomorrow morning. I have an early errand that
I would not miss for anything."